Keith Dixon was born in Yorkshire and grew up in the Midlands. He's been writing since he was thirteen years old in a number of different genres: thriller, espionage, science fiction, literary. He's the author of seven novels in the Sam Dyke Investigations series and two other non-crime works, as well as two collections of blog posts on the craft of writing.

When he's not writing he enjoys reading, learning the guitar, watching movies and binge-inhaling great TV series. He's currently spending more time in France than is probably good for him.

THE BLEAK

KEITH DIXON

A Sam Dyke Investigation

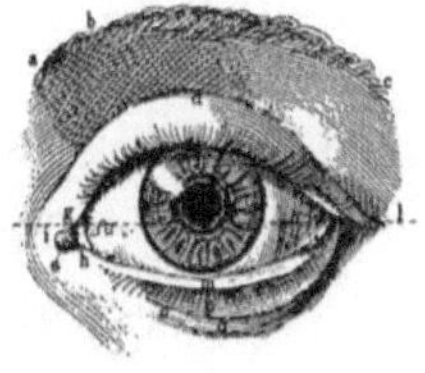

Semiologic Ltd

More information

Learn more at www.keithdixonnovels.com and www.cwconfidential.blogspot.com .

THE BLEAK

CHAPTER ONE

THE NINTH RULE of private detection states that you should never take on a client you think might be nuts.

I wasn't entirely convinced this was the case with the woman who'd called me that morning, but I was certainly tending that way.

As I walked towards Chatwins, the best bakery in the North West, looking forward to a latte and a slice of Victoria sponge in their tea-room, I warned myself against being a soft touch. She'd asked me to carry a folded newspaper in my left hand and told me I should call her Barbara, though I doubted that was her real name. A certain amount of paranoia in the people you deal with in this job is acceptable, but you can take things too far.

Nevertheless, here I was on a cold Monday lunchtime in Crewe, my leather jacket pulled up around my ears and a copy of The Guardian stuffed under my left arm. If nothing else I wanted to see what she looked like. She'd sounded as though she'd been talking to me from a cupboard with her hand over the mouthpiece and her eyes wide and staring. My kind of client.

I crossed the street and was about to open the bakery's door when another customer opened it from the inside and slipped out, holding it ajar. I went through gratefully and was murmuring a word of thanks when she said, 'Costa Coffee, fifteen minutes.'

I had the presence of mind to nod and then continue inside without looking at her. I knew she was slim and dark-haired, a little taller than the average. She'd kept her face turned away from me so I got nothing else except a whiff of floral perfume.

Once inside I joined the queue for bread and bought a brown loaf. Most of the customers were older women and I felt as though they'd all seen the playlet at the door and weren't fooled.

I stood for a moment and looked through the plate glass windows at the passing pedestrians. None of them looked sinister, or even vaguely naughty. When my fifteen minutes were up I went out into the wind again and crossed the pedestrianised town centre, ignoring the siren call of Marks and Spencer's Food Hall and clutching both the bread and the newspaper like any ordinary shopper, a hard act for me to pull off.

She was sitting at the furthest table from the door in Costa Coffee's murky rear section. She watched me come in and picked up her coffee mug so that my provisions didn't knock it over. Her eyes moved past me to watch the door as I pulled out a chair.

She was somewhere in her late twenties or perhaps just thirty, with straight black hair pulled into a severe knot at the back of her head. Her face was oval, her skin nearly as white as the coffee mug she held between her fingers. She was dressed for the office—a simple black skirt and a cream blouse underneath a maroon jacket that had some kind of complicated lapel thing going on. Her lips were rather large but matched the fullness of her round eyes. It wasn't a hardship to sit opposite her.

I said, 'Barbara.'

'What? Oh, yes. I gave you that name, didn't I? I forgot. My mother's name.'

'But not yours.'

'Are you mad? Of course not. Why would I give you my real name when I don't know you?'

'You're the one who called me. It's not like I've been hunting you down.'

She looked away as though gathering herself, going over options.

She said, 'Are you any good at this?'

'Irritating women? It's my speciality. I can get you references, if you'd like.'

'This being-a-private-detective business. Sam Dyke Investigations, or whatever your Yellow Pages ad says. I have no idea what you do, or whether you can help me. Well, actually, it's not me. Well, it is in a way …'

I held up a hand.

'First, why are we meeting here and not in my warm and cosy office? What are you frightened of?'

'I'm not *frightened* … not exactly. But I wanted to meet you in public, out in the open.'

'So now we're in the open you're worried someone will see us. Unless there's something on my shoulder that you can't take your eyes off.'

She raised those large round eyes—which I'd noticed by now were a kind of bluey-green—back to my face.

'I don't know what the hell I'm doing. Things seem to be going crazy around me. Around my boss. That's why I'm here.'

I leaned back in my chair and summoned up some preconceptions and prejudices: secretary, boss. Young secretary, very attractive. Perhaps an older boss who decides to notice her …

She headed me off.

'It's not what you think.'

'What do I think?'

'That I'm having an affair or something grubby like that. It's not.'

'Okay, so what is it?'

'Are you going to have a drink?'

'Should I? Will I need one?'

'It might look less suspicious.'

'Of course, coffee always lessens the look of guilt I wear on a daily basis.'

Nevertheless I stood up and fetched a *latte grande*, then sat facing her again.

I said, 'So tell me. What's going on? And what do you think I can do about it?'

She took one more sip of her coffee, sticking out her tongue to lick a feather of froth from the mug's rim.

'Do you know Midwinter? The company?'

I shook my head. She nodded, as though she hadn't expected me to know.

'It's a kind of research laboratory out near Alderley Edge. Only about two hundred of us work there. Very private. Not secret as such, not working for the government or anything like that. More like environmental research, though there are teams working on different projects too.'

'Scientists, white coats, petri dishes and retorts.'

'Exactly, though I'm not sure what a retort is. My boss would know. Nathan. Doctor Nathan Mustow.'

'So he's one of the scientists?'

'Definitely. Very bright man. I'm his assistant, on the admin side. He's part of a team of people working on something to do with bioaerosols …'

I raised my other hand. I needed the exercise.

'Is there going to be a test on all this?'

'I'm sorry. I don't understand it all either. Nathan told me once that bioaerosols are basically living organisms caught up in moisture in the air. They can be harmless like pollen or a bit nastier, like viruses and spores. His group study how they're carried and when they're active and so on. He's been all over the world doing research. I've written up papers for him.'

'So he's a big cheese in the world of bugs.'

'If you want to belittle him, yes.'

'I'm sorry, I get carried away with my own wit sometimes. So what's the problem? Why have you come to see me?'

Her shoulders slumped and she stared down at the table. Then she lifted her head, and those eyes, and there was fear and sorrow and hesitation all compounded into one forlorn expression.

'I have no idea what I'm doing here. I … I just feel I need to do something. I've worked for him for nearly two years and I think I know him quite well.'

'And?'

'And he's falling apart.'

CHAPTER TWO

I TOOK A sip from my coffee.

I said, 'You're going to have to be clearer than that. Falling apart physically? Mentally? Spiritually?'

'You're not very sympathetic to a new client.'

'If you want a counsellor I can give you some names. It's not my job to give you sympathy.'

She stared at me for a moment. 'You're right, I don't want sympathy.'

'What *do* you want?'

'I'm prepared to pay you to find out what's happening to my boss. Why is he so stressed? Why is he making mistakes? Why is he turning up late for work and then going home early?'

I pushed my coffee mug to one side and leaned forward. I said, 'I have to tell you, this isn't promising. What you've just described sounds like every middle-aged executive I've ever met. What makes you think he's any different to anyone else in a high-pressure job? In this economy?'

'You don't understand—he's just *different*. When I first started there two years ago he was funny, open, helpful. A great boss. I really liked him. He's married to a woman called Isobel, who he really loves, as far as I can tell. When I started there he used to talk about her and what they'd done at the weekend. I was just getting over a split from a boyfriend myself and he was nice without being, you know, creepy. He was thoughtful.'

'What changed?'

'Nothing. At least nothing I could see, at work. He's still married to Isobel. They don't have any kids, so no problems there. No deaths in the family. He's working on the same projects. But about a year ago he started coming in late and looking haggard, you know, as if he hadn't slept. He'd ask me to do something and then a couple of hours later he'd ask me again. He started sitting in his office, staring out of the window. I'd walk in and find him looking at the trees instead of poring over a database on his computer. He seemed to lose his drive and his focus, and I had to start covering up for him.'

'Has anyone said anything to him? His boss? Colleagues?'

'He has reviews every three months with Harry Tuck, the production manager. But I'm not privy to what's said. Everybody else is so caught up in what they're doing that I don't suppose they'd notice if he jumped out of a window. So long as it didn't interrupt their work-flow.'

She stopped, as though expecting me to say something. Perhaps she realised she'd sounded critical and that I'd want her to elaborate. I said nothing and waited, usually the best tactic when you think people are going to reveal themselves.

She said, 'As I'm telling you all this I can see how childish it sounds. All I have is a feeling, an intuition. Things were one way before, now they're another. I should just get over it, shouldn't I, and save my money?'

'Have you spoken to Isobel about him?'

Now she looked shocked, her eyes widening. 'I couldn't do that! I hardly know her. We've only spoken on the phone, when she's rung in to talk to him. And she usually calls his mobile anyway.'

'So you have no idea what his wife thinks. Whether she's noticed any change or not.'

'Trust me, she's a woman. She's noticed.' She leaned back in her chair abruptly, as though she'd made a decision, then reached down for her handbag, which she placed on the table between us. 'I'm wasting my time, aren't I?'

'Pretty much.'

'Well thanks for your honesty.'

'I don't see how I can help you. Most of my work involves tracking down people who've gone missing, or investigating frauds of one kind or another. And paperwork. Don't get me started on paperwork. But in this instance there's nothing there for me to look at. I understand you've had an intuition, and I respect that. I do. But I wouldn't know where to start.'

'I see. Anyway, thanks for your time.' She began to stand up and pushed back her chair.

A thought occurred to me.

'Hold on. Please, sit down.'

She lowered herself to the chair again. 'What?'

'Why all the cloak-and-dagger stuff when I came in? Why the change of venue? What's all that about?'

Her mouth twisted sardonically. 'I'm a bit paranoid, I suppose. The security at Midwinter is crazy and we're always being reminded not to talk about what goes on there because it's commercially sensitive. When you're at the cutting edge you have to be careful that no one bleeds. That's a poster in the ladies' toilet. Good, eh?'

'So … you thought you might be followed? Or that *I* might be?'

'Something like that. I came off campus for lunch, which hardly anyone ever does. There's a great subsidised canteen on-site and we're miles from anywhere, so most people stay put during the day.'

'Sounds more like a concentration camp than a jolly place of work.'

'Oh, it's not jolly.' She stood up again. 'Margaret, by the way.'

'What?'

'Margaret Sellers. My real name.'

I stood and reached out my hand, which she shook.

'Sam Dyke.'

'I know. Of Sam Dyke non-Investigations.'

'Let me think about it. Do you have a card?'

'No, but I wrote my details down before I came here. To make things easier.'

She opened her handbag and pulled out a lined index card. Her name, private email and phone information were inscribed in a neat italic hand in blue ink. I put it into my wallet.

We said goodbye and she walked towards the front door and I followed her, though I stayed inside. She exited and turned left, probably heading towards the car park in Forge Street. She walked briskly, head down, minding her own business and obviously trying not to attract attention to herself. It occurred to me that she was a hell of a secretary to have so much invested in her boss that she'd talk to a private detective. Perhaps she *was* in love with him, a little bit.

Opposite my position, from the parking bays facing McDonalds, a dark Prius pulled out and came towards me. It paused briefly outside the Natwest Bank branch and a pencil-thin man with short red hair peeled away from the cash-point, glanced briefly in Margaret's direction, then climbed inside the back seat. It rolled away smoothly, and not too quickly for me to make a note of its plate.

CHAPTER THREE

IT WAS ONLY a two minute walk to my office but I took my time and went the long way around, skirting the back of Marks and Spencer instead of heading straight across the square. There was something desperate in Margaret Sellers that I never liked to see in people younger than me. I couldn't tell whether she was secretly in love with her boss but couldn't admit it, or whether she was over-dramatising a very common workplace malady. The idea that she might be right didn't appeal to me.

Except …

I hadn't liked the look of the slim man who'd climbed inside the Prius. Body language experts tell us we make up our minds about people within the first four seconds … well, I'd made him in two. At long range. He was jittery, a bit cruel, focused and probably followed orders well. I had no doubt that he was following Margaret and what worried me was the fact that he might have seen me talking to her. He could have stepped into the coffee bar, had a quick look around, and then left.

But probably not.

Margaret would have leaped a foot off her chair had he walked in, assuming she knew who he was. If he did indeed belong to the security set-up at Midwinter, she more than likely knew him by sight.

So perhaps he stayed outside.

But then, what was the point? Why follow her if you didn't see what she did once she was off-site? Why follow her in the first place? What had she done?

I spun on my heel quickly and looked around.

No one.

If I was being followed after leaving the coffee shop, it was being done by people who knew what they were doing. And probably drove dark-coloured hybrid cars.

MY OFFICE SITS over a large store that used to sell furniture but is now empty. The owners couldn't make a go of it any longer, especially after the Crash, when people were more interested in selling furniture than buying it. I missed the gentle hum from the heating units downstairs and the occasional bursts of laughter of the sales reps, having fun together when there were no customers about. I picked up the post that had arrived since I left for my appointment with Margaret earlier and trudged up the stairs to my two rooms. I'd inherited the kitchen I'd shared with the furniture store and doubled my floor-space, though thankfully the landlord hadn't yet seen fit to increase my rent. He obviously didn't want to mess with me.

The post was one piece of junk mail and one bank statement, which didn't make enjoyable reading. I filed it in the big cardboard box I use for all my accounts detritus and fired up my laptop.

Midwinter's website was a limited affair. Pages for Who We Are, What We Do, Location and Contacts.

The Who We Are page showed a photo of the Chairman and CEO, Charles Montgomery, a slightly rotund man in his forties with a gleaming dome of a head and an artificial smile that he seemed unwilling to share with us. He wore the usual Chairman's dark suit and striped tie and could have been an impostor, a bought character from Getty Images for all I knew.

The Contacts listed were a generic email address — info@ — and one phone number which was probably Reception.

The company wasn't exactly clamouring for our attention.

The What We Do page was slightly more informative. There was some bland PR-speak about being on the leading edge of research in the fields of Geoscience and Environmental Science, with renowned researchers from all over the world being part of their team, but there were no specifics. No links to individual pages for scientists. No links to research papers or successful project outcomes. Nothing about any publicity or joint ventures or government funding.

Not very much at all.

I thought again about Margaret and her vague intuitions concerning her boss and his state of mind. It seemed odd to me that she would look to someone in my line of work to help her out. Didn't Midwinter have an HR Department? Could she really not have spoken to Mustow's wife, Isobel? Or his boss … what was his name, Harry Tuck?

I wanted to file the whole thing under 'interesting but crazy,' but something about the way the thin man had glanced at her, that fleeting moment, almost as though he disliked what he saw, changed my mind.

After all, it was my mind and I had every right to change it.

I WAITED UNTIL three o'clock and then rang Margaret on her work number. She didn't sound pleased.

'What do you want? I thought you said you wouldn't do anything.'

'Do you know a very thin man with red hair, possibly owns or is driven around in a black Prius?'

There was a moment of silence that I would probably describe as 'stunned'.

'What about him?'

'Who is he?'

'David Bonetti. They call him Mr Bones, because he's so thin. And his name, I suppose.'

'What does he do?'

'He works for Security. For Jolyon Greif.' She pronounced it 'Griff'. 'What about him?'

'Let's just say you weren't as paranoid as I thought.'

'Oh my god! Was he following me?'

'Or it was a massive coincidence he just happened to be taking out money from the cash-point opposite.'

'I'm going to be in such shit!'

'Take it easy. Did you see him come into Costa after me?'

'I don't think so.'

'And he didn't stay to watch me leave, either. I suspect as far as he's concerned you were just out for a coffee, no harm done. Probably just an exercise.'

'You don't know these people. They're like the bloody Gestapo.'

'Look, can you get me in to see your boss? Do you control his timetable?'

'Up to a point, yes. I can get you an appointment. But why? What would you say to him?'

'I don't know yet. When can we do it?'

She went away for a moment and then came back.

'He could fit you in tomorrow, eleven o'clock.'

'Okay. How do we do it? Who should I be?'

She thought about this for a while, then said Mustow frequently met people from recruitment companies. Often it was under the pretence of talking about recruitment in general when in fact they were just trying to head-hunt him.

'I'll tell him you're from our new agency and you want to get a feel for what kind of work he and his colleagues do. Can you manage that? General questions about the work and the company? You'd have to wear a suit and take notes.'

'I can do that.'

'But don't get too personal. He'll hate me if he finds out what you're up to. I'll have a hard enough job selling the interview to him anyway. I'll tell him HR wanted him to do it.'

'You don't have to do this just because I asked.'

'You're right, I don't. But I came to you, didn't I?'

'Strikes me you're risking a lot for your boss.'

'Life's about risk, Mr Dyke. I learned that a long time ago. I'm not someone who can pull the bed covers over my head and pretend that everything's okay.'

'Then you're a woman after my own heart. Carry on.'

We worked on some more of the details for a while and I thanked her. Then I told her my fees and there was a pause before she said, 'That's okay.' She added, 'When you get here tomorrow you'll have to go to the Security lodge and get a badge. Ask for me and I'll fetch you back here.'

'Will this get you in trouble?'

'I'll handle Nathan. I'm more worried about why Mr Bones was following me. I don't mind taking risks but I dislike that bunch of little Hitlers. I wouldn't want them to think they've got something on me. Do you really think it was, like, practice?'

'In my experience security people don't like change and they don't like the unusual. When they saw you driving out this morning they probably wondered where you were going and thought they'd have a look because they've got nothing else to do. How exciting can it be, herding a bunch of white coats from one laboratory to the next and making sure they don't spill acid on each other?'

'I hope you're right.'

'Me too.'

Though I suspected I wasn't. Hopefully, getting into Midwinter would give me the opportunity to find out exactly what went on there and why Margaret and her boss were being run ragged.

CHAPTER FOUR

ON THE WAY to Alderley Edge, along the main road from Congleton, a small lane snaked off to the right and took me between high hedges before depositing me at a square, brick-and-glass security lodge. A tall wire fence loped away in either direction, sustained by concrete pillars that leaned backwards at the top and held three strands of barbed wire and, every hundred metres, an assortment of surveillance gizmos. The campus looked like it encompassed a large stretch of well-tended park land but from where I sat there didn't seem to be many buildings at its centre. Like any large city, Manchester had its fair share of low-key, high-tech satellite companies, but as far as I knew not many of them had this level of security. I wondered what they had to hide.

A white pole raised itself as I approached the lodge and I slowed to a stop as a bulky man in a general-purpose security uniform came out, carrying an iPad. I saw him use it to photograph my licence plate, then he walked towards my window.

'Your name, sir?'

'Sam Dyke. Here to see Doctor Mustow at eleven o'clock.'

He scrolled down his screen and found my name.

'That's fine. Pull into the Reception building over there on the right and they'll give you a pass.'

He went back into the lodge and another pole in front of me lifted into the air.

I parked in front of the building he'd pointed to and went inside. The heads of two middle-aged women floated above a high counter, a television playing a corporate video behind them. I told one of the heads who I was and why I was there.

'First time on-site, Mr Dyke?'

'Yes.'

'Then we'll have to show you the Health and Safety video. Here's your badge. It'll work on some doors but not all. You'll have to be hosted. Please take a seat over there and we'll start the video.'

I sat on a modernist brown sofa—that's to say, it had no arms—and another flat screen on a stand flickered into life as though it knew I'd arrived. The video began with an overhead plan view of the site, which wasn't as big as I'd expected. Apart from this Reception building and the Security lodge, there appeared to be two main work blocks, one of which contained the canteen, and a separate housekeeping or maintenance building.

An American actor's voice told me about the safety procedures while animated graphics pointed out the fire collection points and instructed me not to wander around without a host or hostess. This was because the work Midwinter was engaged in sometimes involved the use of hazardous materials. More animation pointed out the exits to all the buildings and indicated with glowing icons where there were courtesy phones connected directly to Security in case I got lost.

Finally the actor thanked me for my attention and reminded me that I would now receive a pass, which I should keep, and which was dated to show when I'd seen the video. If I were to return more than a year later I'd have to watch the video again. It's always good to keep up.

I went to the counter and the same woman gave me a laminated pass stating that I'd seen the video on this date.

'You'll need to show that if you come again, love. Think of it like a bus pass.'

'Thanks. Is someone coming to pick me up? Miss Sellers, is it?'

'Park your car round the corner there and she'll be here when you come back.'

I did as I was told, parking my old Mondeo amongst a glitter of Audis and BMWs and Porsches. Science obviously paid well. I didn't see a dark Prius. Maybe Security had their own parking lot.

When I went back into Reception, Margaret was indeed there, looking tall and slim in a tailored trouser-suit.

She shook my hand and introduced herself, a formality for the ears of the Reception staff.

'Let me take you to Doctor Mustow's office.'

'Lead on.'

She was wearing a short winter jacket over her suit, and as we went outside she pulled it tight across her chest and tucked her head down. I thought again how she seemed to want to disappear, as though her body was something to be ashamed of. She glanced briefly at me.

'At least you look the part.'

'Glad you noticed. This is my funeral suit.'

'Remember what I said yesterday. Ask him about his job, what he does, colleagues and so on. Don't get too personal, he won't like it. Try to be subtle.'

'I know how to do this. Duplicity is my middle name.'

Before we arrived at one of the two large concrete and glass buildings I'd seen on the video, we passed through a massive turnstile. It was like those you used to find at football grounds but was set in a large concrete frame and went from head to foot, presumably preventing you from smuggling any illicit packages in or out of the building. Margaret used the pass looped around her neck to trip the mechanism and we squeezed through one at a time. I was carrying a thin briefcase that she passed around the outside of the turnstile and through a small square sensing device. A green button lit and she handed it back to me.

Now we were in a small lobby and again Margaret used her pass to buzz us through a further glass door. She said nothing but looked at me with an expression that said, 'See what I mean about security?'

This was a corporate building like any other — at least in the foyer. Large abstract paintings on the wall. Another TV showing the corporate video. A couple of leather banquettes and a humming coffee machine.

Margaret talked over her shoulder as she led me down a tiled corridor.

'We call this the science block. Over the way is admin. HR, payroll, finance, that kind of thing.'

We went through two more doors that needed Margaret's electronic pass, then turned down another corridor, this time carpeted and hushed. There was an atmosphere of serious industry about the place, as though joy and humour had been caught like suspect parcels by the sensor outside. We'd gone past several blank doors containing small windows and a couple of conference rooms with floor-to-ceiling glass when she finally stopped and opened a door with Mustow's name on it. Inside, it was obviously Margaret's office—filing cabinets, desktop PC, printer. She nodded towards another door to my right, this one seemingly made of a heavy wood and fairly substantial.

'I'll see if he's ready.'

She crossed the carpet, knocked and went in. Moments later she opened the door from the inside and held it open.

I went through and heard it close behind me.

I wondered how I'd begin.

NATHAN MUSTOW WAS a man in his early forties with a large square head planted rather forward on his shoulders, as though he was permanently curious about what was in front of him. He didn't get up to greet me but remained seated behind a wide partner desk with an inlaid green leather top. He gestured to the seat that faced him and I sat down. Then he reached a hand across the desktop and I shook it. His hand was warm and rather thin.

He introduced himself and I gave him my name in return.

I'd expected someone who looked less well-tended and focused. Someone with a wild eye, perhaps, or a suspicion of drool in the corner of his mouth. But instead he seemed the picture of professionalism, his iron-grey hair slicked neatly in place, white cuffs showing beyond the arms of his grey suit-jacket, a look of calm appraisal in his eyes as he took note of my own suit and tie. I opened the leather portfolio I'd brought and took out a notepad and pen.

At this he seemed to relax and leaned back in his chair, swivelling it so that he could turn to see out of the large window to his right. The Cheshire countryside was rampant outside, the trees now thickening and the grass taking on a heavier green. This was the view to which he was paying more attention than he should, according to Margaret.

He said, 'So what's this all about, Sam? Margaret says you're new to the agency and want to get a feel for us. So we can hire even better people. You do know we haven't hired anyone in over a year, don't you?'

'So I'm told. My job is to find people who suit the profile you're looking for. There are always jobs for the right people.'

'Is that true?' He seemed to find this amusing, smiling to himself but not sharing the joke with me. 'Don't you watch the news, Sam? Not many jobs around just now.'

I didn't want to get into a discussion about the economy so I said nothing. My silence seemed to bring him back into the room and he turned towards me again.

'You've seen the job descriptions, I suppose?'

'Yes, at the office.'

'So what more can I tell you? We do science here, Sam. Personalities are redundant. If someone's got the brains, we don't care whether they're train-spotters in their spare time, or go disco-dancing with their granny. They don't have to fit in to a 'team environment' or any other of that personnel crap.'

'Okay, I see where you're coming from. So tell me, what exactly do you do here?'

He was about to say something but changed his mind and I watched him turning wary, almost like a chameleon changing the colour of its skin. His tone of voice became more conciliatory, as though he'd pushed down what he really wanted to say for the sake of diplomacy.

'As it happens, I do work with a team of colleagues. But we largely work on our own, or in small groups of two or three. We don't do any team-building nonsense—no paintballing up a mountain. I won't go into the details of my work because it's irrelevant to what you need.'

'I'd still like to hear you talk about it. Hear the kind of language you use.'

'Well, if you must. My projects are usually focused on biogenic cloud precipitation feedback processes in different ecosystems. The most recent project was based in a region of South America.'

'And what's that for?'

'*For?* You mean, do we get teflon out of it? We're not NASA, you know. We're not expecting to convert research into patents and make a killing.'

'I just wondered what the outcome of the research might be, that's all.'

He drew a sigh. 'Climate change. It's all about climate change. The reduction in the availability of water in certain parts of the world has been dramatic, as you probably know. If we can find ways to manage the ecosystem better by studying how it works now, then we might be able to do something positive. Change something for the better in the future.'

'That sounds like a worthy cause.'

He gave an odd barking noise that I took for a laugh, however strained.

'So I thought. It's turning out to be harder than I imagined. Tell me, Sam, have you ever pushed yourself really hard in order to achieve something, then found that the goalposts had moved just as you got there?'

'I don't really do objectives and goals. I'm more of a spur-of-the-moment kind of guy.'

'In my line of work I can't afford to operate like that. Project management, Gantt charts, timelines. That's what we deal in here, Sam. Predictability of outcomes through structured goal-setting.'

'And is it working? I get the impression you're not happy with the way things have been going.'

He looked at me sharply.

'Where did you get that from?'

'Just your general tone. I'm sorry, ignore me. I'm probably reading too much in. What else can you tell me?'

Before he had the chance to answer, the door burst open and a large man wearing an open-necked polo shirt stepped in, holding on to the door-handle as though he was only dropping by.

'Mustow, need a word. Can you—'

At this point his eyes fell on me and his demeanour changed. He'd had an imperious, take-no-prisoners air about him at first, but when he spotted me he pulled his features into a smile and relaxed his body language. It was an outrageously bogus act.

'Oh, so sorry. Who's this then, Nathan, old chap?'

I stood up and introduced myself. The man shook my hand as though it were the greatest pleasure he'd ever known.

'Harry Tuck, i/c Production. That just means I keep the ranks in line while the big guns are off on parade. To what do we owe … ?'

'I'm forcing Dr Mustow to give up some state secrets so we can recruit more like him.'

'I'm sorry?'

'I'm from Hallows, your recruitment agency. Getting some gen on the goings-on around here. Prep work for a big push on the recruitment front.'

I could bullshit Army-speak with the best of them. Especially when it was as fake as Tuck was.

He was still concerned. He was a man who was probably younger than most people thought, having lined already around the eyes and lost some of his thin blond hair at the front. He was perhaps around forty but looked fifty-five. He had three or four inches on me, and I'm not short.

He said, 'Sorry, Nathan, I don't understand. Recruitment's off the board at the moment, isn't it?'

I felt sorry for Mustow as he shrugged. I'd sandbagged him and I didn't want him to get in trouble because of me.

'I was told to meet Mr Dyke here. I just follow orders, Harry. You know HR, they've got more power than any of us.'

Tuck gave a *'We'll see about that'* look, but smiled at me, as though I should be kept out of the intra-office politics.

'Tell you what, Mr Dyke, why don't I take you on a tour of the premises? Give you some insight into what we do here. Then you don't have to badger our valued employees. What do you say?'

'Well—'

'Excellent. Come this way.'

He had his arms around my shoulders by now, and was not so subtly leading me out of the door and past Margaret, who did her best not to look at us as we left.

Tuck escorted me along a corridor and then used his pass to get us through a pair of double doors into the kind of wide corridor you see in hospitals. He took his arm from my shoulders but stayed close.

'So how long have you been with Hallows?'

'Couple of weeks. Hence the fact-finding.'

'Thought I hadn't seen you before. How's Constance?'

'She's fine.'

'I thought she'd left?'

'She has. We're still in touch.'

I don't know whether this lie satisfied him but he carried on talking anyway as we went deeper into the building. He told me it was less than five years old and was purpose-built. He boasted about the number of Ph.Ds on the staff and the fact that they were working alongside some of the most famous universities in the world. The company currently had researchers off-site on all five continents and was strengthening its own reputation daily. They had several different units working on a range of geoscientific and environmental initiatives.

'Of course you know all this if you've read the client portfolio. But you should also know we're proud of the work we do here. Proud to be adding to the sum of human knowledge. Makes it all worthwhile, don't you think?'

I murmured something approving and he patted me on the back as though I were a child who'd said something clever.

He stopped abruptly by a door with a glass window and pointed through it. A couple of men leaning over a table looked up at exactly the same time, as though our darkening of the window had produced an automatic response.

Tuck said, 'They're working on a backscatter cloud spectrometer. The idea is to get it fitted to commercial airlines so we can get regular info on cloud formation. The Yanks are interested in it, too. Goes for testing in Ottowa in a couple of weeks.'

'What sort of testing?'

'They have an icing tunnel—simulates conditions up to thirty thousand feet. Saves actually having to go up there, up in the icy cold, see?'

He moved me along and showed me another couple of laboratories where scientists in blue lab coats—not white— were deep in their work. At one door he knocked and entered, introducing me to three more researchers who were polite but obviously eager to carry on. I'd expected men and women in their forties, with serious demeanours and no social skills. But most of the people I'd seen so far seemed to be in their early twenties, with bright, alert faces and the ability to look you in the eye.

Finally we came to a heavier door where the glass window was laced with a metal grid. A sign above said, 'Protocol Unit, Biosafety Level 2', and another plaque beneath said 'Rooms P14 - P24. Permitted personnel only'. There were various Health and Safety stickers on the door, including a yellow triangle with four circles within it that said 'Biohazard' underneath. Tuck saw me looking at the heavy door but didn't want to stop.

'Clean rooms. Can't go in there. You're not trained.'

My suspicious nature wondered whether it was about my training, or whether I might get curious about what I saw.

I realised that we'd travelled the perimeter of the building and Tuck was now leading me back towards the entrance. The tour was evidently over. I'd seen nothing that I might not have inferred from a glance at Midwinter's website.

He said, 'Have you met the boss, Stratford Greif?'

'No. Do you think I should?'

'Not necessarily. Dr Greif's a very busy man. Not much involved in the daily grind. Other fish to fry, you get my drift.'

'I thought Charles Montgomery was the CEO.'

Tuck opened a sudden grin, giving him the appearance of a child caught in a lie and trying to act innocent.

'Well of course he is. I meant boss of the Protocol unit. Mr Montgomery is *capo di tutti capi*, certainly. Dr Greif is our immediate boss. Clever man. He'd liked to have met you, I'm sure. But he's always busy. Can't disturb him for a simple recruitment matter, can we?'

We'd arrived at the front door. He stuck out his hand.

'Nice to have met you. Mr Dyke, was it? I'll send Margaret down to escort you out.'

'Thanks. Tell me, isn't Greif the name of … let me think, head of Security?'

'That's right. Jolyon.'

'So they're related.'

'Hard to say, isn't it?'

He grinned at me and walked off with a cheery wave of his hand. I stood and watched him, checking myself for bruises. I was sure I'd just been manhandled in some way.

MARGARET ARRIVED FIVE minutes later and walked me back through the turnstile towards Reception. Once we were away from the science block and into open ground she stopped and turned towards me as if she couldn't wait any longer.

'Well, how did he seem? What did you think?'

'I saw nothing in Mustow to change my mind.'

She threw up her hands.

'I knew it was a waste of time. How much do I owe you?'

'Don't be silly. I'm just saying I didn't see him long enough to get a proper read. That character Tuck came in and gave me a real snow-job. There's lots of weirdness here but that might be in the nature of the beast. Industrial espionage and patent farming being what it is these days, they might be justifiably paranoid. I'm not the best person to judge.'

'What's patent farming?'

'Where somebody buys a patent they don't intend to use and then sues someone who does use it. So Midwinter will be keeping their developments secret to prevent anyone creating a patent around their work and holding them to ransom later.'

'I see. So they're justified in their behaviour, Nathan should snap out of it, and this is all the stupid anxiety of a silly woman?'

'You're putting words in my mouth. I understand why you wanted to talk to someone if you've seen changes in his behaviour. But to be honest, that's probably best done between himself and someone else—his wife or a counsellor. I'm not sure it's even your place to butt in, however sensitive and caring you think you're being. He might not thank you for it.'

This time she didn't bother to reply, just turned on her heel and continued walking towards Reception. I caught up and followed a pace behind in silence, knowing that I'd done enough damage to her self-esteem.

As I drove away from Midwinter, I thought that was the last I'd see of her. And that was a shame, because I like people who stick up for what they believe in.

At least I thought I did.

CHAPTER FIVE

AT THREE O'CLOCK I took a phone call from my son, Dan, who asked to see me that night. He'd had another of his get-rich-quick ideas and, I supposed, wanted me to approve of it.

These meetings never went well.

He'd been brought up in foster homes because I didn't know of his existence until he was eighteen years old. His mother had feigned a miscarriage and left me before she gave birth. This made our initial dealings fraught, but when he moved from London to Crewe and started working with my then girlfriend, things got better. Then she became my ex-girlfriend and things were rough again for a while.

Now he'd made his own friends and been involved in a couple of small start-up businesses that usually involved importing cheap goods from abroad and re-selling them on-line, where he was a whiz-kid.

He'd begun renting a house out near Leighton Hospital, and when he opened the door I was shocked. His hair was neatly cut and he wore a proper shirt instead of the usual sloppy tee-shirt. When we went through into his living room his books were ranged on an Ikea bookcase and the cushions were in place on the sofa instead of being strewn across the floor. The PS3 was disconnected from the television and a stack of DVDs was ordered neatly on the stand below.

I turned to him.

'You can afford a cleaner now?'

'Changing up, Dad. A new world order. Take a pew.'

I sat on the sofa and he sat on the armchair. His eyes still reminded me of his mother, who'd been murdered a few years before, but his features were beginning to firm up. He was developing both cheek-bones and an air of gravitas.

He said, 'I'm going to be upfront with you. I'm going to ask you for money. I'm going to be investing it in an on-line venture and there's a certain amount of risk involved.'

'What sort of venture?'

'Bitcoin.'

I wanted to say, 'What's Bitcoin?', just to hear how he defended it. But in fact I had a clue. There'd been plenty in the newspapers on the subject—sufficient for me to get the idea that I didn't like it. Essentially it was a digital currency that you could use to pay for certain things on-line. And because it was a currency, you could speculate with it on commercial exchanges, buying and selling bitcoins like stocks and shares. So of course people had made and lost fortunes.

I said, 'There's more risk than you're letting on.'

He was taken aback by his old man.

'What do you know about it?'

'I know that hackers have taken over other people's identities and then fraudulently bought bitcoins from innocent dupes.'

'You know I'm not innocent.'

I sighed. 'Tell me more.'

He spent thirty minutes explaining to me how the system worked and how it was possible to make money by buying and selling bitcoins over the Internet. He opened up his laptop and showed me a video of how you did it. He took me to a bitcoin exchange site and showed me a tutorial. He opened YouTube and showed me a series of Americans talking about how much money they were making each month.

When he'd finished I sat back on the sofa.

'How much do you want?'

'I've got a grand. If you can lend me another two grand, at today's prices I could buy ten bitcoins and go from there.'

'Two grand!'

'You'd get paid back as soon as I double it. Then I start again and you're out of it, if you want to be.'

It was pointless to argue. He had a psychological hold over me—my feelings of guilt. I hadn't been there for him when he was growing up, so I owed him. And we both knew that.

He was well organised. He had a little folder with an agreement in it, together with his bank details. I was to transfer the money as soon as I could and he'd let me know when he'd got it, together with daily updates on how he was doing.

'Don't bother with that. Just let me know when you're paying me back.'

'Cool.' He closed his laptop. 'So what's happening on the work front? Anything I can help with?'

From time to time he'd used his computer skills to help me. I'm no slouch but I didn't have his talent. I told him briefly about Margaret Sellers and the non-case that I wasn't taking up.

He said, 'So what was this company like? Was it all science-fiction with sliding doors like Star Trek?'

'More like 2001: A Space Odyssey. Or Alien—in space, no one can hear you scream.'

'And they were all weirdo scientists with big hair and clipboards?'

'No, they were all young and intense. Like a cult. Like Mormons who believed in science instead of whatever the hell it is they believe in.'

Dan stood and fetched us a couple of beers from his kitchen.

He said, 'That pushes two of your buttons, then.'

'What do you mean? What buttons?'

'Religion and intelligence. Brainiac-type intelligence.'

'I'll give you religion—what do you mean about intelligence?'

He grinned over the top of his can.

'You tend not to like people with lots of brains. I think you think they're acting superior. You want to take them down a peg or two with your anti-brain fighting skills.'

'For God's sake ...'

'It's true! I've seen you being sarcastic and snide whenever it seems that someone might know something that you don't. As if you think they're showing off.'

'You talk a lot of rubbish. I might take my bitcoins back.'

'Too late. You've signed the agreement. And as we say in the trading business, your word is your bond.'

'You don't know what you're talking about.'

'Then why else are you not going to take the case? Don't you think you can help this woman? You're usually up for helping a damsel in distress. You're always wanting to show what a good person you are.'

'Jesus, where are you getting this stuff from? Have you been reading Psychology for Dummies—or Nerds, in your case?'

Dan shrugged, enjoying himself.

'You're always telling me about granddad, what a good bloke he was. Isn't there a bit of envy or something there? Righting wrongs like he did?'

I said nothing. What he said about my father was true. He'd been a miner in Yorkshire and had always had a sense of himself and his worth. But this came from an instinctual knowledge of right and wrong. He was the least prejudiced person I ever knew, and he never bad-mouthed or gossipped about anyone. Even when denigrating the Coal Board he blamed the organisation, not the people in it. He'd set the bar pretty high for me in terms of the moral position that I ought to aspire towards.

I said, 'The difference between him and me is that people looked up to him. And as you've proved so clearly tonight, that isn't true in my case. Nobody listens to me or cares a hoot what I think. Now drink your beer and shut the hell up.'

MY WATCH SHOWED twenty minutes after midnight when I left, two thousands pounds poorer than when I arrived. It was only a ten minute drive back to my place from Dan's and I spent it feeling confused. He was right that I wasn't happy about blowing Margaret off. My bank balance could have used the income, but I was more upset that she'd think no one cared. I was in no doubt that Mustow was in a stressful position. What I didn't know was what I could do about it. If he was suffering because of the demands of his job, then he needed a counsellor or someone from Human Resources to talk to. The more I considered it, the more I thought it odd that Margaret Sellers had asked me to get involved. It was hardly her business if Mustow was having a tough time coping with work—unless he was mistreating her in some way, which I didn't think was the case. Perhaps there was more to their relationship than she'd admitted.

My house is on the edge of Crewe, down a track that's shielded on both sides by tall trees. The house itself had served at one time as a repair garage, the previous owner having installed a hydraulic lift and pit in the downstairs rooms. I'd converted that area into a gym and built out over it from one of the upstairs rooms, adding a floor-to-ceiling glass window so I could look out over the portion of Cheshire farmland that was my view.

Because it's off the main road and there are no street-lamps close by, any unusual lighting is easily seen. So when I started to pull in to the drive, before my headlights turned into the track itself and illuminated the house, I saw the flicker of a flashlight to one side of the building straight away. I stopped immediately, killed the car lights and switched off the engine. I did nothing for a couple of minutes and let my eyes acclimatise to the darkness. It might have been nothing, a passing headlight from a car at the bottom of the field a quarter of a mile behind the house.

But I didn't think so.

You get to know your own house and its peculiarities when you're out of the urban ruck.

I moved the courtesy light switch so that it wouldn't come on, then quietly opened the door and stepped out. I pushed the door closed but didn't slam it.

Then I began to edge down the track, the soft earth sucking quietly at my shoes. It was an overcast night with no moon, but there was a hearty breeze that agitated the treetops and sounded like a hundred brooms sweeping a gigantic floor. I hoped it would cover my approach.

As I got closer I saw that there was light playing inside my downstairs office. Whoever was inside had closed the curtains but it wasn't enough to prevent the flickering light from being visible. I bent down and found one of the substantial rocks that I'd used to line the edge of the path, painted white to show up under my car's headlights. I held it inside my jacket and advanced further.

From about ten feet I saw that my front door was ajar. I had a couple of good locks on there, but they'd apparently served no purpose tonight. The burglar evidently wanted to get in without breaking a window and leaving any disruption.

I was close to the door when I heard a low whistle from my right and turned. I couldn't see anything but there was a change in the atmosphere, as though someone had moved. I brought out the rock from under my jacket and pushed quickly into the house. I turned on the switch inside the door and the entrance was flooded with light. Quickening my pace I took a couple of swift steps and opened my office door. It was dark inside and I didn't see the person who pushed me back immediately and spun me around, tripping me so that I fell face-first back into the entrance hall. The rock in my hand tumbled away.

Then a boot landed in the small of my back and whoomped some of the air from me.

It took me a moment to scramble to my feet but he was already out of the door and running, much faster than I could, with the speed of a young man. He was thin and tall but moved with agility. I saw a vague shape down the track and knew it would be his partner, the look-out, waiting for him. No doubt there would be a car just around the corner. I watched them vanish into the darkness like heavy-booted wraiths.

I'd never believed in coincidence, and this wasn't going to change my mind.

IT LOOKED LIKE I'd come back in time to disturb the burglars because, as far as I could see, nothing had been taken. They must have been watching the house for hours and seen that I wasn't home, so chanced their arm. It was either that or risk breaking in when I was asleep in bed, a much riskier undertaking.

Although I've never been particularly friendly with the police, it was my civic duty to report the break-in to keep the crime figures accurate and in case it was part of a wider pattern of burglaries in the area. A half hour later two bleary-eyed cops arrived and asked some desultory questions and gave me a crime number. Nothing had been taken, nothing had been broken—not even the locks on the front door—and so there was correspondingly nothing they could do.

One of the policemen was called Vickers and knew me by reputation as there aren't that many private detectives in the area, especially someone working by himself and not part of a corporate investigative group. He was the older of the two policemen and had the somewhat blasé and superior attitude they develop when trying to minimise the extent of a crime.

Putting his notebook away, he said, 'You're not working on anything that might have set this up, are you?'

'I don't have a case at the moment.'

'You haven't done anything that might have prompted someone to take a look around, then?'

'What do you mean?'

'You know what I mean. Nosy buggers like you get on people's nerves. Maybe someone wanted to repay the compliment, have a look at your stuff for once.'

'I haven't done anything to anyone and don't have any active cases at the moment.'

He looked at me as though he didn't believe me, which he was absolutely right to do. I barely believed myself.

He added, 'So you won't be doing anything silly.'

It was an instruction more than a question.

I said, 'What do you mean?'

'Going after them yourself, like.'

'How would I do that if I didn't see them and don't know who they are? That's your neck of the woods. All I saw was one tall thin person, probably young from the way he moved. And another one seen from the back, looked a bit thicker around the middle but ran pretty quick. Aren't you going to send forensics and squads of CSIs to look for a vital thread of cotton?'

The younger of the policemen laughed.

'It's probably kids larking about. Saw a dark house and thought there might be something they could nick. I don't think we'll be spending the police budget on it.'

'Glad to know I rank so highly in your list of priorities.'

'We're here to serve.'

Part of me wanted to punch him on the nose, but instead I thanked them both and saw them out of the house, closing the door before they'd reached their car.

I needed to get some sleep if I was going to be awake early enough to call Margaret. I had to tell her I was on the case as soon as I could, and before she hired some other hapless detective.

Perhaps I shouldn't have waited so long.

CHAPTER SIX

MARGARET DIDN'T ANSWER her phone at work after twelve rings but it was then picked up by a woman whose voice I didn't know. I asked for Margaret.

'I'm sorry, sir, she's not here. Can I take a message?'

'Do you know where she is?'

'I believe she's gone home. If you leave your number I can get her to call you when she's back. Is there anyone else who can help?'

I said no and hung up.

I found her home number on the index card she'd given me and tried that next.

No reply at all this time, not even an answer-phone.

Now I was worried. She'd written her address on the index card so I climbed into my Mondeo and programmed it into my GPS.

The day was bright and warmer than it had been for weeks, as though the weather was giving us a taster of the spring and summer to come. The GPS took me out of Crewe and wanted to take me on to the M6 North towards Knutsford. I knew the motorway would be a nightmare at that time of the morning so I went up the A50 instead, through Holmes Chapel, a quieter route that ran parallel to the motorway and was almost as quick.

As we drew closer to Knutsford I started paying attention to the GPS again and it took me right off the main road and into a lane with large red-brick houses set back from their front hedges, steep-roofed and with wide tarmacked drives sweeping into and out of the properties. They looked like executive houses for the financiers and consultants who worked up the way, in Manchester, and I couldn't figure out how someone like Margaret—a secretary or admin assistant—could afford one of these top-of-the-range billets.

The GPS led me to a property that was as big as its neighbours, with a car port attached to one side and a large, quartered window set into the gable above the front door. There was no car under the car port, but there was also a built-in garage so it was possible Margaret was at home with her car safely stowed. The curving drive was edged with flower-beds that were not yet showing much activity. However, some of the bushes lining her fences were greening up and the garden had the sense of being well-tended and I wondered whether the house and environs benefited from Margaret's devotion and attention to detail.

I parked and knocked on the door. There was no reply. I saw a bell-push and when I pressed it I heard it sound further back in the house, but no one answered.

I stepped back and looked up at the window above my head, wondering if I'd see Margaret peering down at me.

But no.

I was considering making my way around to the back when the front door opened at last and she stood there, staring at me. Her hair was not the sleek bob I'd seen that first morning and her make-up, if applied, looked as though it had been scrubbed off. She was even paler than usual, her eyes red in their corners.

She said, 'You heard?'

'Heard what?'

Her shoulders slumped and she stepped back.

'Come inside.'

I passed her and went into a large entrance hall with a wide staircase on one side and a room to my left that looked like a sitting-room. There was a scent of furniture polish in the air, and through another door I saw a gleaming oak table and an upright piano.

Margaret went into the sitting-room and sat down on a deep cream-coloured sofa. She looked up at me as I followed her in.

'Nathan was found dead in a hotel room in Manchester last night. There were two empty bottles of whisky and a syringe.'

I sat facing her and saw that she was crumbling a paper tissue between her hands.

'What was in the syringe?'

'Too soon to say, apparently. Christ, he worked around chemicals all day. Could be anything.'

'Who found him?'

'Room service. Apparently he'd ordered something and after trying three times to deliver, the waiter rang the room, got no answer, so talked to his manager. Eventually they used a pass key and got in.'

'Who told you all this?'

'Jolyon Greif gathered those of us who worked with Nathan together this morning, first thing. That's as much information as the police had told him. They must have contacted his wife and she put them on to someone at work.'

'And you were sent home?'

'I was a mess. They could see I wouldn't be able to work today. I've only been back ten minutes. I've been sitting on this sofa staring into space.'

I looked around the room. There was a television in one corner and a table to the left of the chair I was sitting in. There were family photos—Margaret about ten years younger with a couple of older people either side of her, presumably her parents. Margaret on a horse. Margaret on a beach, again with the parents.

She saw me looking.

'This is their house, my parents. They died together five years ago next month. Car crash. They both worked at AstraZeneca, up the road.'

'They were scientists?'

'More like project managers, administrators. Senior management types. Been there a long time, careful with money.'

'And you didn't follow them, didn't do science?'

'Anything but. I gave up university after one year. I don't do well under exam pressure. So I did secretarial skills instead. Then they died, left me the house and enough money so I don't have to work.'

I'd been wondering how she could have afforded to pay me on an assistant's salary. Now I knew.

'But you do work.'

'I did. I don't think I can go back now.'

I said, 'Were you in love with Nathan?'

Her eyes narrowed.

'That's a cruel thing to say.'

'Is it?'

'You're suggesting I'm upset just because I was in love with him. As it happens, I wasn't. He never looked at me twice and besides, he was much older than me. I've had boyfriends, you know.'

'Okay, I'm sorry. Have the police been in touch yet?'

'No—will they be?'

'I suppose it depends on the autopsy. They might scratch around a bit anyway.'

She lowered her head into her hands.

'God, I feel like shit. You don't think me getting you involved in this had anything to do with him killing himself, do you?'

'How could it? It's unlikely he knew anything about me.'

'I just don't trust Jolyon Greif. Harry Tuck must have had a word with him, because Jolyon asked me lots of questions after you went. How you came to be seeing Nathan, how was it all set up. Why were Hallows sending you along to speak to Nathan and nobody else … I was lying my head off. If he checked up with Natalie over at HR he'll know I was lying.'

I hesitated. I wondered whether I should tell her about the attempted burglary of my house so that she would at least be warned. Instead I changed tack.

'You just mentioned Jolyon Greif. Is he related to the boss of the unit Nathan worked for? Tuck asked me whether I'd seen him.'

It took her a moment to organise her thoughts.

'You mean Stratford Greif, Head of Protocol Development? Well of course he's related. It's not that common a name. It's supposed to be pronounced "Griff" but he's a weird one so everyone calls him "Grief". As you can imagine.'

'They're what—brothers?'

'I don't know. That's what everyone says. Do you think he's involved in this? We don't see him very often. One of those aloof, introvert types. Harry Tuck reports to him, and Jolyon seems to see him a lot, which you'd expect as they're family. Nathan would be dragged in from time to time for a word. And someone told me that some of the younger scientists are favourites. He holds little get-togethers after work. Half a dozen of them have gin and nibbles in his office.'

'A little club.'

'I wouldn't know. I don't care what they get up to.'

She sat up suddenly and turned to look out of the window that was behind her back. We could see my car parked on the tarmac and beyond it the main road into Knutsford. A heavy agricultural machine trundled by, an orange light rotating on its highest point.

She turned back to me.

'What are you doing here anyway? How did you know I'd be home?'

'I didn't. No one at Midwinter would tell me anything. I phoned but you didn't answer, so I took a chance.' Suddenly it didn't seem fair to keep her in the dark. 'Listen, someone tried to burgle me last night.'

'Oh my god!'

'I got home before they managed to take anything. But for me it's all too coincidental. I wanted to tell you that I was going to help you, and Dr Mustow. How that works now I don't know, but I think I should do something.'

'Surely it's too late? What can you do for Nathan now?'

'Nothing practical. But if we could find out whether his suicide was real or faked, that would help, wouldn't it?'

I LEFT HALF an hour later, just as the sunshine decided to take a break and return us to the rainy March we knew so well.

My route took me back through Holmes Chapel, a large and prosperous village in danger of turning into a small town. It was late morning so the traffic had died down.

There was a point where I turned off the main road to circumvent the centre of the village, then took a quick left and then right to get me back on to the A50. This short-cut was known by all the locals because it avoided lengthy traffic-lights in the centre of the village where four roads met.

In the small lane that fed back to the main road there was a severe right-hand bend that went around the edge of a converted barn, then crossed a small river by means of a stone bridge. Once I'd crossed the bridge I stopped the car and reversed it quickly so that it covered the exit from the bridge, which was only a car's width in size.

The black Prius behind me came to a halt as it rounded the bend and saw me there. He idled the engine but didn't reverse.

I climbed quickly from my Mondeo and went up to the driver's window. Mr Bones was driving this time. He lowered the window as I approached.

I said, 'Can I help you?'

'Not much.'

'I'd appreciate it if you stopped following me. I don't take kindly to it.'

'You can do what you want. It's a free country.'

'So I'm free to take your plate number and report it to the cops.'

'Good luck with that. Are you going to move?'

By now another car had turned the corner behind him and was blocking the road. I'd seen Bones notice it in his rear-view mirror.

I said, 'Do you want to step out of your car so we can talk about this face to face?'

'Just get out of the fucking way.'

'Okay, Mr Bones. Don't get all twisted up. Tell Chairman Montgomery I'd like to speak to him. See if you can organise that better than a burglary.'

Now he stared ahead, a muscle playing high in his cheek. His side window went up.

I walked back to my car and drove off. When we reached the main road I turned left towards Crewe and he turned right, back towards Alderley Edge and the safety of Midwinter.

CHAPTER SEVEN

I'VE FOUND THAT once I start a case it tends to move quickly. I hadn't exactly started on this—whatever it turned out to be—but things still moved along at a lick.

I was having a late lunch in my office at home when I saw a dark saloon car coming down my track. It halted and two men got out. One looked to be in his forties, average height, stocky but strong build, with a round but rather cruel face. His partner was younger but taller and more bulky. Muscle. They both wore dark suits over black tee-shirts, like Hollywood bodyguards, and glanced at the trees and the fields surrounding my house as if they didn't know what they were. Eventually satisfied, they moved towards my front door. They made walking look like wading through treacle.

I waited until they knocked. I was enjoying my cheese and tomato sandwich and was in no hurry.

I let them knock again before going to the door. The older of the two men was front and centre. He didn't smile or hold out a hand.

'Mr Montgomery said he'd see you.'

'And who are you?'

'Head of Security, Midwinter Enterprises. This is George.'

'Hi, George. Step back a bit, you're blocking the light.' I looked the older man up and down. 'So you'll be Jolyon Greif. The head honcho. I'm amazed you haven't got square eyes, staring at all those security monitors.'

He didn't seem surprised that I knew his name. He struck me as someone it was very hard to surprise.

He said, 'You wanted to talk to Mr Montgomery. Will you come with us?'

'I'll fetch my tiara. Hang on a sec.'

I closed the door in his face and put on my jacket. I had a roll of coins that I kept in a drawer under the telephone. I slipped it into my trouser pocket and checked that I had my mobile phone with me too.

Fully kitted-out, I opened the door.

'So nice of you to wait. Shall we go? Your car or mine?'

Greif and George had stepped back, one either side of the door like an honour guard. Or a prison convoy.

'Ours is more comfortable.'

They waited until I moved outside, pulling the door shut behind me, then followed me to the back door of their long vehicle.

I said, 'Front or back?'

'Keep it up, smart man. George and I just love clever-dicks, don't we, George?'

George must have considered this to be a rhetorical question because he said nothing and climbed into the driver's seat. I went to the back and Jolyon Greif got in the door on the other side so he was next to me. I half expected a gun barrel to be sticking into my ribs.

George turned the car and we headed out of Crewe again, down past the football ground and then over the railway bridge by the station. I debated offering him directions but thought better of it. Let him find his own way. It was their petrol.

I turned sideways to look at Greif, who was staring at the back of George's head as though it was the most fascinating sight.

I said, 'Must have been tough for you this morning.'

Greif said nothing.

'You being responsible for Security and all, and here you have one of your people found dead in a hotel room. A suicide no less. So it seems. What do you think was going on with him?'

Greif spoke to the back of George's head without looking at me.

'We all knew Nathan had troubles. It's a terrible tragedy.'

'Your thoughts are with his wife?'

'Absolutely.'

I turned to look through my own window at the passing scenery. I'd already seen it twice today, coming and going, but the lot of the private detective is to perform an excess of pointless travelling.

I turned back to Greif, who still hadn't moved. The Cheshire countryside obviously held no charm for him.

I said, 'What were you hoping to get from my house last night?'

'I have no idea what you're talking about.'

'Of course you don't. But if you did, what would it be?'

I saw George's eyes flicker in the rear-view mirror but he didn't say anything. He was one of those who let his muscles do the talking, I guessed. Perhaps he thought I was getting near to the knuckle with his boss and he was trying to warn me not to push too hard.

I said, 'There were these two thugs, see, who I caught breaking into my place. They were quite good but in the end a bit amateurish. Like lads who hadn't done it before. They had the gear to break in, but they didn't know what to do when they got there. Where to look. How to look without being seen. That kind of thing.'

Greif turned his round, cold face towards me.

'Did they get away?'

'Yes, as a matter of fact. They were lucky. I reported it to the police afterwards. Bloodhounds are being primed as we speak.'

He nodded.

'Hope you get the little bastards. Don't know what the world's coming to. Can't trust anyone, can you? People passing themselves off as something they're not. Wheedling their way into your confidence, poking around in your business.'

I nodded back at him, sagely.

And that was the end of the conversation until we arrived at Midwinter. This time the two wooden poles rose at the same time and George drove us around the back of the building I hadn't been inside on my previous trip—the admin block, as Margaret had called it. There was a bay containing half a dozen black cars, including the Prius. George parked next to it and Greif opened his door and got out.

Before he opened his own door, George turned in his seat and poked a large finger at me.

'You talk too much, squire. Very dangerous habit. Can get you into all sorts of trouble.'

'Why, thank you, George. I was beginning to think you were dumb. As in unable to speak, of course.'

I climbed out while he was processing this and joined Greif, who was already walking towards a glass door in the back of the administrative building. A small white camera overhead peered at us as he buzzed us in. A click said the door was unlocked and he pushed it open.

I followed.

MORE HUSHED CORRIDORS, but livelier than the science block. When a door opened you had the sense of real life going on behind it—voices, laughter, the clacking of a printer. We passed a young man and then a young woman, both of whom glanced at Greif with a kind of guilty smile on their faces before squeezing past, papers in hand.

Then we were in a hushed lift, just Greif and I, rising six floors and exiting into a space that was more light and airy than the warrens beneath: high windows on the outward-facing walls, more corporate art on the others; a deep-pile carpet in beige on the floor; a large conference room with glass walls and twelve comfortable leather seats around a wide boardroom table; a secretary of a certain age sitting behind a counter with a high drop so that we could only see the top of her greying head as we approached.

Greif said, 'Is he in, Mary?'

'He's expecting you, Mr Greif. Go straight in.'

Greif went to a door marked with Montgomery's name and knocked on it, then stood back so that I would precede him into the room.

The door was opened by a portly man with a bald head whose picture matched the one I'd seen on the website. So he wasn't a fake from an image library after all.

But I wondered what kind of fake he might be nonetheless.

He stuck out a hand and pumped mine, then looked around me to Jolyon Greif.

'Thanks, Jolyon. Stick around, will you? I'd like a word after I've spoken to Mr Dyke here.'

He ushered me in and offered coffee or tea, which I refused. His office was the size of a smallish ballroom in a Georgian mansion, with a large panoramic window showing green Cheshire countryside and the distant white bowl of the radio telescope at Jodrell Bank. The facing wall was taken up entirely with bookcases, full of actual books, not golf trophies, while the wall behind his desk was filled by a gigantic abstract painting that looked vaguely scientific, a mixture of galaxies and atoms and electron clouds. The furniture was black leather wrapped around curved steel. He gestured towards a chair while taking a seat behind his own desk.

He said, 'Sit down, Mr Dyke, and let's talk.'

I sat. 'What is there to talk about?'

Before he replied he spent a long time looking down at his hands, which I noticed were trembling slightly. I had the impression of someone operating way out of his comfort zone. Although I'd only just met him, he seemed more flushed and red in the eye than the Chairman of a growing enterprise like Midwinter should be.

He said, 'What do you know about Midwinter, Mr Dyke?'

'Everything that your website has to tell me. Which is to say next to nothing. You're a very secretive bunch.'

He seized on this.

'Yes, indeed. Our investors are very keen that their, ah, investment is kept under wraps. Nothing that we do here is potentially harmful or dangerous, I want you to understand that from the beginning. But there are commercial considerations that we simply have to take into account. We can't allow information about our procedures to, ah, escape the building, so to speak.'

'What's this got to do with Nathan Mustow's death?'

He leaned back in his chair as though shocked. Perhaps he was.

'As far as I'm aware, nothing. Are you suggesting there was anything unusual about poor Nathan's suicide?'

'I'm not in a position to suggest anything. But you should know that some people have had suspicions about his state of mental health.'

'You mean Margaret? Yes, we know. She's spoken to one or two people.'

'And you did nothing about it.'

'What could we do? Nathan played a very large part in some of our most important projects. His line manager spoke to him and reported to me that as far as he could tell, everything was fine. Nathan was a little tense because at least three of his projects were coming to fruition at the same time. He had many stakeholders to appease, to, ah, satisfy.'

'This sounds like bullshit.'

'In what way?'

'I don't think you have any idea what your so-called Security people are doing here. Or Harry Tuck. I've only been around the place a couple of days and already my house has been burgled, there's been a suicide of someone I spoke to just yesterday morning and both myself and at least one other person has been followed by that red-headed pencil-neck, Mr Bones. I think you've lost control.'

His anger got the better of him and he stood up. He made to come around the table and then thought better of it and walked to his massive picture windows instead.

'I'm willing to forgive the fact that you came on to our site yesterday on false pretences, as I think Margaret's intentions were, ah, noble. But I'm afraid I can't have you talking about some of the best staff on this campus in that manner.'

'Who said this "Margaret" was the one who got me involved?'

He turned back to me.

'Don't be childish, Mr Dyke. It took very little of Jolyon's time to find that there was no request from Hallows for one of their people to come and interview Nathan yesterday morning. Which left only Nathan himself or Margaret—who placed the appointment in his electronic diary—as culprits. I'm told Nathan knew nothing other than what Margaret had said to him, so we can rule him out, can't we?'

'It appears he ruled himself out.'

'That's very coarse of you.'

'You're right, I'm sorry. I'd forgotten your sensibilities were so refined you'd be more worried about catching and punishing Margaret than finding out what happened to Nathan Mustow.'

His anger apparently under control, he took his seat again, this time leaning over his desk towards me. His ruddy complexion had calmed somewhat and I noticed his eyes were both deep-set and intelligent.

'What can we do, Mr Dyke, when matters are in the hands of the police?'

'You can let me talk to your employees. Give me a free pass to walk around or at least interview some people. Keep Jolyon Greif and Mr Bones and George off my back. And Harry Tuck, for that matter.'

He appeared to be considering it, his eyes roaming over my face.

'I'm afraid that's not possible. You'd require security clearance and a certain amount of procedural training before we could let you just "walk around," as you put it.'

'Then give me a minder. Someone to make sure I don't blow the place up but who doesn't prevent me from talking to whoever I want to.'

He leaned back and took a deep breath.

'As I understand it, private detectives have to keep to a strict code of practice.'

'Well, there are guidelines. We're not licensed yet, but we will be soon.'

'So you'd sign a piece of paper that we drew up for you? A contract?'

'I'm not sure. You're not my client.'

'I see. Who is?'

'I don't have to tell you that.'

He spread his hands. 'Of course not, but I can guess. I tell you what: the most important person here, I think you'll agree, is Isobel Mustow, Nathan's poor wife.'

'Yes. I haven't met her yet.'

'Well, you get her signed permission to investigate her husband's death and I'll see what I can do. I hope you understand that I'm admitting absolutely no liability here. But I want us to be seen to be doing the right thing by Nathan. I don't want any doubts arising as to our involvement or otherwise in his death. And if the coroner rules it to be a suicide, which I'm sure he will, then you'll stop your investigation immediately.'

I stood up and stuck out my hand.

'That sounds like a fair deal.'

He stood too and shook my hand firmly.

'I'll call Mary and get her to organise one of our taxis to take you home.'

BY THE TIME I made it out of Montgomery's office, Mary was already talking to the taxi company and giving them my name. It would take them ten minutes to have someone here.

Jolyon Greif was still waiting, standing in a corner talking to Harry Tuck. I had the impression that they were keeping away from Mary as well as anyone else who might have passed through.

Tuck noticed me and broke off from Greif. The casual golf shirt of the previous day was gone and he was smartly dressed in a pinstripe dark-blue suit, white shirt and a dark tie with some kind of yachting motif patterned on it. I supposed that clients or investors had been on-site.

He came up close, as extroverts do, and looked down at me. His habitual bonhomie seemed to be struggling with his urge to give me a good telling-off.

'Deceptive little oik, aren't you?'

'Sorry if I hurt your feelings.'

He threw back his head and stared at the ceiling as if restraining himself.

'It's not me who was hurt, was it?'

'Are you saying there's a connection between my visit and Mustow's suicide?'

He jabbed a finger in my chest.

'We don't know, do we? And we likely never will. I wouldn't like to be in your shoes if it turns out to be the case. Rum business all around.'

Jolyon Greif had joined us by now. The pair of them gave off a kind of angry musk, as though my presence had provoked a feral response.

Greif said, 'At least we won't be seeing you again. I hate your kind, you know. Grubby little plods, taking a dirty pound just to stick your noses in where they're not welcome.'

I looked from him to Tuck and back again. It was good to savour the moment.

'I've got bad news for you. Montgomery has just agreed to let me on-site to talk to Dr Mustow's colleagues. See if there's anything I can find out, any reason why he would have wanted to kill himself.' I turned to Greif. 'You might have to escort me around while I do some digging.'

There was a pause and the atmosphere cooled several hundred degrees.

Greif said, 'No one will talk to you. They have nothing to hide.'

'Well if they have nothing to hide then there's every reason they *should* talk to me, isn't there?'

'But they won't.'

'We'll see.'

'Yes, we will. I think that's your taxi.'

CHAPTER EIGHT

CHARLES MONTGOMERY WAS not someone who was given to feelings of paranoia. Nor was he a manager who felt that he had to be kept informed of every minor change or development in the functioning of the organisation of which he was the nominal head. But he had often felt that there were people in this organisation who kept things from him, probably for his own good—or so they thought.

After Dyke had left he felt a bitter taste at the back of his mouth and knew that its cause was the fact that he'd been deceived. Dyke was blunt but, Montgomery felt, fundamentally honest. His methods might have been underhand in the first instance, but given that the Security at Midwinter was now the most formidable and zealous that he'd ever witnessed in twenty-five years of executive management, he understood why Dyke—and presumably Margaret—had resorted to sleight-of-hand. Mustow was a good man, and if there was something in Midwinter that needed investigating or ultimately changing, then it would be investigated and, if necessary, changed. His duty was to the investors who had entrusted him with the management of the operation, not to the petty tyrants and power-hungry dictators who felt that their own view of the company was the only one that counted. After all, he was here first. It was still his company.

He switched on his intercom and asked Mary whether Jolyon Greif was still there.

'Yes, sir, and Mr Tuck is with him.'

'Send them in.'

The men knocked and entered a moment later, bringing with them the conspiratorial air that Montgomery had noticed before whenever they had shared a room. It was as though each one had passed their ideas or thoughts through the filter of the other before they actually spoke.

He said, 'So what the hell is going on here? Jolyon, have we heard anything more from the police?'

'Not a thing. They won't tell us anyway. Isobel Mustow will be the first to know if they want to say anything to anyone. Which they won't.'

'So we wait for the, ah, coroner's report? The autopsy?'

'We have no choice.'

'Have we done anything for Isobel?'

'Mary sent some flowers. Natalie in HR has been in touch.'

'I should speak to her.'

Jolyon Greif shook his head.

'We're the last people she wants to speak to. Can I be frank?'

'As you like.'

'Why are you letting Dyke into all this? He's a little toe-rag who shouldn't be truffling around looking for something that he won't find.'

'I don't see that I had much choice. How bad would it have looked if we prevented him from asking a few questions after one of our own killed himself? People would have wondered what we were hiding. Our investors would have been suspicious that we weren't being open. We have to be as open as we can afford to be, given the, ah, circumstances.'

Harry Tuck pushed his hands into his pockets and walked over to the picture windows with a proprietorial air that irritated Montgomery.

'I disagree, Charles. We should keep people like that at arm's length. Let the police do their job. They won't find anything more than a sad tale of a sad man who couldn't handle the pressure. We all knew that. We knew he was close to going AWOL. Losing it. We talked about it, remember?'

'Don't tell me what I remember, Tuck. I rely on you to manage your people, Nathan Mustow included. It seems you singularly failed in that regard. I know you two like to operate like a little in-house mafia to keep your secrets safe from me, and I accept that as part of doing business in an organisation where secrecy is paramount. But please don't think that I don't know what you're doing, and please don't think that I'm not aware of the manner in which you manipulate me to get your own way.'

A grim smile had appeared on Tuck's face, though he hadn't turned away from the view outside the windows. The fading light was beginning to reflect their images back to them and Montgomery turned away from his own reflection, disliking the chubby, balding man that confronted him and didn't mirror the person he felt he really was.

He said, 'We're in a bind here. Nathan's projects are fundamental to our success in the next three months. With him gone I've had to re-jig roles and responsibilities. How is Stratford, by the way? Has he said anything?'

Jolyon Greif said, 'You know him. A grunt. A recalculation. Then let's move on. A minor inconvenience, nothing more.'

'Good. I hoped it wouldn't upset him too much.'

Harry Tuck said, 'Ha! Take more than a death in the family to get Stratford's attention. Nuclear bomb, maybe. Colleague's death, not so much.'

Montgomery realised that he had been standing throughout the conversation and he suddenly felt weary. He went behind his desk and sat down. He badly wanted this day to end.

'Dyke told me his house had been burgled and that Mr Bonetti was following him. What do we know about this?'

The two other men exchanged a glance.

Greif said, 'I don't know anything about the burglary. Coincidence, I'd say. I told Bonetti to check him out after I discovered who he was yesterday. He was probably over-enthusiastic. You know what he's like.'

From the window, Tuck said, 'A terrier. Little rottweiler. Good man to have at your back.'

'But a bad man to have dealing with the general public. Greif, tell him to be more discreet. Dyke has to get permission from Isobel Mustow before he can carry on with his investigation, if that's what we must call it. If he does get her permission I want you—and any of your people who deal with him—to be respectful and honest. At this point, we can't afford to send the wrong signals to anyone who might be watching our, ah, performance. We're already on the back foot. Let's try to keep our guard up until all this dies down and our products come on-stream. Agreed?'

Both men murmured a low-key agreement. Montgomery wondered how long it would be before one or other of them broke his word.

He had no doubt that they would.

I CALLED MARGARET that night to check in and see how she was doing.

She said, 'The police were here. I'm sure they thought Nathan and I were having a rabid affair. They were very insulting, in a quiet way.'

'Take no notice. They're paid to be sceptical.'

'Even when it was obviously a suicide?'

'Do you think it was, in your heart of hearts?'

She paused and I wondered whether it was the first time she'd really considered the option that Mustow might not have ended his own life.

She said, 'Put it this way: given the stress he was under, and given all the other things I told you about his behaviour, should I be surprised? Haven't people killed themselves with less provocation?'

'Maybe. You don't sound convinced.'

'Perhaps I'm not.'

'I have something to ask you. I saw Charles Montgomery today. I persuaded him to let me into Midwinter to poke around a bit. Just fact-finding. I wouldn't tell him who my client was, but he guessed. Do you still want me to do this? I'd have to start charging, though part of me wants to stay on their backs anyway, just to see Tuck and Greif squirm.'

'Yes, do it. They've told me to take some time off, so I don't have to be around. I might not even go back, actually. I think I was only staying on because of Nathan, poor man. He needed looking after.'

I let that go without comment. It was probably best for her state of mind if she didn't pursue that line of thought. If she started feeling sorry for Mustow she might find herself stuck in a pattern of thought she couldn't escape.

Instead I asked if she had Isobel Mustow's phone number, which of course would have been the number for her boss before his demise.

'Why do you need that? Shouldn't you leave her alone?'

'It's one of the conditions set by Montgomery before he'd let me on-site. She has to agree.'

'She'll never do it. She'll want the police to investigate, surely.'

'If the coroner rules it as a genuine suicide, there won't be a police investigation. If I can persuade her to let me ask some questions then maybe I'll find something out.'

'She'll be feeling terrible right now.'

'I agree. And the people she'll be feeling the most terrible about will be Midwinter Enterprises. That's why I have to ask her as soon as possible.'

She gave me the number and shortly afterwards I rang Isobel Mustow.

THE MUSTOW'S HOUSE was a fake-Georgian redbrick demi-mansion ten minutes this side of Wilmslow, the satellite town of Manchester known as a refuge for millionaire footballers and their managers. A two-car garage stood to one side, one of its doors lifted upwards, the boot of a BMW sticking out as though the driver hadn't been able to get the whole length of the car inside. The windows sparkled in the sunlight and the house itself glowed with a kind of serenity that I doubted was a true representation of what was taking place inside.

A thin woman with a gaunt face answered the door, pulling it open only far enough to show that it could quickly be shut if I offended her in any way.

'Mrs Mustow? My name's Sam Dyke. I rang last night.'

The woman looked me up and down as if checking for signs of my bad intentions. Then she stepped outside and pulled the door behind her without closing it.

'Isobel's inside. I'm her sister. I told her this was a bad idea. What are you trying to do, make it all worse for her?'

'I'd rather talk to her if that's okay. I'm not here to do her any harm, I promise you that.'

'How do we know that's true? A private detective? We've seen all about you on the television. Hacked any phones lately?'

I said nothing, letting her anger wane of its own accord.

She stared at me for ten seconds that felt like a minute, then finally turned on her heel and went inside, holding the door open for me.

The hall went straight through to the back of the house, and through the kitchen door I could see beyond, into the greenery of a spring garden. The sunshine outside made the gloom inside worse by contrast.

Isobel's sister turned left off the hall and led me into a room at the rear containing French windows, through which I had yet another view of the garden—a long stretch of lawn, a summer house at the bottom and a wooden gazebo with trailing wisteria—not yet in bloom—draped over its cross-beams. She closed the door behind me and I sat down.

The room itself was comfortably furnished with leather sofas and chairs in the current style, a wooden CD rotating stack to one side of the chimney breast and a Marantz player on the other. No television. A wide bookcase holding several series of books by American crime writers—Pelecanos,

Lehane, Burke, Parker. Music and reading—an introvert's relaxation.

The door opened again and another slim woman stepped into the room. I could see the resemblance to her sister in the bone-structure and, at this time, the haunted look in her eyes. Like her husband, she was in her forties and had an elegance in the turn of her wrist and the length of her neck that made her an ideal match for Wilmslow.

I stood up, shook her limp hand and introduced myself.

'Thank you for seeing me.'

'I hope this won't take long. I have some more people coming. The funeral director. The vicar. Have you ever been through this, Mr Dyke? It's a surreal experience, and one that I wouldn't wish on anyone.'

'I had to organise my father's funeral, but I suppose that's different.'

She nodded and seemed to be contemplating at length the potential differences between the two situations.

She said, 'Did you feel that you'd laid something to rest afterwards? I mean, metaphorically?'

'Not really. It was a case of practicalities. I still missed him, if that's what you mean. Still do.'

'How interesting. Now, how can I help you?'

'Can we sit down?'

'Of course.'

I waited until she'd lowered herself carefully on to an armchair, smoothing her skirt beneath her knees, and then I took my seat again. She was wearing a chocolate brown blouse beneath a black jersey and had found time to match her small round ear-rings to the simple necklace and its heart motif that hung from her slim neck. I guessed at times like this the habit of careful accessorising was a useful distraction.

I had to be careful how I got into this because I didn't want to land Margaret in any more trouble.

I said, 'As you know, I'm a private investigator. I've done a lot of work for government agencies, so I wouldn't want you to think I'm one of those people you've probably seen on the television, doing unsavoury things for newspapers. I'd like to think I'm more ethical than that.'

'Wouldn't we all?'

'Indeed. Now I've spoken to Charles Montgomery at Midwinter, and he would like me to carry out an investigation at the offices, just to find out what might have been troubling your husband at the time of his death.'

Isobel Mustow folded her hands on her lap and shifted her eyes from my face to look through the French windows into her garden.

'And does he—or do you—believe that the source of Nathan's troubles lies in his work?'

'Of course it's too soon for me to say. Did the police mention whether Nathan left a note?'

'No, nothing was said about that.'

'Has there been any suggestion as to why he was in that hotel? Was it work-related?'

'Am I part of your investigation, Mr Dyke? Has it started so soon?'

'I'm sorry. The police won't talk to me about the case. I was just wondering whether there was anything I should know.'

'They have told me precisely nothing except the bare facts. That's what they deal in, I suppose.'

'I take it there'll be a coroner's inquest.'

'So I've been advised. I don't know why I'm seeing the funeral director today because I have no idea when the funeral might be. I have to wait until I'm told. The same for the vicar. We're all in limbo, Mr Dyke.'

'So do you have any objections to me carrying out an investigation? Do I have your agreement?'

She coughed slightly and shifted her position on the chair. Her eyes came back to meet mine.

'You can do whatever you wish, Mr Dyke. I have nothing but contempt for Midwinter Enterprises, Charles Montgomery and all of the Greifs that work in that viper's den. In the last eighteen months I watched my husband change from someone who enjoyed his life, enjoyed his work and enjoyed whatever spare time he had left to spend with me. He changed into someone whom I barely recognised. He didn't eat well. He didn't sleep well. He spent more time at the office than any sane man should. So if you by chance find any evidence that Midwinter or any of its senior management is responsible for my husband wishing to end his life, you have my blessing to do what you see fit.'

There was a pause while we both considered what she'd just said. I had opened my mouth to ask a question when she continued.

'In fact, I'd like to thank you, Mr Dyke.'

'For what?

'After I received your phone call last night, I started thinking. I had been singularly unimpressed by the policemen who'd been to see me, especially in respect of their thoughts about the suicide itself. I decided that I should take action myself, so I have recruited a private investigator of my own. That's another of my meetings this afternoon.'

I felt my temperature rise, usually a bad sign. Working with someone else on this would only complicate matters as far as I was concerned.

I said, 'I'd worry that we might get in each other's way. I mean, if there are two of us working on this.'

'Please, I'll ask you to set aside any professional jealousies you might have. I'd like you to work together if it becomes necessary. Those are my rules.'

'I understand that. Will this other investigator know these rules, too?'

'I'll make them clear.'

'Of course you must do as you like. Does this other person know about me yet?'

'Yes. We'll talk more about that this afternoon, now I know what your objectives are.'

'I see. Then I have another question for you.'

'This must be your last. I have things to do.'

'You mentioned that Nathan started to change eighteen months ago. What happened then?'

'I might have the time-scale a little wrong, but it's close enough. Nathan started to become stressed shortly after the management at Midwinter installed another head of the research unit. He came trailing lots of glory and, I understand, had built an extraordinary reputation. Which corporations always like, next to any funding he might have brought.'

'This would be Greif?'

'Indeed, Stratford Greif. I'm sure you'll come across him in your investigation. An odious specimen who adopts the pose of the intellectual shrinking violet in public. But whatever you do, don't turn your back on him. You might later find it peppered with knives. Or worse.'

'Thanks for the warning.'

'One more thing.'

I had risen to leave. 'Yes?'

'As I seem to be issuing warnings, watch out for The Bleak.'

'I beg your pardon?'

'You'll hear people talking about it as though it's an after-hours club. It's not. In fact, I believe it was the source of Nathan's misery for the whole of the last year. I can say no more because I know no more.'

'The Bleak? As in the bleak midwinter … frosty wind made moan—the song?'

'Yes, just a bit of fun. A jokey pun on the company name. That's what they'd like you to believe. Don't.'

CHAPTER NINE

THE FOLLOWING MORNING, Friday, I confirmed with Montgomery that Mrs Mustow had given her approval for my engagement, and on Monday morning I turned up at Midwinter's gates, showed the signed note from Isobel Mustow and my Health and Safety pass to the ladies in Reception, and was then escorted into the Admin block by Natalie, the head of Human Resources.

On the walk up the pathway to her offices, I said, 'Thanks for organising this at such short notice. It must have been a pain. I appreciate it.'

She was a brisk professional woman in her early thirties who had showed no sign of irritation or anything else when I'd spoken to her on the phone. She would have had very little time to arrange the interviews but hadn't complained. If Chairman Montgomery wanted it, she delivered—that was the unspoken message.

'We've organised them into one-hour sessions. A couple in the morning, then a lunch break and another couple in the afternoon. If anyone can't make it we've arranged back-ups. There's a machine in the room so you can make yourself tea or coffee when you want.'

'Am I going to have a chaperone?'

She smiled. 'Not necessary. You can't get in anywhere you're not supposed to. Your pass will get you into the toilets and the canteen. Anything else, give me a buzz.'

She showed me into a room that contained a six-seat table, a white dry-marker board, a cupboard containing stationery supplies and the aforementioned hot-drinks dispenser. An octopus-shaped conference telephone squatted on the centre of the table until I snaked it out and put it on the window-sill.

My first interview came in. He was a man in his mid-twenties called Preston. He didn't take a seat immediately but poured himself a drink into a brown plastic cup, then took off his blue lab coat before pulling out one of the aluminium-framed seats to perch on.

I introduced myself and said that in light of Dr Mustow's suicide, I'd been called in by the management to see if there was anything in his working environment that might have contributed to his taking his own life.

'So you're what, some kind of HR consultant? Specialist subject—death?'

He grinned at me as though I'd also see the funny side of my job.

With as much gravitas as I could muster, I said, 'I'm an investigator. Management takes this very seriously.'

He leaned back, cup in hand.

'Oh, I know, I know. We've had the pep talk. I've given my ten quid for the flowers. But life goes on, you know?'

'Did you know Dr Mustow? Have any dealings with him?'

'Of course. He was my boss.'

This caught me by surprise. I expected this level of callousness only from people who hadn't known him.

'So you saw him on a daily basis?'

'More or less.'

'Did he seem … depressed, or different in the last few days?'

'If you want psychology, Mr Dyke, you've come to the wrong department. I'm fluid mechanics. I didn't notice any difference in him, but then I wouldn't. I don't notice the difference in anyone. And I tell you something else,' —he leaned forward portentously— 'you won't find anyone else here who does, either.'

He leaned back, as though he'd taught me a lesson.

I said, 'Don't you think that's a little cruel?'

He shrugged. 'Nathan was all right. As a boss. But he wasn't my best friend or anything. We're here to do a job, to get results, to make the darling investors happy. This is a community of scientists. You won't find a more rational body of people within a radius of a couple of hundred miles. But we're like jackals. We leave our dead behind. No pun intended.'

'Jackals are actually very sociable animals who look after each other.'

'Really? Is that true?'

I had no idea, so I just shrugged meaningfully, as though my expertise in that area shouldn't be questioned.

I said, 'So he was all right as a boss. What did that mean? How did he act towards you?'

Preston sighed and looked at the ceiling as though trying to dredge up a significant memory.

'He was sweetness and light. He never shouted at you, never found fault with your work. He got in earlier and stayed longer than any of us.'

'Other people have said he seemed stressed recently. What did you make of that?'

'I have no idea what stress is. I think it's something older people get when they're losing it.'

'Don't you believe it's a medical condition?'

'Who knows? They haven't found a stress gene, have they? It's all in the mind. You have to be strong in this day and age.' He leaned forward. 'My view is that stress is for people who can't solve the problems they create for themselves. It's a sign of mental weakness, in my view.'

'You're a man with a lot of views.'

He threw up his hands.

'I'm entitled to my opinions. I'm as well-read as the next man. Except in the stress literature, obviously.'

He grinned and I wanted to punch him. I'd been having that reaction a lot lately. Perhaps I was stressed.

The rest of the interview was equally meaningless. Preston avoided answering any questions that might have involved revealing an emotion or any signs of sensitivity, preferring to talk about his project and his timeline and his milestones. I had the impression that Mustow's death and the subsequent disruption was nothing more than an irritation, a disturbance in the space-time continuum that surrounded his project.

Forty-five minutes later we shook hands and he left. I would swear I heard him whistling as he walked down the corridor.

THE SECOND INTERVIEW was with a woman named Harcourt. She was average in height, had mid-length brown hair, wore spectacles with the designer's name written on one of the arms, and was almost as intransigent as Preston. If I'd expected a little more compassion or fellow-feeling from a woman, I was wrong.

I began to wonder whether I'd walked through a magical mirror into Stepford, where all individual thoughts and ideas were strangled at birth.

'Nathan was *all right*, but he didn't really relate to the rest of us. Know what I mean?'

'No, explain it to me.'

'He was older. He was married. He didn't do any fun things. Hated team-building activities … or even just having fun.'

'Was he always like that? Or was it something that grew over time?'

'I've only been here twelve months. How would I know?'

'Didn't you talk amongst yourselves? Everyone talks about their boss. I did.'

She seemed to feign a casual lack of interest.

'Nah, not really. We're too busy. Stratford drives us hard.'

'Did he drive Nathan hard, too?'

She thought about this for a while.

'I can't really say. I didn't see so much of him. Just filed a progress report every week. Then a bunch of us would talk it over with Stratford. Nathan didn't come to those meetings.'

'He was your boss. They're his projects. But you say he didn't come to project meetings?'

'To be honest, I'm not sure Stratford wanted him there. He could be a real killjoy. Stratford pushes us but he's motivational. You wants you to do your best work for him.

With Nathan it was ticking a box so that he could show we were on track. It didn't seem important to him.'

'And it does to Stratford?'

'Oh, absolutely. The most important thing in the world is to finish his project on time.'

AT LUNCHTIME NATALIE directed me towards the canteen on the ground floor. It was exactly as I'd expected, a catered set-up in an echoing room where plastic tables and chairs skittered across the floor and young women in pale blue uniforms and little peaked caps stood behind counters with fixed smiles.

I chose a goulash and a baked potato, took a yoghurt for dessert and an orange smoothie to wash it all down with. It cost next to nothing because of Midwinter's subsidy. I wished I'd bought more.

I saw the two members of staff that I'd spoken to earlier sitting at a table with four other blue-coated young people, huddling over and probably talking about the weird consultant they'd met that morning. Preston even lifted his fork in my direction in a kind of ironic salute. How he managed to invest a fork with irony, I don't know. Probably years of practice.

I'd almost finished when the chair opposite was pulled back and Harry Tuck sat down facing me. He wore the large smile I'd seen him using before—the one that told you he was being insincere.

He pointed at my empty plate.

'Enjoy that, did you?'

'Very nice.'

He nodded, the smile widening.

'Don't get too used to it. Chances are you won't be eating here often.'

'If you say so.'

'Oh, I do.' He leaned forward, his eyes glittering. 'What do you think you're going to find, exactly? What do you think people are going to tell you?'

'I won't know until they tell me. That's the way it is in this game. One minute complete ignorance, the next, enlightenment. Private detection is almost a spiritual act.'

'Is that right? So you're prone to religious conversions, seeing the light, that kind of thing.'

'A seeker after truth, me. I might even meditate if the mood's right.' Now I leaned forward. 'Tell me, Mr Tuck. What exactly are these conversations about? Are you trying to intimidate me or put me off? What are you so frightened of? Because I have to tell you, they're having exactly the opposite effect to what you probably think. You should take a leaf out of your staff members' book.'

'What do you mean?'

'They're so laid-back they're almost flat out. They think they rule the universe through cool. I think you should take lessons. Get some of whatever Stratford Greif is giving them.'

As I hoped he would, he tensed.

'Why do you bring him into it? What have they said?'

'It'll be in my report. You'll have to wait and see whether Charles Montgomery lets you read it.'

'Of course he'll bloody well let me read it ...'

'Good for you. Tell me, were you in the forces? Army? Air force?'

He frowned. 'No, why?'

'Your manner. Very brusque. Matter-of-fact. I just wondered.'

'My father. Died in the Falklands.'

'Sorry to hear that. Must have been hard for a youngster.'

He shook his head. 'I don't need your bleeding-heart sympathy, Dyke. I hardly knew him anyway. Just another stranger who stayed in the house from time to time.'

He caught himself as though he'd revealed something private. He slapped the table with his hand and stood up.

'Enjoy your yoghurt. I like the strawberry ones myself. Tell you what, why don't you just let the police do their jobs and forget all this stuff, all this whining? Isobel Mustow needs that poker taking out of her arse and I don't think you're doing her any favours by raking up work issues.'

'Are there work issues?'

'I was speaking hypothetically. That's what I do, Dyke. I work on hypotheses. And I hypothesise that you won't be doing much more of this investigating lark. Have a nice afternoon.'

He walked away, stopping abruptly at another table to have a chat with a couple of people who stared up at him with round eyes, as though he was about to eat them.

CHAPTER TEN

SHE HAD ENDURED the day as best she could, but all of the conversations were beginning to take a toll. Although Sarah had taken some of the weight from her shoulders, Isobel found herself longing for the comfort of her bed, the isolation of her bedroom and the tranquillity of sleep. Since Nathan had died she'd found it difficult to grieve openly — she knew that would come, probably at the funeral — but it seemed to have left her exhausted by the slightest exertion. At least the next phone call would be the last before she could take herself off and leave her sister downstairs to watch television or telephone her own husband.

When the phone rang she felt herself jump slightly. She had become sensitive to abrupt noises in the last two days, like a cat that had been mistreated when young. All of her own fears and suspicions seemed translated into aggressive physical sensations, to the point where ordinary light almost hurt her eyes.

'Isobel Mustow.'

'Hello, Mrs Mustow. We agreed that I should call you now, if you remember. I'm sorry I couldn't get there in person.'

'That's quite all right. I'm not sure I could have handled another person in the house today.'

'I'm sure it's been dreadful for you.'

Isobel was soothed by the detective's voice, which was authoritative and calm.

She said, 'I outlined the circumstances this morning, on our first call. Now you've had time to think about it, is it something you think you can help with?'

'Yes, of course. I'll send you a contract in the post outlining our respective roles and responsibilities. I'll attach my bank details and you can make the deposit on-line, if that's all right.'

'I can do that. I have to tell you something else.'

'Yes?'

'It appears that there's another investigator involved. I'm not sure who he's working for, but I understand he's investigating Nathan's colleagues and staff. I believe that Charles Montgomery is covering himself—making certain that no blame can be laid at his door.'

'What would you like me to do?'

Isobel sighed and found herself looking into her garden. It was so lovely at this time of year, when things were just beginning to bud. Just beginning to show signs of growth. She would really have liked to spend time out there, but it seemed so selfish, given everything that had to be done for Nathan's funeral …

'Mrs Mustow?'

'Ah, yes, I'm sorry. I was just thinking.'

'What would you like me to do about this other investigator?'

'I would like you to work with him. His name is Sam Dyke. He seemed very competent, if a bit … masculine.'

'He might resent me working with him. Given the circumstances.'

'I don't care whether he does or doesn't. He's only being allowed to talk to Nathan's people under my sufferance. If I withdraw it, then his investigation ends.'

'I see. What else can you tell me about Dyke?'

Isobel described him and sensed that the other detective was making notes.

'Did you happen to notice what car he was driving?'

'I don't know cars. It was a dark maroon colour and seemed a little dirty. It was quite long, not a sports model or a hatchback. Is that enough?'

'I'm sure it is. I should be able to find him if he's hovering around Midwinter and its crew.'

'Yes. Tell me, how long do you think you'll need for your own investigation? How long do these things usually take?'

'There's no such thing as "usually," Mrs Mustow. I'll probably be doing the same kind of work as this Dyke character—trying to talk to people where I can, see what the company is doing, a bit of on-line research. Maybe follow some of the senior people to see how they spend their time.'

'What do you learn from that kind of behaviour?'

'Quite frankly, I don't know. It all depends on the subjects. If it's your belief that Dr Mustow was being pressurised above and beyond what his job required, leading to his suicide, then it may be that there are external pressures playing on Charles Montgomery and the other senior people too. Investors may have a part to play. But given the nature of the work as you've described it, maybe there's something else. Government agency involvement, perhaps, from the UK or America.'

'That hardly seems likely.'

'But we can't rule out anything. This kind of hi-tech research is big business now, Mrs Mustow. There are potentially millions riding on the decisions made inside small offices in remote research facilities. Fortunes can be made and lost.'

'And lives?'

'And lives. Definitely.'

Isobel pondered that for a while after she hung up. Since marrying Nathan all those years ago she had felt herself become more and more withdrawn and—there was no doubt—less open to experiencing new things. Nathan's work had often taken him away but she hadn't compensated by finding new friends or groups of people with whom she could relax or 'be herself,' whoever that was. Now that he was gone she wondered whether she'd go back to Suffolk, back to the family farm still run by her sister and her husband. But she'd escaped it once and didn't relish returning.

What she did know—and surprised herself by knowing it—was that she wanted the people at Midwinter to suffer. Nathan had been the centre of her world for so many years and now he was gone. Someone would have to pay for that or she would never have any peace.

IN THE AFTERNOON I met two more people from Mustow's team. The idea was that today I'd see people who worked for him and the next day I'd meet his peers and colleagues.

The afternoon couple turned up at the same time but I sent one away—a young man who looked like a surfer: streaked blond hair, good tan, carried himself easily. I told him I preferred to see people on an individual basis.

He shrugged and said, 'No probs. Catch you later.'

The man who stayed was perhaps a little older than the others I'd seen so far. He was somewhere in his late twenties, had an open face and seemed respectful. His name was Jones.

It soon became apparent that as with the morning interviewees, I wouldn't get anything useful from him. He answered my questions but offered nothing extra, no insight, no additional details. For a scientist he seemed incurious about what his boss might have been thinking or feeling, as though it was such an unknown territory there was no point enquiring. I began to wonder whether I was completely wasting my time even talking to these people. It seemed that Nathan Mustow had been no more than an incidental figure in their lives.

Then he said something that made me sit up.

'Of course, Nathan never came to any of the after-hours meetings. He didn't seem interested in us or The Bleak at all.'

I tried to appear blasé and only casually interested.

'What did he have against The Bleak?'

'He didn't connect with any of its ideals. Stratford said that he was too set in his ways to understand what we were trying to achieve.'

'Explain it to me, if you would, so I'm clear.'

He turned a pen end over end between his fingers.

'It's nothing earth-shattering. We recognise that there's a very special group of people here. Yes, we're clever by most standards. But we're also committed to the improvement of our society. So we've just formalised that commitment, made a little club, if you like.'

'And what does the club do?'

He burst out laughing.

'Drink, mostly. Stratford's got this amazing stuff that he has imported from France. Not wine as such, some kind of *eau de vie*, you know? Takes your head off.'

'So The Bleak gets together after hours, drinks and talks about how to improve society? Is that it?'

'More or less.'

'So why wouldn't Dr Mustow get involved?'

He shrugged.

'We guessed it was because he was married—Isobel was a bit strait-laced. He wouldn't want to arrive home rolling drunk at midnight.'

'So it wasn't because he disagreed with your "ideals"?'

'Why should he? Who wouldn't want to improve society if he could?'

AFTER JONES HAD left I made a few notes prior to the surfer re-appearing for his interview. I'd just finished when the door opened and an older man came in. He was dressed in navy-blue trousers under a black jacket with a nehru collar that was buttoned up over a white shirt, making him appear a little like a priest. He was slim, nearly six feet tall and had dark eyes that, I soon noticed, rarely blinked. He closed the door gently and stood with his hands folded before him, an expression of calm enquiry on his face. He was probably in his mid-forties, though his hair was so black it almost seemed blue. I suspected he'd given it a little chemical attention. When he spoke his voice was quiet but deep.

'I'm Stratford Greif. I sent Kenneth away. I'm here to take his place. Does that suit?'

I felt I should stand up, so I walked around the desk to shake his hand. He offered it up limply, then moved to the chair the furthest away from my own—one that was at the opposite end of the conference table—giving him the air of someone who was in charge, notwithstanding his role as interviewee. He folded himself carefully into the chair and sat upright, his elbows on the table.

He said, 'I admit I'm not entirely sure why you're here, Mr Dyke. I thought in circumstances like these, I mean suicides, it automatically becomes a police matter.'

'It depends on how things look. They try hard to find reasons why it might not be a suicide, see if anything's being covered up or hidden. I won't be interfering in any way with what they do. But after talking to Charles Montgomery he seemed keen to know whether there was anything that Midwinter could have done differently. Anything to spot the signs that Dr Mustow wasn't happy.'

Greif spread his hands.

'He only had to ask me. I could have told him, and you.'

'Told us what?'

'That poor Nathan wasn't coping particularly well with the pressure. Mr Tuck and I were in constant communication about him, trying to assess whether we should intervene.'

'And did you?'

'Not sufficiently, it seems. Mr Tuck tried to keep on top of the situation but we were of course nonplussed when we found out he'd taken his own life. Such a waste.' He added, 'We're not entirely certain that your visit here under false pretences didn't increase the pressure he felt. Are you aware of that?'

This was interesting. I felt my pulse-rate quicken.

'I'm not sure I take your meaning.'

He leaned back and crossed his legs, though his eyes never left me.

'Suicide isn't that rare, you know. Research shows us that more people die globally through suicide than through war and murder put together. And people in Nathan's age range are at particular risk.'

'What's that got to do with me and my visit?'

'It's also been shown that when someone has, shall we say, a degree of mental instability, then one culminating incident can push them over the top.'

'Was Mustow mentally unstable?'

'He'd been exhibiting some of the signs of schizophrenia for several months. Hallucinations, delusions, changes in his behaviour.'

'That's not the story I had from his wife.'

'Isn't it true that our partners see what they want to see and ignore the rest?'

I pretended to write a note to give myself some time. Greif's confident analysis of Mustow's mental condition seemed to me as much a delusion as anything that Mustow himself might have experienced.

I said, 'If you or your colleagues had been witnessing this breakdown in his behaviour for so long, why didn't you get him some help? Call in HR? A counsellor?'

'It's a fine line, Mr Dyke. He was still functioning pretty well in his role and to be honest, we needed his expertise. He had three projects under his wing that we couldn't afford to leave without a lead scientist in place.'

'Which is the situation you find yourselves in now.'

'Acknowledged. But we had two months' more work out of Nathan than we might have had.'

'You mean, you managed to squeeze more value out of him before he killed himself.'

'That's a cruel way of putting it, but yes.'

His voice throughout our conversation had barely been raised above the volume required for it to cross the table to me. His eyes had scarcely blinked. His body language was still, almost catatonic.

I said, 'What's The Bleak for?'

For once, a flicker in one eye. He cleared his throat, though even that sound was quiet and unaggressive, as if he didn't want to trouble the atmosphere with a minor disturbance.

He said, 'You may have noticed the people who work here are young. It's one of the criteria we have. Young minds are curious and not burdened by an excessive devotion to how things have been done in the past. They will try things that older minds dismiss as impractical. We cherish that, Mr Dyke. We delight in intelligence and its ability not only to solve existing problems, but to find new problems to tackle. Do you know there are several forms of intelligence? A man called Gardner proposed that there are nine different types, including visual-spatial, verbal-linguistic, interpersonal, musical and so on. We want our people to be high-functioning in as many of these intelligences as possible, and that means that we have to give them the opportunity to practise and develop along those spectra. Another theory of intelligence suggests that there is a core intelligence that enables an individual who is high-scoring on that dimension to excel in a variety of fields. In other words, if you're bright in one field, you're likely to be bright in another, too. The Bleak is an attempt to harness and harvest the products of these intelligences, to enable our people to share their ideas, their thoughts, their insights. I admit it's fuelled somewhat by the addition of relaxants like alcohol, but its aim is to allow our people to be the best possible thinkers they can be. We will benefit from their development—but of course so will they.'

'It's a drinking club for smart-arses.'

Now he smiled, thinly.

'That's a very narrow view, if I may say so. I expected more from you. I understand you've done very good work so I'm disappointed to hear you talk like that.'

'I'm sorry I disappoint you. But you do realise that this so-called club sounds like the worst kind of high-handed, self-serving nonsense?'

'I'm not sure you're seeing it correctly. It's a lot more casual than you're implying. For example, myself and Jolyon will sometimes bring along our guitars and sing songs. Hardly self-serving.'

'Unless you sell CDs afterwards.'

He didn't crack a smile this time. Obviously he limited himself to one expression every ten minutes.

'Despite what I just said, we do take our role in society very seriously, Mr Dyke. Not everyone is fortunate enough to be gifted with intelligence sufficient to effect a change in the world.'

'Is that your intention?'

'Who knows? I would only say that we see it as an obligation, a duty of care, if you like.'

'And do all members of The Bleak think this way?'

'I would like to believe so.'

'Then I'd suggest it's not only because they're bright and have a burning obligation to help mankind — but that you're involving them very early in their careers in a like-minded group and they'll adopt the manner and behaviour of their leader. That is, you.'

'If you say so.'

'I've worked in institutions, Mr Greif. I know what peer pressure is like. And I know what it's like to want to belong, to be part of the group that will have you.'

'Psychologists call it being part of an in-group.'

'Psychologists have a word for everything.'

'Indeed they do. It helps them organise the world into a form that makes sense for them. Because like the rest of us they're probably appalled by the random nature of life and the living and wish to impose some order on it, even if it's only through the naming of parts.'

'And do you want to impose some order on life and the living?'

He spread his hands out again, as he had done at the beginning of the interview.

'I might see it as an obligation, but I don't feel it as a necessity. Life and the living can look after themselves very well without my intervention.'

He stood up and went to the coffee machine, put in a little pouch, pressed a button and waited for it to complete its cycle. He brought his plastic cup back to the table.

'Tell me, Mr Dyke, what do you believe?'

'What do you mean?'

'What motivates you on a daily basis? We all have something that lies deep inside us and drives our actions. What's yours?'

'I'm paid by clients to find out the truth for them.'

'Ah, the truth. And are you successful?'

'I make a living.'

'You see, I don't believe there's one truth. Or I should say that it's likely your truth is not the same as my truth. We might both be searching for something, and we both call it "the truth". But it's not one thing. It varies. It's malleable. You wouldn't recognise mine and vice versa.'

'So what's your version of the truth?'

He sipped his coffee, then frowned at it. 'That is truly disgusting stuff. My truth is that we all have potential that we usually fail to achieve. This world is a great deadener, don't you agree? It conspires to keep us in place and kill our aspirations and our better selves. My truth is that we can all do better, and be better. Despite the influence of the society and culture that surrounds us.'

I stared at him. 'What are we doing here, Greif?'

'Having a conversation. Getting the measure of each other.'

'And what are you concluding?'

'That you're no match for us intellectually, despite some native cunning.'

Until that point I hadn't realised that he and I were actually engaged in a competition. Then I saw that we were. And that he didn't seem worried at all.

CHAPTER ELEVEN

WHEN GREIF LEFT it was late afternoon and I had no stomach for any further cagey conversations with people who thought they were more intelligent than the rest of us. Especially me.

I told Natalie that I wanted to leave and she escorted me out of the building and down to Reception, where I handed in my clip-on badge, then walked around to the Visitors' car park and waited.

Ninety minutes later I saw Harry Tuck walking to the employees' car park and a couple of minutes after that his white BMW slid past me. He passed through the first Security pole, which was already raised, then paused at the lodge and had a word with the guard, who laughed at something he said before going back inside to raise the second pole. I was close behind at this point but didn't merit a joke with the guard so the poles went up quickly enough for me to keep track of Tuck's direction.

He went north, towards Manchester, and fifty minutes later we were in the streets behind Christie's hospital, slowly working our way through the rush-hour traffic. His car was easy to follow but I wasn't worried about him seeing me behind him. In fact, I wanted him to know I was there.

He eventually turned into one of the hundreds of 1930s semi-detached houses that cluster together in that area of south Manchester. He had a short driveway leading to a garage, but he parked on the driveway and climbed out, glancing over his shoulder at me as he did so.

After a few minutes he appeared inside one of the bay windows looking out at me, talking on a mobile phone.

Half an hour later, changed into black jeans and a zip-up fleece, he came out of his house, reversed the car out of his drive and drove off quickly without so much as glancing in my direction.

Now we were getting somewhere.

THIS TIME WE drove south for about twenty minutes, heading towards the golf club that ran close by the M60. It was too early in the year and too late in the day for a round of golf, so I guessed Tuck was heading somewhere else. He turned off the main thoroughfare and took us along Dene Road, a normal-seeming suburban street which eventually narrowed and became an upscale residential area where many of the houses were equipped with electronic gates. He turned into the drive of a house that looked as though it had been renovated as a faux-Mexican ranch house—white square pillars and brilliant white walls—but was also festooned with quartered fake-Georgian windows and a two-car garage.

I knew from a list I'd acquired from Margaret that this was Jolyon Greif's house, and parked in the forecourt was

Stratford Greif's Bentley Continental Flying Spur. I'd arrived early at Midwinter and watched them all arrive and taken note of their rides. It was an easy win. I could have asked Natalie but I doubt she'd have told me.

This turned into a long meeting. None of the men had wives so there was no urge for them to go home, I supposed. Maybe they were playing pool in one of Jolyon Greif's many rooms. Perhaps they were watching French films on a wide-screen TV. Or perhaps they were talking about little old me, sitting outside in a car watching them.

They must have found themselves in a bind. They would know that I had absolutely no evidence of any wrong-doing by any of them. And yet I was suspicious of them all, largely because they'd acted suspiciously. They couldn't exactly call me off because that would be Charles Montgomery's say-so. And at the same time they had to show respect to Nathan Mustow and his widow, proving to the world that there were no problems at Midwinter that might have driven him to his early grave.

Stratford Greif was definitely the coolest customer amongst them, but I hoped the strain would be getting to him. That was all I was doing—showing them that I was around, that I didn't take them at face value. That there were doubts …

At a quarter to eleven, Harry Tuck came out of Jolyon's front door, turned his car in the driveway and accelerated away. I followed him at a distance.

CHAPTER TWELVE

IF ASKED TO describe himself, Jolyon Greif wouldn't have used adjectives detailing his height, weight, hair- or eye-colour. He'd have thought of those personal qualities that, to him, were more important: loyalty, commitment, persistence and, perhaps, cunning. Since leaving the Greater Manchester Police Serious Crime Division a couple of years ago he'd found those qualities less useful. Nowadays he was asked to be nothing more than a silent partner while Stratford and his people went about their business.

He was okay with that because he approved of their objectives. Police work had proved to him that changing hearts and minds needed a concerted effort, and that arguing the toss wasn't effective—what changed people's minds was direct, clear and focused action. Stratford and his group were smart, and they were smart enough to know that all their intelligence wouldn't win the argument. They had to use demonstrations of their ideas, not write letters to the papers.

His job was to keep them secure and intact until they were ready to start operating.

So when Harry Tuck left via the front door, Jolyon slipped out of the back, duck-walked to his own car to keep below the height of the fence, and watched as Dyke started up and followed Tuck home. It was late and traffic had eased off so it was easy to follow Dyke, especially as Jolyon knew the route that Tuck would take.

He had known people like Dyke while working in the job. They were mostly scurrilous ex-army types who couldn't find anything else to do with their worthless lives. Or they were accountants, never happier than when sitting in front of a spreadsheet adding up columns of figures to see who'd defrauded whom. None of them had what he would call a purpose, a reason for waking up each morning. As far as he was concerned, getting paid for strolling through someone's love-life or financial transactions wasn't work for a grown man.

They turned into Tuck's street and Tuck pulled on to his drive. Dyke parked further down the road and Jolyon drew to a halt himself, a hundred yards further back. He saw Dyke's courtesy light come on. He was probably writing something in a notebook, or perhaps grubbing around looking for a sandwich.

He thought back to what he and Stratford and Tuck had discussed earlier that night: ways of disincentivising Dyke. They hadn't been able to persuade Charles Montgomery to discontinue Dyke's work at the office—he was too caught up in the public relations angle, what people would think. But they needed to persuade Dyke that it wasn't worth his effort to keep turning up and getting nowhere with his questions.

Jolyon had persuaded the others that men like Dyke only understood one level of conversation—threat. Subtlety or appeals to reason didn't work with stubborn men, as he knew himself. You had to show an intent that was much more … committed than the simple nosiness of a paid-for grubber.

His phone rang.

'Can you see him outside my house?' Tuck's voice was still irritated, as it had been all evening.

'I've got him. He's not doing anything. He's just showing us his dick. It's long and wide.'

'I don't need that kind of language, Greif. Just see that this nonsense stops.'

'Sorry if I offended your sensibilities. Just stick to the plan we worked on. He'll get the message quick enough.'

'Or your name's not Mac the Knife?'

'Something like that. Go to bed. Rest your weary brain. Turn up tomorrow and let be what will be.'

Tuck hung up. Jolyon went over the conversation in his head. He amazed himself with his own turn of phrase from time to time and liked to re-live them, smiling slightly at his own eloquence. He particularly liked the dick comment.

His phone rang again. This time it was Stratford.

'I think I've been followed.'

'Not by Dyke. I'm looking at him.'

'I don't care. When I left your place I saw a pink something-or-other slip out of the parked cars behind me. It stayed with me all the way home. When I got back it drove slowly past my house, then parked down the road.'

'Is it still there?'

'Stayed ten minutes after I turned the lights out, then went. I hope you're handling this. We're too close to fail now.'

Jolyon pushed down his temper.

'It might have been coincidence. As far as we know there's only Dyke on the case. He's never worked with anyone before and there's no reason to believe that's changed. Go to sleep. We'll talk tomorrow.'

'We may have to broaden what we talked about tonight. I can't be having this.'

'We'll talk tomorrow.'

He hung up and threw his phone on to the passenger seat, where it bounced once and then fell to the floor. He left it.

He stared again at Tuck's house, where all the lights were now switched off. Dyke seemed settled in for the night, though Jolyon couldn't imagine what he hoped to learn from watching a dark house.

He started his engine and drove home. There was more thinking to be done.

CHAPTER THIRTEEN

I DIDN'T HAVE anything else to do, except sleep, so I settled in outside Harry Tuck's house and waited. Patience is the number one characteristic of private detectives. That, and a strong bladder. I'd had nothing to eat or drink since lunchtime so I thought I was probably all right in terms of my toilet needs.

Tuck knew that I was following him so I wasn't expecting him to set off for a clandestine assignment. But I hoped that I'd worried him enough to keep him awake. If he came to his bedroom window at one o'clock in the morning to see if I was still there, I'd won a little battle. It's petty victories like that which make my life a never-ending joy.

Of course he would have been within his rights to walk across the street and tell me to bugger off; it wouldn't have meant anything in relation to Nathan Mustow's death. No guilt could have been attributed to him if he simply wanted me out of his thinning hair. But the fact that he hadn't said anything suggested to me that the three alpha males in this private conspiracy had something on their conscience.

I'd followed Tuck because despite his bluff manner, I suspected that he was the weakest in resolve of the three of them. Jolyon Greif was stone-faced and tough; you could see it in his flinty eyes and lack of expression. Stratford Greif was cut from the same fibre, though he operated at a higher intellectual level than Jolyon. They wouldn't submit to panic easily. Harry Tuck was different. The Greifs worked on strategy, I guessed, while Tuck was their man for tactics: a smaller view of the world.

I was contemplating how long I should stay outside Tuck's house when my passenger door was abruptly yanked open.

Before I had time to react, a young woman stepped into the car and lowered her backside on to the passenger seat. She wore tight jeans, a leather bomber jacket zipped up the front and had shoulder-length straight hair that was a deep mahogany brown. She trailed in with her an expensive scent mingled with an acid note of sweat.

Once she'd settled in she stared straight ahead, looking down the road at the pools of light thrown by the street-lamps, which were partly covered by overhanging trees and so gave a greenish hue to the pavements.

Then she turned to me and laughed. It was a pleasant laugh, her mouth opening slightly to show even white teeth.

She said, 'I'm Belinda.'

'Hi, Belinda.'

'You're probably wondering who the fuck I am.'

'Crossed my mind. It's okay, you'll tell me eventually. You've started well with Belinda.'

'It's Belinda McFee, incidentally. You're Sam Dyke, and you've been following the guy in number 43 over there, Harry Tuck.'

'Observant.'

'Yep. I'm guessing that you're just trying to put the wind up them a bit. Tuck and the others, the Greifs.'

'Do I know you from somewhere?'

'Nope. I've been following you. And I've just come back from Stratford Greif's house. I followed him from Jolyon's just to see he went home. That's some flash car he's got. Hard to miss.'

I began to realise who she might be.

'Who gave you your information, Isobel Mustow?'

'Well done, Sam. First prize. Yes, I'm the other investigator she told you about. Didn't expect me, did you?'

She was right. In fact I made it a principle not to meet other people in my trade, but my expectations were that they'd be mostly men with some kind of police or military background. Men who were either easily bored and wanted some excitement in their lives, or who had lots of experience in their previous jobs of following paper-trails, reading reports and looking at accounts ledgers. Young, attractive women were a breed I hadn't expected to come across. I'd have gone to more meetings of the local Detective Wine Club if I'd known.

I said, 'Did Isobel tell you I wasn't happy about the arrangement?'

'Not in so many words. Look, Sam, get over it. We've both got jobs to do here. She's not your client so you have no say in the matter.'

I sat back and looked down the street, mirroring her posture. She'd certainly been professional so far and had fooled me. I'd seen Jolyon Greif following me but I hadn't noticed anyone else.

I said, 'Which is your car?'

She turned and pointed back down the street and I shifted in my seat to follow her gaze.

She said, 'That bright pink Volvo on the right. Stupid car really, but I like it.'

'And are you sure Stratford didn't see you?'

'I don't care, as I'm sure you didn't. We're not here to watch, are we? We're here to put a fright in them.'

'Tell me something about yourself.'

'What, my star sign? Well, I'm a Leo—'

'Your background, history. Something that will let me trust you.'

'Oh, my *CV*. You don't want all that boring stuff. Short version, I'm twenty-eight years old, spent some time in the Army, driving big trucks around in Germany and delivering stuff from one base to another. Came out three years ago and got a job with an agency in Leeds. But it was dull doing government work, as I'm sure you know. Had a boyfriend but found him having it away with my best friend in the back of his Meriva. Gave him a black eye and a piece of my mind and went home and packed a bag. So then I came back over the Pennines and set up on my own about six months ago. Do I pass the entrance exam?'

'What sort of work do you do now you're here?'

'Same as you. Divorce, benefit fraud, tracking missing persons. What would we do for a job if people weren't such dickheads?'

'I don't do divorce work.'

'No? Why's that?'

'Too messy. Screws up people's lives.'

She laughed again and glanced my way.

'Oh my god, *scruples*. It's a job, Sam. You're not a priest. You don't get to make judgements on what's right and wrong.'

'I just take home the cheque?'

'If you're lucky enough to have someone pay you, of course.'

'This isn't going to work.'

'Aw, have I said something wrong? Trodden on your ethics?'

I leaned over her and opened the door.

'Don't get in my way and I'll try not to get in yours. Agreed?'

'Here's my card, have you got one? Just in case we need to confer on strategy.'

I looked at her and knew she was making fun. I suddenly felt like the starchy uncle who wouldn't play with the kids. We exchanged cards and I saw that her address was local to where we were sitting.

I said, 'You didn't come far.'

She shrugged. 'I'll go anywhere, me. Just a bit of luck, this time. So what do we do tomorrow? Tell you what. I've already followed Stratford tonight, so why don't we do the same tomorrow?'

'Have you any idea what you're doing?'

'Not really. Isobel Mustow doesn't trust these people further than she can throw … oh, I don't know, a cat. And I can tell you're the same. You've been interviewing people at Midwinter, haven't you? Found anything useful?'

I sighed. More of the joyless uncle.

'I don't have to tell you anything about what I've found out.'

'No, but you wanna, don't you? Gossip about what you've heard.' She smiled and rocked her head from side to side on her shoulders as though egging me on. 'I just know they're a bunch of big-brained scientists and that Isobel thinks her husband's suicide was dodgy. He'd never have done it, she said. So why did he? They must have some theories. And you must have some suspicions, otherwise you wouldn't be out here on day one following these management-types around as though they've got a stash of weapons or gold bullion somewhere. Something's tickled your fancy, hasn't it?'

'I'm just a seeker for truth and justice.'

She laughed again and stepped out of the car, leaning in before she closed it.

'You get good old Harry tomorrow and I'll watch Stratford. Jolyon's just a soldier, following orders. See you soon.'

She closed the door quietly and I felt myself exhale. It was bad enough dealing with the Midwinter crew and the bright sparks of The Bleak without having to baby-sit an investigator who seemed completely oblivious to the potential threat posed by people like Stratford and Jolyon Greif.

There was that killjoy uncle again.

I drove home.

CHAPTER FOURTEEN

THE FOLLOWING DAY continued in the same pattern. I negotiated with Natalie and managed to talk to three people in the morning. In appearance they were different—two men and one woman, for one thing—but in attitude and character they could have been poured from the same mould. These were Mustow's peers and colleagues, slightly more senior than those I'd seen the day before. They were confident, distant and acted as though they belonged to a club that I wasn't even good enough to read the rules of, never mind join. They revealed nothing about the work they did and were polite if rather uncaring about the fate of Nathan Mustow. I was beginning to wonder what Mustow had done to create such a depth of indifference in other people. Margaret had obviously liked him and found him a good boss and a decent man. But the people I was talking to now sounded as though they were discussing a distant cousin they'd met once at a wedding and didn't much like.

At lunch-time I ate alone again, though the number of people who knew who I was seemed to have grown. There were several looks of appraisal as I walked by but no one met my gaze. I doubted they were checking out my sartorial style. Harry Tuck didn't appear and I didn't know whether he was avoiding me or had genuine reasons for missing lunch. He may have been so angry with my following him that he could barely trust himself to be civil.

Another three interviewees in the afternoon and I was ready to give Mustow an award for putting up with these people. The last was a woman in her late thirties who had an immobile face and an unforgiving nature.

When I asked whether she thought he might have been stressed by the nature of his work, she grimaced, the first sign of any kind of feeling that she'd demonstrated.

She said, 'If he wasn't stressed then he wasn't doing it right. We're *all* stressed, Mr Dyke. We handle it. We're a community of rational people who understand the demands of our work and the financial pressures on the organization. Just because we wear lab coats doesn't mean we're removed from the real world. If Nathan couldn't handle the stress, then he should have got out sooner. He didn't do himself or us any favours by remaining in place if he wasn't up to scratch.'

'That sounds a bit harsh.'

'Does it? He was one of the most senior people here. Part of his job was to act as a buffer between those of us at the coal-face and those in management.'

'You mean like Stratford Greif.'

She turned her head away and for a moment I thought she wasn't going to answer. Then she turned back to me and laid a single finger on the table, as though holding down a key on a piano.

'Things changed around here, Mr Dyke. Eighteen months ago Stratford Greif joined this organisation and the level of commitment and professionalism rose instantly.'

'But.'

'Yes, but. Something was lost. Charles Montgomery had established a working environment which suited us all, those of us who work in the labs and those who work in the offices. Now the balance has shifted and I'm not entirely certain it's for the better. That's where Nathan Mustow could have shown his mettle.'

'But if the company is more professional and committed, where's the problem?'

She raised her finger from the table and leaned back in the chair.

'I rather think that's something for an investigator such as yourself to find out. Don't you?'

THAT NIGHT I picked up Tuck's car when he was a couple of miles down the road from the Midwinter facility. I followed him to a Sainsburys car park and watched him go inside and come out twenty minutes later with a plastic bag of supplies. Then he drove home and I parked outside as it grew dark around me.

At a few minutes before nine he came out to his car again and climbed inside. He reversed out of his drive and set off north, towards central Manchester. We hadn't got very far when my phone rang. It was Belinda. I hated to use my phone while driving—quite apart from its illegality—but I thought it might be important. I replied and pressed the loudspeaker button, laying the phone on the passenger seat.

She said, 'We're moving. Stratford's heading north. How's your boy?'

'Same here. Maybe another meeting. I might see you soon.'

'Not unless I see you first. Kissy-kiss.'

I closed the connection and focused on watching Tuck's white BMW. The sun had gone down about fifteen minutes before but it had been a cloudy day and the light had faded fast. I drove closer to him than I would have liked but he was in no hurry.

We turned eastwards gradually, the sky ahead of us much darker than the lighter sunset in my rear-view mirror. We drove through Levenshulme: acres of red-brick former council houses—some showing the red cross of the English flag in their gardens—bricked up off-licences, shops for sale. The parks we passed were untended and ragged-looking, as though no one had been near them for years. We drove past a primary school surrounded like a prison by a bright blue wire fence; keeping children in or predators out, I wouldn't have liked to guess.

After a few more turns the roads widened out and we were suddenly entering a semi-industrial zone marked by a series of single-storey warehouses. Tuck indicated and then passed between two large rusting gateposts into a former retail estate, the buildings now boarded up and padlocked. I switched off my headlights and followed. He slowed and turned down one of the narrow lanes that gave access to half a dozen of the low buildings. They were metal-sided with full-width front entrances into which a door had been cut. Glancing around I noticed that there was no lighting on the estate and that all of the warehouses were shuttered and locked. The place must have closed down some time before, judging by the aerosol graffiti and long grass sprouting up along the pathways.

Tuck drew to a halt outside a warehouse that was painted steel grey and seemed as defunct as all the others. I looked around as best I could from my position a hundred yards further back. There was no sign of Stratford Greif's car, nor the pink monstrosity that was Belinda's.

Tuck got out of his car, glanced around without resting his gaze on me, then walked towards the warehouse. He hesitated briefly in front of the door cut into the front, then turned and headed left, towards the side of the building.

Reaching into the glove compartment for my heavy torch, I climbed out and followed.

THE ESTATE WAS silent. There were no trees in the grounds so there was no rustling of the wind, no sunset bird-calls. A car swished past on the road a couple of hundred yards behind me. The area was reasonably remote and we were deep inside the estate. I wondered what the hell Tuck was doing here and whether Belinda was close by, too.

Tuck had been gone about a minute by now so I quickened my pace across the cracked tarmac and approached the warehouse. His car engine ticked quietly in cooling as I passed it. Down the side of the warehouse there was a row of bushes used to separate each warehouse from its neighbours. They seemed to be intended to create a sense of individuality or privacy for each warehouse owner. The gap between the bushes and the side of the warehouse was about a metre, wide enough to walk through without rustling.

I held my torch loosely in my right hand but didn't switch it on. There was a residual light from the streetlamps far behind me, and the general glow of the city to the west and north. It was enough to see by. I approached the front of the warehouse and listened. There was no sound. No footsteps inside, no hum of machinery. It was possible Tuck was heading for another entrance and I was now losing more time.

I stepped to the side and, touching the rough metal siding for guidance, made my way past the corner of the building, edging between the wall and the bushes.

There's a moment just before an act of violence when your senses become more alert than usual. A shift in the pattern of the air—caused by bodies disturbing the acoustic field—tells you at an almost pre-conscious level that something has changed. Depending on your experience and your personal proclivities, you prepare to be hit, or you move to prevent yourself being hit.

I was in the second camp.

So the gentle tread of a step on the grass, the slightest change in the wind on my cheek, a shift in the pattern of light and shade, made me move my upper body a fraction of an inch before a heavy object hit my head.

Instead it caught my left shoulder, which was okay because that's my weakest arm anyway. It felt like a club, not a metallic implement like a wrench, but a wooden bar of some kind. If it had hit me on the head it might have shattered my skull. Instead it deadened my shoulder and weakened my left arm, which I flung out in reaction, connecting with nothing.

By now my fighting brain was coming on-line. I've done a little martial arts training, mostly to keep fit and in shape, but of course the conditions in which you fight are highly regulated and formalised. Here all I could do was depend on some reflexes and hope to get a grip on something in order to shift my weight and get a fall, or perhaps a punch. I could make out two shapes, none of them Tuck's. One of them was shorter than the burglar I'd confronted at my house a few days before, the other one was about the same height and build. They were moving quickly and I was backing away at the same time, trying to get out into the open at the front of the warehouse.

One of them lunged and grabbed on to my left arm and the other man stepped forward. I still had my torch in my right hand, but I didn't have space or time to swing it. I held it up because I sensed the wooden bar or baseball bat coming towards me again. It clattered into my torch and someone said, 'Shit.'

Perhaps two seconds had passed since the first blow to my shoulder.

It was all moving fast. The man who had my left arm had succeeded in twisting it behind me and he had moved out of my sight and reach. I began to feel vulnerable. The man with the bat was readying himself for another hit, taking a step forward with one leg and positioning his body with his arms turned away and high, raised in a striking position.

I saw all this even as I was still struggling to walk backwards, forcing the man behind me into the open ground. He rabbit-punched me in the kidneys, though, and I bent over, the pain searing like a burn.

The man in front of me said, 'Hold him!' and I sensed the second hit coming.

I changed my direction. Instead of going backwards, I pushed forward, into his face, reducing the arc of his swing. He was forced to take a step back and stumbled over the root of a bush, throwing out his arms to regain his balance.

Which is when I stepped backward again, into the man who'd been holding my arm. He'd been yanked forward with me, then found my back pushing into his face, toppling him over. He went down, with me on top of him, and suddenly we were back at the front of the warehouse, in the open and with room to manoeuvre.

I scrabbled and turned to bend over the man who'd fallen beneath me, ready to punch him hard in the face. He was wearing a balaclava covering his face but still I thought I caught a glimpse of red hair bunched up beneath it and opened my mouth to say something.

Which is when the other man hit me on the back of the head with his club and I fell forward and forward and forward into the black hole that had opened before me.

CHAPTER FIFTEEN

IT HAD ALWAYS been Belinda McFee's belief that she was as good as the next person. Her relationship with her father had been fraught after the age of fifteen, where they seemed to disagree with each other over everything from make-up to her choice of favourite rock band. But he had at least instilled in her an egalitarian outlook that demanded respect. Being in the Army, driving trucks alongside men twice her size, with twice her experience, had conditioned her to stand her ground. True enough, she had a smile on her face as she said no, but she wouldn't be cowed and she wouldn't be intimidated.

She was discovering this was a useful characteristic to have as a fledgling private investigator in what was still, largely, a male occupation.

But what she was doing now was the reason she'd chanced her arm in this profession. Driving two hundred yards behind a man who considered himself important, perhaps a cut above the rest, an intellectual—but who,

Belinda suspected, had the moral character of a snake. After the first contact from Isobel Mustow, she'd researched Greif on-line and found nothing much written about him at all. After getting his doctorate he'd had a couple of minor research posts, then did some teaching at a university in London before getting a gig with a large multi-national pharmaceutical company. Why he left was a mystery, but then in fairness there was no reason for it to be anything but commonplace: he'd left one job and started another. Then he'd moved again and this time he was with Midwinter Enterprises. What could be more harmless?

But since talking again to Isobel, Belinda had dug further. She'd telephoned the university in London and talked to the people in staffing there. They had become very tight-lipped very quickly, and gave no clue why he'd left his teaching post. From the reaction of the woman she'd spoken to, she didn't think it was a case of him leaving for a better job. For instance, he'd quit half-way through term-time, when a professional would at least have waited till the end of term before leaving for a new job, no matter how better paid it was.

Another couple of phone calls to previous employers had produced a similar sense of unease—people weren't just reluctant to talk about a former employee, with all the privacy issues surrounding such a conversation. They sounded, and felt, faintly disgusted with the subject-matter: Stratford Greif himself.

So she was interested to see exactly what he was up to. She'd considered whether he might be a sexual predator, someone who leaned on his students, or his colleagues, to offer up sexual services in return for advancement of one kind or another. That didn't wash. There would have been a stink about it across the Internet, somewhere. She'd considered whether it was something like plagiarism, which might have sunk the career of an aspiring academic. That didn't work either—as far as she could tell, apart from his Ph.D thesis, Greif hadn't published anything, anywhere. Plagiarism would only erupt as an issue if someone had found their work copied in another place with a sufficiently wide circulation to make it worth pursuing a case. And that hadn't happened.

She wondered what Dyke made of it. She'd liked him immediately. He hadn't seemed surprised when she burst into his car the day before, nor had he put up too much of a fight about her involvement. He didn't seem territorial like that.

And he was quite hunky in his leather jacket and dark hair, with a bit of a sparkle in his eyes, as though he found most people and most situations faintly comical.

Ahead of her, Stratford Greif's car turned off the main road and headed into what appeared to be the site of a deserted factory. The gates were wide open and the door of the factory had been peeled back as though by a super-hero in a cape. Perhaps they'd started to tear down the site but thought better of it. Belinda cruised to a halt and killed her lights, groping in her glove compartment for her binoculars—a tongue-in-cheek present from her dad when she'd started work as an investigator.

Greif stopped in front of the factory's Reception office, a small brick building that showed no lights or other signs of occupation. Greif didn't get out of his car.

Later, the irony wasn't lost on her that the men came into her car the same way she'd got into Dyke's. One minute she was staring through her binoculars at the Reception block, the next, both of her car's front doors were pulled open and she was dragged from her seat, dropping the binoculars as she felt her jacket being hauled up around her neck.

She let herself go slack so the man had to do most of the work. She was actually going to enjoy this.

The man held her up with her back to the car door. He wore a balaclava and black clothing and his small eyes moved around inside the cut-outs in the wool. She heard her passenger door slam behind her and moments later the other man came around the front of her car. He was taller and thinner but also wore a balaclava and dark clothes.

The tall one said, 'Now what do we do? I don't like duffing up a girl.'

The one holding her didn't reply but punched her in the stomach. She doubled over, breathing deeply, taking her time.

The man who'd hit her said to his associate, 'It's a job. Do it. You want the bonus, don't you?'

Belinda hadn't wasted her time just driving trucks while in the Army. She'd taken the opportunity to learn. And one of the things she'd learned from an instructor was Krav Maga, the Israeli self-defence technique derived from street-fighting.

The technique emphasised fast, pre-emptive strikes and aiming for an opponent's most vulnerable physical areas.

She was doubled over and her assailant was two feet in front of her, probably thinking that the fight was over. Gathering her strength, she acted as though she was stumbling forward but drew back her fist and punched him hard beneath the belt. The man grunted and bent towards her, and as his head lowered she stood quickly and raised her own palm upward into his face. She caught his nose, pushing him up and back, hooking her leg behind his. The speed of the attack caused him to fall back hard on the concrete paving.

By this time the other man had started his move towards her. She saw his arms reach out and she ducked to her left, knocking his arms downwards with her own and simultaneously kicking at his genitals with the heel of her foot. He bent backwards from the waist to avoid her kick and as his face came towards her she smashed him across the nose with her right elbow. She felt a bone give. He groaned and fell sideways.

The first man was struggling to his feet. Belinda crouched and punched him in the cheek twice, quickly. He lay still.

She stepped back to her car and looked at the men, both curled on the floor and groaning. That felt good. She turned to duck through the door of her car when her heel slipped off the curb. Her foot turned awkwardly and a spasm shot through her lower leg. She yelped but fell into the car, pulling the door shut and locking all the doors from the inside.

Then she started the engine and drove away, nursing her left leg.

She'd gone to all that trouble to disable those men and then twisted her ankle. How stupid.

CHAPTER SIXTEEN

IT WAS THE pain in my head that woke me up.

I was face down on the concrete, sprawled out like a cartoon man, my arms raised, my hands flat on the ground, my face turned sideways so that I could feel the contours of the paving slabs.

My head throbbed like a timpani, with the occasional clash of symbols piercing through for the high notes.

Before I opened my eyes I listened. There was barely a sound. The faint soughing of the trees beyond the industrial park. A distant car dopplering by the entrance gate. Maybe the vaguest of hums from the centre of town.

I called on all my reserves of strength and moved my hand. The timpani became transformed into the whole percussion section. With triangle. I think I groaned.

Slowly I came to a sitting position and felt the back of my head. There was blood, and a lump. I looked around, checking my eyesight. Everything was clear, so perhaps I'd escaped concussion. Perhaps they didn't want to damage me permanently after all. They would hardly have left me here if that were the case. I'd be fighting chain-link inside a tarpaulin dropping to the bottom of the Manchester Ship Canal had they really wanted to prove a point.

But it was a message nonetheless: leave us alone, or see what you get.

For a bunch of scientists, they acted awfully like Mexican cartel thugs.

Eventually my legs worked and I stood, woozily. My car was where I'd left it, though of course Tuck's was gone. There didn't seem any point going back to the warehouse to see whether there was anything going on there—it was patently a trap to get me isolated.

Which made me think.

I found Belinda's number on my phone and called. Straight to voice-mail. Damn.

I phoned Dan, who impressively answered on the second ring.

'Yo, Dad. You can't have your money back. But it's moving up. You made a good decision.'

I suddenly realised I had nothing to say. There was an awkward pause.

He said, 'What's up?'

'Nothing. I was going to ask you something but realised I already knew. Nothing important.'

'You're weird. Anything I can do for you?'

'No. Stay safe.'

'Always.'

I hung up, realising that wanting him to be safe was in fact the reason for the call. I'd wanted to check that he was okay, as though Midwinter's thugs might have sent someone to him as well as trapping me.

Which was crazy.

Or maybe not. I phoned Margaret Sellers. She answered after half a dozen rings—just enough to make me anxious.

I said, 'It's me, Sam.'

'Yes? Is there something to report, or whatever it is you do?'

'No … well, yes. But nothing specific.'

'So you're reporting something non-specific. How much is this costing me?'

I grinned at the phone. I liked her bluntness.

'I just wanted you to know I was still alive.'

'That's good to know. Was there ever a doubt?'

'Possibly. Anyway, you were right about Midwinter.'

'Right in what way? They made Nathan kill himself? Or they're a bunch of arrogant bastards?'

'At least one, maybe both. Look, I've got to go. I'll be in touch soon.' I paused. 'Do you think I could persuade you to go away for a few days? Or stay in a hotel?'

'Why? Am I in danger?'

'I don't think so. But I'm not sure. Two guys just jumped me when I was following Tuck.'

'Oh my god! Was he there? Did he know?'

'No and yes. He'd left the scene of the crime, but I'm pretty sure he set it up.'

'You have to report it to the police.'

I blew out air and realised my head was still hurting.

'Nothing to say. I don't know who it was and there may have been no connection to Tuck, just a tragic coincidence. Anyway, I don't want to give him the satisfaction of denying it all then convincing Charles Montgomery to take me off the case because I'm imagining things.'

'All right, if you say so. I've seen how stubborn you can be. Are you all right?'

'Passable. I've got to go. Check something out.'

We said goodbye and hung up. I rang Belinda again, mobile and office, and went straight to voice-mail again.

I picked up her business card and checked the address. I put it into my GPS and drove out of the industrial park, trying not to get blood on the car seat.

BELINDA McFEE'S HOUSE was a respectable semi-detached red-brick in Fallowfield, the street crowded with trees that were just beginning to leaf out. The houses weren't grand enough to have driveways so the pavements were lined with cars that were half on the road and half off. I found a space fifty yards past the house, a position where I could watch the front door. I'd seen the place was dark when I passed so she wasn't back yet.

I'd been waiting ten minutes when the pink Volvo turned in at the end of the street and crawled along, looking for a parking space. As it happened, the only space left was next to my Mondeo. She juggled into the gap and climbed out. She was trim and lithe in the same jacket and tight jeans from the day before, but it seemed to me she was moving a little slowly. She closed her car door and leaned back against it, then turned her head pointedly towards me.

I locked my car and approached.

'They were waiting for me. Two men.'

'Same here.'

'You okay?'

'Better than them. I know a few things. How about you?'

'I'm going to bleed all over your carpet.'

She grinned. 'No carpets. Nice shiny polished floorboards. Let's go in.'

We crossed the road and she let us in. A standard-issue 1930s semi, tiled hallway with staircase on the right, door to the front room with open fire on the left, a dining-room at the back—used by Belinda as an office by the look of it—and kitchen to the rear, straight down the corridor from the front entrance.

She said, 'Let's have a look at you then,' and led me to the sink in the kitchen. I noticed she was limping. She found a clean cloth and wetted it, then gave it to me to dab the back of my head.

I said, 'How's it looking?'

'Bob down.'

I bent at the knees so she could see better. She parted my hair with her fingers.

'It's not too bad. It's stopped bleeding. We'll put something on it.'

'What's with your leg?'

'Twisted my ankle. I was so excited I'd beaten up two villains I forgot to look where I was walking. It'll be okay.'

TWENTY MINUTES LATER we were seated in her front room, curtains drawn, coal fire sputtering into life, cups of tea in hand. There were some small oil paintings, landscapes, grouped together on one side wall, a large mirror on the wall at my back, behind the sofa, and a Panasonic flat-screen TV in the corner. In the other corner, a round table with a lamp and a couple of family photos. A larger one of Belinda in fatigues messing around on a Churchill tank, somewhere in Germany judging by the road signs behind her.

I said, 'You do those paintings?'

'My dad. My mum died when I was three so I was looked after by his sister, my auntie Grace. He worked in a textile factory all his life. Made to retire a couple of years ago, when he was sixty. He found out he liked painting, went to some classes. Does it all the time, now. Even sells.'

'Who'd have thought it, eh?'

'You've got it. It's like he's had a testosterone removal. Left him all soft and woolly. Smelling of linseed oil.'

'My dad got tougher as he got older. More pissed off with the government, with the people running the coal mines. He couldn't handle the lies.'

'This was Yorkshire, was it? I can hear it in your voice.'

'That's your time in Leeds. Beating up boyfriends in the back of vans.'

'You listened. I'm impressed.'

I took a sip from my tea.

'So how are we going to do this?'

She knew what I meant.

'I suppose we should share what we know. You start.'

'Why me?'

'You were hired first. More to share. I'll add what I know afterwards.'

I couldn't fault her logic, so I told her what Margaret Sellers had told me about Nathan Mustow and his behaviour in the last year. I told her about my interviews with the scientists and managers at Midwinter, about my meeting with Stratford Greif.

She said, 'What's he like? I've not met any of these people yet but I've read about him.'

I hesitated. I didn't know how to describe the cool menace that Greif had projected.

I said, 'He fancies himself like a Bond villain, I think. Icy cool. Superior. Always ahead of you, so you can never outsmart him.'

'And is that true?'

'Well he's obviously bright. And I have no idea what he's up to. Or the rest of them. Harry Tuck is the one who puts himself about, but Stratford is the one they're frightened of.

The young geeks there like him but there's as much fear as admiration.'

'What about Charles Montgomery?'

'Can't really make him out. He let me inside to ask all these questions, so I think he probably has no idea what's going on.'

'Do we?'

I shrugged. This was the question that had been bothering me. We had a man who'd committed suicide and nobody knew why; a culture of secrecy in a private research organization; and a handful of goons working overtime on their security duties. It was fragments, bits and pieces. Had Mustow really committed suicide? If not, what had happened to him? If he had put the syringe in his own arm was the pressure at Midwinter to blame or was there some other cause? I had nothing to offer but conjecture that was the result of my suspicious mind.

And the fact that I'd been hit over the head by a wooden club.

I said, 'What's your contribution?'

She leaned forward on her chair, then grimaced as her ankle turned.

'Ouch. I'm really glad I hurt those guys, otherwise I'd be feeling stupid. Anyway … Stratford Greif is a weird sort of intellectual. He comes from a wealthy family who seemed to have been living in Eastern Europe when he was born. His mother was English and he took her name when he finally settled in the UK. He's bilingual, English and Russian. Got his first degrees in the old USSR, before the wall came down. Then came over here and got his doctorate in Manchester. Since he graduated he hasn't held a job down for long, but I can't find out why. Nearly twenty years. Nobody from the places he's worked will talk to me about it. You'd think he was exercising some strange hold over them. He seems to have left every job under a mysterious cloud.'

'Sexual stuff?'

'I don't think so. I'd have found it on the net somewhere. But he's obviously doing something that pisses people off enough for them to get rid of him.'

'What kind of jobs were they?'

'Academic, research scientist. Respectable gigs, so he must be clever enough to get through the interviews. His Ph.D is in some difficult science subject that had a title so long I could barely read it, never mind remember it. I can't find the text on-line, just the title.'

'So what do you think's going on? Why are they so keen to put us off?'

'When I worked in Leeds they taught us to follow the money. But I'm not sure that's the case here. He already has money, lots of it. He doesn't need to work. He doesn't own Midwinter, so it's not as though he might be defrauding investors and running away with the investment capital or siphoning off the funds.'

'All we really know is that the group at the top don't want us investigating Nathan Mustow's death. I've had nothing but ear-ache about that from Harry Tuck. Which means that we might find out something they don't want us to know.'

'Which means there *was* something dodgy about it.'

We both sat back in our seats.

I said, 'I don't know about you, but I really hate it when people don't want me to know something.'

'I bet you're really bull-headed, too. I knew a lot of Yorkshiremen like you.'

'It's not that. Well, it might be that. But I don't like it when people lie.'

'You sound like your dad.'

'I suppose I do. But that's not a bad thing.'

'So what do we do next?'

'We have a rest. I let the bump on my head go down. You let your ankle get better. Perhaps we do some more research.'

'We should tell the clients. Keep them informed.'

'Why would you want to do that? The more they know, the more they worry.'

'It's in my contract with Isobel. Don't you follow the guidelines?'

I smiled thinly.

'I didn't write 'em. I don't have to follow 'em. They're guidelines, not rules.'

'I bet you make your own rules.'

'Only when I have to. And even then I sometimes break them.'

CHAPTER SEVENTEEN

I SPENT THE next day at home. My head hurt and I even considered going over to Leighton Hospital to let them have a look at it. But by late afternoon the headache had gone and anyway, I was tired of sitting down and watching reruns of Top Gear.

I tried contacting someone who could tell me about Nathan Mustow's suicide. The police wouldn't talk to me and neither would the coroner's office. I rang Belinda.

I said, 'If you've got a spare moment …'

'Nothing but. What would you like?'

'It would be nice to know some details about Nathan's death. What did the guys who found him say? When did he die? That kind of thing. Do you have any way of getting hold of that kind of info?'

'I'm ahead of you, big boy. I've got a contact in the GMP, from my time in Leeds. We worked with them occasionally.'

'Handy.'

'I spoke to him a few minutes ago. They're still working on the analysis of the syringe. It looks like it might be sodium thiopental.'

'What's that?'

'It's what they use in lethal injections in the States. I looked it up. Remember when they used to use a cocktail of three drugs for executions? Well some states are now using just this one. In bigger doses. It's also used as a truth drug — you know, what they give people in Hollywood films to make 'em talk. Usually called Sodium Pentothal.'

'So these people on death row tell the truth until they die?'

'Don't be silly. In big enough doses it can kill you, but in smaller doses it lowers your resistance to talking freely. You talk more, but perhaps not more truthfully. They're doing research but at the moment the jury's out as to whether it works or not.'

I sensed she was enjoying lecturing me, but I didn't mind.

I said, 'But that's not confirmed yet. It could still be anything in the syringe.'

'Correct.'

'Any news from witnesses, people at the hotel?'

'My man says no, nothing. Nathan came in, registered, went upstairs. Had a briefcase but no bag. An hour later later he ordered room service but was dead before it arrived. If it wasn't suicide, someone else must have gone up first, or went later and knocked on his door to be let in. The outside window doesn't open. Do you know the place?'

Margaret had told me the name of the hotel, out near the airport, but I didn't know it. If it was near the airport the windows would have been hermetically sealed against the noise.

I said, 'I've never been there. The question is, why did Nathan take the room? He obviously wasn't planning on staying overnight. So this was a meeting of some kind. A meeting that Margaret knew nothing about, because she kept his diary. A meeting that Isobel, his own wife, knew nothing about. So it must have been organised by him personally, either through a phone call or a personal conversation.'

'My thoughts exactly. The Greifs and Harry Tuck are still in the frame for this.'

'Absolutely. How's the leg?'

'Bearable. How's the head?'

'Healing. Speak tomorrow.'

We hung up.

Margaret Sellers didn't answer her home phone so I called her mobile.

She said, 'They've told me I'm not to talk to you.'

'Where are you?'

'At work. I know, I know … I said I wouldn't come back. But I couldn't stay home. I was more worried there than I am here.'

'Who have you spoken to?'

'Jolyon Greif called me out of the office for a word. They've put me in with the other admin people for the time being, now that Nathan's not around. He gave me a talking-to in the corridor outside. He said they understood why I'd done it, called you in. I must have been worried about Nathan and they understood. But I was to have nothing else to do with you.' She paused. 'I hate that man.'

'Then leave. You don't have to stay there. I don't trust any of them.'

'I've got to go.'

'Can I come around tonight? There are things we need to talk about.'

'After eight.'

I hung up moments after she cut me off. I couldn't understand why she'd gone back to work there. But then I could. It was probably the only family she had at the moment. Both her parents were dead, her boss had apparently committed suicide, she hadn't mentioned any other family. It was possible she had no one to talk to outside of the people she worked with. Where else would she go?

IT WAS GETTING dark by the time I turned up at her door. She opened it before I knocked, and I realised she must have been scouting the road, perhaps fearful of who might arrive.

She was wearing a cream blouse and a blue skirt and looked more feminine than I'd seen her before. The image of her that had stayed with me had been attractive but stern, which of course was her work front. She looked up at me with those big blue-green eyes and stepped back so I could enter.

We sat in the front room again and now I could see the resemblance between Margaret and her mother in the family photos. The same dark hair against pale skin, the faint look of puzzled disapproval in her eyes. Her father, by contrast, was open-faced and hearty.

I said, 'I'm sorry to keep calling like this. I thought I should keep you up to date with what's happening.'

'Like what?'

'Well, for one thing, Isobel Mustow has hired a separate investigator to look into Nathan's death.'

'Who?'

'It's a young woman called Belinda McFee.'

'Is she any good?'

'I think she can handle herself, yes. I don't know what she's capable of in terms of investigation, though she worked with a big firm in Leeds. Would you like to meet her?'

'Not particularly. I'm fed up with the whole thing, now. I'm sorry for Nathan but I shouldn't have got in touch with you.'

'Do you want me to stop? You're the client.'

She was sitting next to me on the sofa, almost like a child who wanted someone close. As I looked at her, her face crumpled and she dropped her eyes, beginning to sob. I wasn't ready for this—it wasn't the Margaret I'd seen up till now. Her hand came out and rested on mine. I was touched by her vulnerability and left my hand where it was.

She said, 'I don't want you to stop. I'm all over the place. I don't know who my friends are. I … I just don't seem to have a place to go to any more. A nice big house and it's empty. I mean, there's no soul here. I don't know what I'm doing.'

'You've hit a road-block. You'll get past it. Everyone does.'

'Will I? Will everything be all right again? Can you promise me that?'

'You know I can't. No one can.'

She nodded as though I'd told her something she already knew. Then her hand tightened its grip on mine and she pulled herself closer to me so that her leg was touching mine.

Before I knew it, her arm had come around me, up to my neck, and was pulling my head down towards her. I smelled her hair and the same floral perfume I'd smelled in the doorway of Costa Coffee. Then her lips were on mine and I stopped remembering things, suddenly caught up in the urgency of the present, the way things fitted together, the feel of cloth, the smooth velvet of skin, the muskiness of sex.

I was overwhelmed by the here and now.

I LEFT AT dawn. She was still asleep, a pale arm laying over the eiderdown, black hair splayed on the pillow like an ink stain, a Rorschach blot into which I could read no meaning. I didn't have to leave … but I did. I didn't want the awkwardness of the next morning. I'd crossed a line, and we both knew it. We needed time apart for the heat of the situation to die down.

When I drove out of Margaret's gateway the sun was casting long shadows and the air was chill. I turned on to the main road, and looking in my rear-view mirror I thought I saw a black Prius squatting like a giant bug on the road. But when I looked again, it was gone. Paranoia strikes deep in the heartland. Paul Simon said so.

CHAPTER EIGHTEEN

WHEN I GOT home I couldn't sleep and I couldn't work, so I did a bit of both and then gave up.

I felt bad about sleeping with Margaret, even though she'd been an equal partner in the decision—hell, she'd instigated it.

Or had she?

Had I put on my shining armour for that night and simply taken advantage of her? I couldn't work out what I was playing at. Of course she was attractive, and spiky, which always drew me to women. But she'd also been needy and in a weakened psychological state, defences down. I wasn't proud of myself. There'd been a kind of bruised aggression in her that I'd wanted to tame. But the closer I'd got to her, the more I'd seen it was just a front—as all strong characteristics are. I'd bulldozed through the front and found the softness behind, the softness that she'd learned to hide to protect herself from hurt.

Now I was likely to hurt her again.

Laura, my previous girlfriend, had left me because she felt I didn't try hard enough to see her point of view. I was too bound up in my job and in other people's lives and didn't have room for her. I knew she was right but couldn't seem to do anything about it. I wore my selfishness like a thick overcoat that didn't let in the cold but was impossible to peel off.

Fortunately I didn't have to beat myself up for long because Belinda rang shortly before noon.

'Are you up for a visit?'

'Where to?'

'I want to see Isobel again. I know it's not in your book of rules but it's in mine. Keep the client updated.'

'Aren't you worried she'll take you off the case when she finds out what happened to us?'

'Be professional, Sam. If that's what she wants, we do it.'

'But it's not what I want.'

There was a pause at her end.

She said, 'You're being difficult today. What's happened? Bump on the head change your personality?'

'Let's say I see things differently to you. You've come from a big company with rules and regulations and contracts. All very commendable. Keeps you in the good books of whoever the hell it is that's supposed to be regulating us. But until they tell me to stop doing what I'm doing, I'm going to carry on looking after the best interests of my client.'

'Are you suggesting I'm not?'

'It looks like you're protecting yourself, not thinking about how to help Isobel Mustow find some peace.'

'That's very hurtful. You can be a right bastard, can't you?'

'Sorry. You're pretty new to working for yourself. You'll soon find out that no one owes you any favours.'

'I know that. I wasn't born yesterday.'

I paused. 'Okay, I don't mean to be getting at you. I haven't known you long enough to be really insulting. Sorry if it came across hard. I guess for me, once I take on a case it becomes almost like a mission. I want to believe in what I'm doing, not just do something for the money.'

'You could make good money as a bouncer. Give up on all this ethical shit.'

I laughed. 'Don't think I haven't considered it, when times were hard. What time do you want to meet there?'

'Oh, so now you're coming?'

'Only so I can give you some feedback and a report on your performance afterwards.'

'I've already spoken to her. I'm to be there for five o'clock. See, I don't need your permission anyway.'

THE PINK VOLVO was already in Isobel's drive when I arrived, though the BMW with its nose in the garage was gone. Perhaps the sister was gone, too.

Isobel let me in and we found Belinda out in the back, sitting in a veranda that I hadn't seen on my last visit. I sat on a bamboo chair and Isobel offered me tea, which I accepted. The tea cup was exactly as delicate and transparent as I would have expected.

She was looking as wan and drawn as before though there was more life in her actions now, as if the initial shock wave had rolled over her and she was trying to stand on her own feet.

She said, 'I'm glad you two are working together on this. It shows a good deal of professionalism. Is your client happy with the arrangement, Mr Dyke?'

'She knows about it, yes. It's immaterial to her what Miss McFee here does.'

Belinda said, 'Thanks very much.'

I turned to her and shrugged.

Isobel said, 'So you're both here now. What do you want to tell me?'

I glanced at Belinda, who was wearing a formal jacket and slacks today, her hair pulled back in a pony-tail. She might have been the manager of an equestrian riding school. Until she began speaking.

She said, 'The other night, Sam and I followed two members of the Midwinter senior management team, separately. When we got close to our targets, we were both attacked by unknown men. We could report the attacks to the police, but we have no evidence and we don't want to expose what we're doing by reporting it and then having Midwinter deny any involvement. They'd claim we were fantasising and then block any contact with them, probably claiming we were harassing the company.'

Isobel looked from one of us to the other.

She said to Belinda, 'Is that why you're limping?'

'Not exactly. I tripped while getting away from the men who attacked me. But they didn't do any damage. Trust me, they're in a worse condition than I am.'

Isobel turned to me. 'What happened to you, Mr Dyke? Are your attackers in a worse condition, too?' She looked down at the cup in her hand. 'I can't believe I'm talking about violence like this.'

'No, they caught me out. I've got a bruise on the back of my head. But I'm okay.'

She sat back in her chair and sighed, staring up at the glass ceiling of the veranda. The weather outside had turned cool and cloudy, but we were as warm as the Bahamas behind the glass.

Isobel said, 'They've told me the inquest might not be for six months. Can you believe it? The coroner's issued an interim death certificate so we can at least bury Nathan. I thought this was going to be one shock and then I'd start to get over it. But I'm beginning to see it stretching out before me forever.' She brought her attention back down to us and I saw a hint of steel in her eyes. 'So what do you want me to do? Why are you here?'

Belinda said, 'You don't have to do or say anything. It was in my contract, if you remember, that I'd keep you up to date on all developments. Let's call this a progress meeting.'

'I see. And what about you, Mr Dyke? Are you having progress meetings with your client?'

She said this with such an odd inflection on 'client' that I wondered briefly if she knew about my relationship with Margaret Sellers. But there was no way she could. She might guess it was Margaret who was the client, simply for lack of other candidates, but she couldn't have known anything about what had happened between us. My paranoia was really ramping up.

I said, 'Unfortunately I'm not as scrupulous as Miss McFee. My client and I are operating on a handshake agreement.'

'Isn't that dangerous? What if your client refuses to pay up afterwards?'

'That's a risk I take every time. People are more honest than we might believe.'

'Or they think you'll have so much information about them after the investigation that they daren't risk upsetting you.'

'I hadn't thought of it like that. You might be right.'

We talked on in this vein for a while and I realised it was a pleasant distraction for Isobel, taking her away from thinking about her husband. Belinda seemed willing to go along with it so I let them carry the burden of conversation while I sat drinking more tea and examining the lawn and gardens.

Eventually Isobel seemed to tire and I glanced at Belinda. She took the cue and stood up.

'I should be going now. Sam, perhaps we should talk again.'

I stood and shook Isobel's hand. Then I remembered something.

'I've been told that when Nathan checked into the hotel he was carrying a briefcase but no overnight bag. That suggests he wasn't going to stay the night. Have the police given you back the briefcase and its contents yet?'

She looked perturbed.

'No, they haven't. This is the first I've heard of it. There's been a very nice man in touch with me, much nicer than the two policemen who came first. He's some kind of liaison person, I suppose. He hasn't said anything about a briefcase.'

Belinda said, 'It might be an idea if you checked whether his briefcase is still here.'

'Of course. It'll be in his downstairs study. Just a moment.'

She turned and went back into the house. Belinda and I looked at each other and then followed casually. We found her in a small room at the front, on the other side of the hallway to the sitting room. There was a bookcase brimming with piles of paper and textbooks, a small computer desk and chair, and a larger yellow chair in shiny leather that had a wooden base so you could swing around on it. Isobel was looking behind the chair and then moved to search beyond the far side of the bookcase.

'It would be here if he left it. But it's not. So presumably he took it with him and either left it at work or the police have it.'

'What does it look like? An ordinary black briefcase?'

'As a matter of fact, no. It's a kind of maroon and it has a pale patch on one side where someone spilled a drink on it and leached out the colour. You wouldn't mistake it for another one.'

I said, 'The police would have finished with it by now and returned it. Especially in what looks like a suicide.'

'What do you mean, "looks like"? Have you found something that suggests that it might not have been? I know I've always thought he was driven to it by that awful company, but I never really thought it was anything but his own hand that ended his life.'

Cutting off Belinda, I said, 'We don't know anything. Did the police at least tell you how he was found?'

'Yes. There were two empty bottles of whisky and an empty syringe. That's a dreadful image I've been trying to erase from my head. What could it have been in the syringe?'

I warned Belinda with my eyes not to mention what she'd discovered from her police contact.

I said, 'We don't know. We'll have to wait for a toxicology report from the inquest. As a scientist I suppose he would have known what he was doing with poisons and so on.'

'Oh yes. That was rather his speciality. Bioaerosols and their ability to carry airborne organisms. He worked with viruses and frightful material all the time. That's why they're so security-conscious at Midwinter. The place is piled high with them.'

CHAPTER NINETEEN

IT WAS GONE seven o'clock by the time I got home and I thought I deserved a drink. I was mixing a gin and tonic in the kitchen when the doorbell rang.

I peered through the spy-hole and saw Jolyon Greif's broad chest and the bottom of his face. I opened up. Greif had two men with him this time—the muscular George and another man who was taller but thinner, with a pockmarked face and short hair. A thick plaster crossed his nose. Greif saw the glass in my hand.

'Nice to kick back and have a good time.'

'What do you want? Am I to go on another pleasant drive through the countryside with you?'

'Can I come in?'

I stared at him a moment.

'You can, the Chuckle Brothers can't.'

He nodded curtly and stepped forward.

I led him through to the sitting room, the one with the ceiling-to-floor glass wall that showed the fields stretching behind the house, a pale sunset just establishing itself on the horizon. Ignoring the glorious view, he sat on one of my armchairs without invitation.

'You know we can't let you back on to the site now, don't you?'

I sat facing him, interested in spite of myself.

'Why's that?'

'You're a clown, Dyke. You've come into this like a bull on steroids. You've upset a lot of people, a lot of important people in the company. We'd be letting down the investors if we let you carry on. Mustow's suicide is in the police's hands now, and that's where it's going to stay.'

'Which people have I upset? They all seemed surprisingly cheery to me, considering their boss had just died. They couldn't wait to get back to their Bunsen burners.'

'That's because you don't understand the scientific mentality. They're cautious. They like things to stay the same. They don't like disturbances around them. Obviously Mustow's death was one disturbance. That doesn't have to be exacerbated by another one—i.e. you.'

'Does Charles Montgomery know about this? Or has it all come from your brother or whoever he is?'

'Charles will know first thing tomorrow.'

'Who are the investors, anyway?'

'Public knowledge, if you care to look. I'm not going to do your work for you.'

I took another sip of my drink, then put it down. Greif carried with him such a sense of corruptibility that it was almost palpable. His haunches and backside squatted on my furniture with elephantine certainty, immovable, as though nothing I could say had sufficient weight to contradict him. To him, I was literally a lightweight.

I said, 'Last night wasn't a clever ploy, you know. It might have seemed like it, but it hasn't worked.'

His expression didn't change. 'I have no idea what you're talking about.'

'Of course you don't. I didn't expect you to. I'm talking to entertain myself. But my colleague and I aren't giving up so easily, if that's what you thought would happen. We have clients as well as you do.'

'I'm very happy for you. It's good to have a job. Just practise it elsewhere from now on.'

'Or what?'

'Or I'll be unhappy. And so will George and Spike.'

I almost laughed. 'Spike? More like Beanpole. And tell Mr Bones that the next time I see his red hair in reach I'm going to grab a handful of it and put it through a wringer.'

'That's very colourful language. Did that bump on your head make you talk as though you'd swallowed a thesaurus?'

'What bump? How did you know about that?''

'I saw it when we came through. Looks very painful.'

'If I can borrow one of your phrases, I have no idea what you're talking about.'

He stood up.

'Time I left. Things to do, places to be.'

'Don't let me keep you.'

'Remember, you won't be allowed on site any more. So we don't want to see you around. You can tell your client that as well. Maybe she'll cancel your contract. That would be too bad.'

I saw him to the door and closed it behind him.

AFTER I'D FINISHED my drink and warmed up something to eat, I phoned Dan.

He said, 'You are keen. Two calls in less than a week. What can I do?'

I told him what I was working on and gave him the names of Stratford and Jolyon Greif. Belinda had told me some things about Stratford but I wondered if there was more.

Dan said, 'Are you looking for anything in particular? Why these two?'

'Because they're the ones who seem to be front and centre on this. Belinda McFee told me that Stratford has something of a mysterious past. But she could only get so far. I wondered if you could get further.'

'And Jolyon?'

'He's just an arrogant bugger and I'd like to know more about him. Why he's working at Midwinter, perhaps. Is it just because Stratford's there?'

'Okay. Anything else?'

'Perhaps you could find out who's investing in them. I'm sure I could find out on-line but you'll do it quicker than me.'

'Why is it important?'

'Two reasons. First, are they complicit in everything that's going on? Are the Greifs and Montgomery carrying out their wishes? Second, if they're just honest angels with money to burn, would it interest them to know what's going on, if we had tangible proof of something taking place that shouldn't be?'

'Investors don't usually care, do they, so long as there's no publicity around their investment and they're linked to it.'

'What happens there is so secretive I'd be surprised if the investors knew the whole truth. I think they're being told just enough to keep them happy. But I think Greif and his personal team are writing their own agenda, whatever that is. I don't think he gives two shits about Midwinter and Charles Montgomery in fact.'

'I'll see what I can do.'

I thanked him and hung up. As I'd been talking to him, several things had become clearer. Primarily that Stratford Greif was without doubt running his own team under cover of Midwinter's umbrella. The more I thought about it, the less I thought Charles Montgomery had the first clue what was going on.

Secondly, if the Greifs were running their own research program, using their own people, even their own security … what the hell were they doing behind those locked doors at Midwinter? And what was so important to them that they didn't seem to mind using violence, threats and possibly even murder to cover it up?

CHAPTER TWENTY

THE NEXT MORNING I rang Margaret and spoke to her briefly, just to show that I wasn't ignoring her, then drove to Belinda McFee's house. I don't like being static and I had no reason to be in the office, so I thought the drive would clear my head.

She opened the door in a night-gown. As it was eleven o'clock in the morning, I was a little surprised.

She said, 'Stop gawping. My ankle played up last night after I got home so I thought I'd stay in bed all day. Until some idiot came knocking on my door.'

'Sorry about that. Can I come in?'

She didn't answer but stepped back, looking out into the street after I'd passed her. Without her heeled boots she was an inch and a half shorter than I remembered, but she had the heft and physical presence of an athlete.

She offered tea and I agreed, wandering through into her front room. The sofa was covered with blankets and there were magazines strewn over the floor. A bag of Maltesers was open on the small table at the end of the sofa. The television was playing silently in the corner—some lurid interview programme by the look of it.

She came in with the teas, put them down and switched off the television. She didn't seem to be limping any more.

'You could have phoned. I'd have prepared my boudoir.'

'I'm going to see my client later. Thought I'd see how you were and what you made of yesterday.'

She sat down on her sofa and I took a chair opposite.

She said, 'Isobel's tougher than she looks. She's got that upper class fearlessness. You get the feeling that if anything went wrong she'd ring the Prime Minister and give him an earful.'

'That might be true, but she's out of her league here.'

'So what do we do, white man?'

'First, what about your ankle? Are you back on your feet?'

'More or less. What are we, Friday? It'll be okay again by Monday. It's got better each day.'

'Okay. As for what we do, it's getting tricky. Jolyon Greif and a couple of heavies came to see me last night. Said my free pass into Midwinter had been pulled. They don't want me in there any more, stirring things up.'

'What reason did they give?'

'They said I'd upset some people. I didn't believe them because it's so unlike me. There must be another reason, if I could just figure out what it was.'

We talked back and forth for fifteen minutes, discussing our next steps. I told her that I had Dan working on some research and she said she'd been trying the Internet too but had found nothing more. As it was close to the weekend we decided that we'd be better prepared if we rested over the next two days, then tried a different tack. Though at this point we had no idea what that might be. Whatever the Greifs were doing, they were doing it behind closed doors. Short of kidnapping one of the young scientists and sweating it out of them, I didn't see what else we could do.

After a while I realised that she was tired—perhaps the bedclothes on the sofa were a sign that she hadn't been sleeping well.

She saw me looking at the state of the room and turned a speculative gaze on me.

She said, 'I used to know people like you in the Army.'

'Handsome daredevils you'd follow to the ends of the earth?'

'A couple of captains I came across, at different times. Different backgrounds, different experiences. But they shared this need to be doing the Right Thing.'

'I don't get you.'

'Well the Army's as full of tossers as any other organisation. Stands to reason. But now and then you come across someone who believes in their bones that they're making a difference, and that the decisions they make are going to be very influential. Whether it's organizing the sleeping arrangements in a bivouac or outlining a strategy to outflank the enemy. They take themselves just seriously enough to be thought of as competent, but at the same time there's a kind of fervour about them. Nearly a zealousness. Is that a word?'

I nodded. She went on.

'They wanted to be doing good. Be on the side of the angels. And I think you've got something like that in you, too. From what you said the other day, perhaps you take after your dad.'

'He'd never want to be seen as a do-gooder.'

'Well that was him. I'm not so sure about you. I think you want to help people and doing it for money makes it seem okay, a proper job. You'd be embarrassed otherwise. I bet you don't charge enough, do you?'

'I think I might be offended by that.'

'Don't be. It's as near to a compliment as you're likely to get. Tell me, why did you come here, really? You could have rung.'

'I told you, I'm in the area to meet my client later. Just thought I'd see how you were.'

She raised her eyebrows.

'Okay, tough guy. Don't let your guard down. You never know when someone might come barrelling through it. Is that a word?'

'It it wasn't, it is now.'

WHEN I LEFT Belinda's house it was lunchtime, so I found a McDonalds and went large on some kind of chicken meal. I wadded up the cardboard leftovers, stuck them in the waste-bin in the car-park, then phoned Dan.

I said, 'Just wondering if you've found out anything on the Greifs.'

'Give me a break, you only asked me last night.'

'I hear the Internet's supposed to be fast. Quicker than ordinary mail and carrier pigeons, apparently.'

'I've only been up an hour.'

'Partying?'

'The States are five hours plus behind us. Eight in some places. I have to stay up late to trade in real time. So I don't get to bed till the early hours.'

'You're young, you can take it.'

'Not when I've got other stuff to do. It's not all about you, you know.'

I grinned at the phone. I quite liked riling him. He was usually so superior and calm I liked to take him down a peg or two.

He said, 'Anyway, I've got something. Not much.'

'I knew you could do it.'

'Something on Jolyon. Apparently he used to be a cop. Fairly high up in the GMP but took early retirement.'

'Any hints?'

'Of being a bad apple? No. It was just a note in one of the police bulletins they send out to locals, keep them informed of how their tax money is being spent. Photos of him shaking hands with a dignitary and getting an award.'

'When was this?'

'Couple of years ago.'

'So then he retired and went to work straight away with Stratford at Midwinter. Strengthened Stratford's hand. I wonder if they even had security there before he turned up? That's something I can check. Keep on it.'

'If I can keep awake. Leave me alone for a bit. I'm making you money here.'

We hung up. It was getting on for three o'clock now and I was supposed to be at Margaret's house. I wondered how we'd talk to each other, given the outcome of our previous meeting. I decided I'd be strong and manly.

It was what I did best.

HOW MARGARET HANDLED it was to refuse to look me in the eye. She opened the door and stood back, then closed it behind me. I went into the room where we'd previously talked and sat down. After a few minutes she came in with two cups of tea. She looked good, her hair washed and fluffed, her face less pallid than usual. She wore a dark skirt that came to just below her knees and a black tank-top over a white blouse with a high collar. Her lipstick was pink and lent her face a vibrancy I hadn't seen in a while.

She said, 'Let's just forget what happened before, eh? I'm embarrassed and it probably breaks one of your client relationship rules. It was very nice but we don't have to carry on with it.'

I coughed. 'That's very nice of you. I don't feel good about it because you weren't in the best frame of mind. I shouldn't have done it. You—'

'I knew what I was doing, Sam. You didn't take advantage of me. I needed it, on several levels. Now let's just drop it.'

Her tone seemed final.

I said, 'Okay.'

'This is coincidental, but I've got something for you.'

She reached to the table that contained her family photographs and picked up a small brown envelope that she handed to me.

'For what you've done already. I've added some more for next week. I hope a cheque's okay.'

I put the envelope inside my jacket pocket without opening it. 'That's fine. Very generous. Thank you.'

She smiled for the first time. 'If you're going to get beaten up on my behalf, the least I can do is pay your hospital bills. Do you go private?'

I shook my head. 'National Health, me.'

We both sipped from our tea like librarians discussing the disposition of a new rack of shelves. I resisted the urge to raise my little finger. As so often before, I marvelled at the weird situations my job placed me in. Meeting people in extraordinary circumstances, getting to know their lives at a fundamental level, but always operating on a commercial basis. I understood why there was always this drive from some people in my job to make the role as 'professional' as possible. Like undertakers, we met people under stress and needed a code of conduct that managed our emotional engagement. Otherwise we'd be forever swimming in an ocean of turbulent passions and most likely would become unbalanced ourselves.

I said, 'I've got something to ask you. I asked you before but we didn't really finish the conversation. I want you to consider going away for a while. I have a feeling Stratford Greif is ramping up for something and I'd feel better if you weren't around.'

She looked down at the tea cup that was juddering slightly in her hands.

'I've committed to staying there. I had an interview with Natalie from HR today, checking I was okay. I told them I'd carry on.'

I don't think I kept the frustration out of my voice.

'That's your choice. But I don't think it's a good idea, given what we're finding out.'

She looked up defiantly. 'You haven't found anything yet, have you? It's all just speculation. I'm beginning to think I made up the whole thing. Actually, I don't know what I think. Everything is the same at work. Nobody mentions Nathan. Nobody sheds a tear. Everything hums along exactly as it did before.'

'Don't you think that's odd? Wouldn't you like to know what really happened?'

'We'll never know, will we? Unless you've got a time machine and can get back into that hotel room with Nathan.'

'I don't trust any of them. Jolyon was a policeman with Greater Manchester Police. I wouldn't be surprised if he has a word with some of his friends and any investigation into Dr Mustow's death quietly goes away. I've been banned from the site and at the moment they think they've done enough to keep us all at bay. If you keep working there it'll just make them more nervous, thinking you might know something. They might do something stupid.'

'Are you trying to scare me?'

'Of course not. But you have to be rational about this. Why walk back into the lion's den?'

'Well what do you expect me to do? I can't stay here, staring out of the window. Smiling at the neighbours as if nothing's happened.'

'Don't you have any friends or relatives out of the area? Somewhere you could go, just for a week, maybe two. Then come back when I've had a chance to suss out what's really going on.'

'A week?'

'Maybe two. I can't be sure how long it will take to get a handle on things, but usually not much more than that.'

She put down her tea-cup and smoothed out her dress.

'I have a cousin in Derbyshire. We visit each other once a year. I could ask.'

'Please. Do it now. I don't want you to change your mind.'

She stared at me for a moment, then stood up and left the room. After a while I heard her voice from the back of the house. She laughed a couple of times and shortly afterwards came back in, now smiling.

'That's done. I can't go till Tuesday because she's got other guests who aren't leaving until Monday afternoon.'

'Okay. I guess that will have to do. I might check in with you over the weekend.'

She closed her eyes and leaned back in her chair. 'It's a good idea, actually. I don't think I've realised how tense I've been. Caroline will make me laugh. She and her partner are like a double-act.'

'Thank you for doing that. Let me know when you're leaving.'

She opened her eyes, those large orbs that were mostly blue with a hint of green around the edges. I hadn't seen the depth of trust that they could hold until now.

She said, 'I'll call.'

CHAPTER TWENTY ONE

SHE CALLED ON Sunday morning, while I was cleaning up my back garden from its winter desolation. Her voice contained a sparkle that I hadn't heard before.

She said, 'Just to let you know I'm all set. I'm staying in today, do some final washing. Then a bit of shopping tomorrow in town, ready to go Tuesday. I just wanted to say thank you. I realised I'd paid you but hadn't actually said thanks.'

'No need. It's supposed to be my job.'

'I still say thank you to the plumber and the window-washer.'

'You're a very polite human being.'

'No I'm not. I can be a pain in the backside, irritable, quick to take offence. I know my shortcomings, Sam. So thank you for ignoring them.'

I wondered if she wanted to say something more but couldn't work out how to say it. Clients often cling to you when you've solved problems that, to them, were insoluble.

I hadn't solved her problem, true, though I had the feeling that I'd got closer to her than most. Maybe I'd done enough to lighten her load, at least temporarily.

I said, 'When you're away don't think about Midwinter or what's going on here. If there's anything to be found, Belinda and I will find it.'

'What do you really think is going on? Why all the aggression and secrecy? If it was Jolyon Greif's thugs who attacked you the other night, what was it for? I don't understand what they think they're up to.'

'My opinion is that it's some kind of self-aggrandising secret society. Stratford Greif considers himself a cut above everyone else and he's gathered a little club of people who'll worship his advanced intellect. Jolyon is along for the ride and the pay-cheque, and the other muscle-men are just paid grunts who get a kick out of wearing uniforms and driving black cars with tinted windows. Everyone likes to think their job is special in some way. Greif is just allowing his tribe to have grand notions about themselves. Maybe it's a motivational thing.'

'So what happened to Nathan? Why did he kill himself?'

I sat down in my kitchen and looked through the patio doors at the wreck of my garden, the half-filled pond, the scrubby herbs, the earthenware pots of bent-over shrubs. Philosophising about someone else's life and death seemed rich coming from me.

'If he did kill himself, we'll probably never know why. If he didn't, and Midwinter had anything to do with it, then we'll find out and hold them to account. Those are the options at the moment. If Midwinter was the cause of Nathan's death then it would have been Stratford Greif's hand behind the scenes. I can guarantee that. He's working up to something and he didn't want your boss letting down the side at the last minute. Nathan was stressed, which made him a pressure point. And to relieve a pressure point you either open a valve or smash the whole device.'

'So you think they made him kill himself, or actually did it themselves, just to keep secret whatever it is they're doing?'

'It looks like that to me.'

'I'm glad I'm going away.'

'Good. And I don't expect to see you back until I let you know.'

'Yes, sir.'

We hung up. I continued to stare at my chaotic garden, wondering what I was doing. I had few gardening skills, but I knew one thing.

When you break a plant it stays broken.

I DIDN'T WANT Jolyon Greif to think he'd won a round, so first thing Monday morning I drove to Midwinter and parked in the lane a little way back from the first security pole. The day was blustery and fresh despite a low sun, so the guard stayed inside his lodge, probably huddled over a paraffin heater and leafing through copies of *The Economist*.

After a short while he came out, took a photo of my licence plate with his iPad, and walked towards my door making the internationally-recognised, if now dated, 'wind-down-your-window' movement. I complied.

'Hello, sir, what can we do for you?'

'I'd like to speak to Charles Montgomery.'

'Have you got an appointment?'

He was scrolling down the list on his iPad and apparently not finding a likely name.

I said, 'He'll want to speak to me. Tell him Sam Dyke wants a word.'

He sized me up, then walked back to his lodge. I had no doubt who he was calling, a guess confirmed when I saw Jolyon Greif, George and Mr Bones walking down the slight slope of the entrance road and edging around the security poles. The slope made them appear to walk with heavy-footed purpose, though that might have been deliberate and intended to intimidate me. It didn't work. Greif nodded towards the lodge and came straight towards me. I got out of my car so he wouldn't have the superior angle.

He stopped in front of me and said, 'I used the word "clown" to describe you, didn't I? I was too soft. Village idiot is more like. How many times do you have to be told that you're not wanted here? Do we have to forcibly eject you?'

I looked at George and Mr Bones. George would be a difficult object to shift, but Mr Bones was six inches shorter than me and slim as a pipe-cleaner. Of the two, though, I wouldn't turn my back on Bones.

I said to Greif, 'I wanted to ask Mr Montgomery whether he knows what's going on in his laboratory.'

'He knows perfectly well what's going on. Research. Brain-work. Something that would be a mystery to you. Just turn your fucking car round and go home.'

'Or what? This is the public highway. I've got every right to be here.'

'Now you're just being childish.'

Mr Bones stepped forward. He'd been chewing on the end of a match like a Hollywood gangster. He took it out of his mouth and pointed it at me.

'You've lost this one, Dyke. Go home like a good boy and you won't get hurt. Again.'

I don't like to use violence—much—but this time I felt I was justified. I snaked out a hand, caught his wrist and turned it so that he had to swivel to avoid it snapping. I lowered him and he fell to his knees, turning and turning so that he was forced to look up at me.

I sensed George taking a step forward and I let go of the red-headed man's wrist. He sprang to his feet and brushed down his trouser knees, almost as red in the face as he was above the hair-line.

He muttered, 'You bastard.'

I said, 'Don't you know it's rude to point with sharp objects.'

Greif had remained immobile throughout this, as though wearied by his own man's performance and unwilling to intervene. His round face with its thin mouth and blank eyes turned from me to Bones and back again. If he and Stratford were brothers, they were different physical types but shared the same steady intransigence, as though nothing could shock or surprise them or make them change their minds.

He said, 'You've had your fun, Dyke. Just go away. There's nothing to see here. You're not getting in. Go home and water a plant or read a book.'

I'd made whatever point I wanted to make. I opened my car door and Greif took a step back to give me room. Mr Bones took half a step forward in his place and took the matchstick from his mouth again.

'Your little helper didn't turn up for work today. She knows what's best for her. Take a lesson.'

Greif said, 'Bones,' and flipped his head, gesturing for him to move back. Mr Bones continued to stare at me, a malevolent grin twisting his mouth to one side. His gestures and expressions were those of someone who'd learned how to be tough from watching a training video. They had no foundation in strength or technique. Finally he glanced up at Jolyon and took a pace back towards George, who had barely moved the whole time. I suspected it took a while to get the mass of his muscle travelling forward, like a refrigeration truck engaging first gear, so he didn't expend energy on trivial movements.

I climbed in my car and didn't look at them as I made a three-point turn in the narrow lane and drove off. In my rear-view mirror the three men stood in the road like tombstones.

CHAPTER TWENTY TWO

I DROVE FOR a mile then pulled into a lay-by and phoned Margaret on her mobile. She'd said she was going shopping in town, presumably Manchester, and I hoped she'd take her phone with her. There was no reply—I was sent straight to voice-mail.

There'd been something on Mr Bones' face that I was just becoming aware of after the event. A knowingness, a brief air of superiority, as though he was privy to something I wasn't. I'd been so pumped up by the encounter between us that it had taken some time for his expression to make an impact.

Now I was worried.

I worked out where I was in relation to Margaret's house and recalculated my directions. I was less than twenty minutes away, even driving through the winding roads of that part of the county. I did a three-point-turn in the road and headed north briefly before turning west towards Knutsford.

My route took me past the white skeletal structures of Jodrell Bank's two radio-telescopes—the larger of the two now pointing straight upwards like a gigantic begging bowl asking for celestial offerings. I wondered if Charles Montgomery could see me beetling along this road from his perch on the sixth floor of Midwinter a few miles behind me. What would he be thinking? Did I impinge on his thoughts at all? Did he care about Nathan Mustow's death beyond a few platitudes, or was he like Stratford Greif and the Bleak members, apparently insensitive towards the death of one of his colleagues? I'd worked for people not dissimilar to him in the past—managers who bent with the wind, trying to show a reasonable side to their behaviour, if only to maintain reasonable relations with the staff, but who in the end would give nothing by way of compromise. I wondered what he really thought of Stratford Greif and the little empire he seemed to have built behind the locked biosafety doors. I hoped for his sake that he wasn't unaware of what Greif was doing.

The roads were clear, the sun still relatively low in the sky, the trees that lined one side of the road casting sharp-edged shadows over the tarmac. I overtook a lumbering farm vehicle and then turned right, coming out near the golf club at Woodside. A couple of middle-aged men were thwacking drives on the practice range, taking Monday off, having a good time as the season started to lengthen.

Ten minutes later I was turning into Margaret's driveway. I stayed calm as I knocked on her front door and tried her door-bell. I told myself not to be surprised when there was no reply.

I took out my phone and called her again, then tried the land-line. I heard it ringing somewhere just inside the door.

I remembered seeing a handset on a small carved table in the hallway.

To the left was a small iron gate leading to a path that ran between the house and its neighbour. It was padlocked but was only waist-high, so I climbed over and padded around to the back of the building. Behind the house ran a long, well-tended garden of lawn, flower beds and a bare wooden gazebo standing skeletally to one side. There was a slabbed patio that you got to via the kitchen door. I tried the door without luck. I couldn't see anything inside the kitchen through the door's mottled glass window, so I moved sideways and peered with a hand to my eyes through the window of the kitchen, which ran the whole width of the back of the house.

What I saw hit me like a punch in the gut.

I ran back down the side of the house, climbed the gate again and opened the boot of my car. I took out a small tool-kit. Back over the gate and at the kitchen door again I used a key and a lightweight hammer to bump open the lock, then pushed the door open and stepped inside.

Margaret was face down on the table, her eyes wide, one hand splayed out unnaturally by her head. I checked for a pulse at her neck but there was nothing. A syringe was still attached to her wrist, a small amount of clear liquid still visible inside, pooled in one corner of the glass. Her other arm hung limply over the edge of the table. She wore a dark blouse underneath a thick pullover—clothes for outdoors, not for staying inside a warm house.

I sat at the table facing her and closed my eyes. She hadn't committed suicide, whatever this was supposed to suggest. It looked as though they'd used the same method as with Nathan Mustow, perhaps to create a fiction that Margaret had followed her boss because she was in love with him.

People at Midwinter would say that she'd been unhappy, that there were suspicions that she and Mustow had had an affair, that she had been despondent after Mustow's death and unable to concentrate. After all, she was a single woman without a current partner …

But it was all a lie. For some reason, the Greifs had wanted Margaret dead. Perhaps it was another attempt to warn Belinda and me to keep out of their business, to tell us this was what happened if you got in their way. They knew we'd been stubborn at the first time of asking so we needed a stronger message.

On the other hand, perhaps it was more than a warning. Perhaps it was a set-up. An attempt to implicate me …

I sat up straight and looked around. Where had I been when I stayed with Margaret that night? What had I touched? My fingerprints were on file because of the work I used to do for the government.

On full alert, I mentally retraced my steps for the visits I'd paid. I looked under the sink and found a large soft cloth, then went upstairs and began in the bedroom. I wiped every surface that I might have come into contact with. Wardrobe doors, bedside table, bed-head, alarm-clock, door handles. Then into the en suite bathroom and did it all again—taps, toilet-lid, shower door. I wiped everything with fervour, trying to erase every possible sign that I'd been in the house.

Downstairs again I wiped more door knobs, the table tops, the edges of the doors. I found the cups in a wall-cupboard and wiped every single handle of every cup. I wiped the sink taps, the draining board, the tops of the kitchen table and chairs. I went to the kitchen-door and wiped its handle and its edge.

Then I went to the front door and wiped off the bell-push and the knocker.

A thought occurred to me and I looked for the sort of table or set of drawers that might have served as an office. I found it in a room upstairs, a writing bureau with a fold-down top. In a drawer on the right was a cheque-book, the last stub showing the amount she'd paid me and my name next to it: S. Dyke. It was easier to take the whole thing, so I stuffed it in a pocket. I hadn't cashed the cheque yet and now never would.

Downstairs and back in the kitchen I balled up the cloth and put it in my other jacket pocket. I couldn't see a suicide note but wondered whether one was being 'arranged' somewhere.

I went to Margaret again and touched the top of her head. It was cold and hard, as though the absence of life had drained her body of any softness or gentleness she might have possessed. I walked around to the other side of the table and looked one more time into her large blue-green eyes, now dimmed. Something welled up inside me but I tamped it down. There wasn't time for that now.

I made certain the kitchen door was locked again and left through the front door. Neither of the neighbouring houses overlooked Margaret's front garden because of the way each house was laid in its own hollow, so I had good expectations that I hadn't been seen, so long as no one had actually observed me driving in to begin with. I pulled the door shut behind me using the cloth from my pocket, then climbed into my Mondeo and drove away.

It took me some time to find a pay-phone in Holmes Chapel. It was in a pub where a midday crowd was beginning to gather, braying at each other with all the confidence of middle-class people who could afford expensive meals. I whispered to the voice at the other end of the line that the police should go to Margaret's address. They'd find the body of a young woman inside.

I didn't leave my name before I hung up.

I sat in the pub for half an hour, staring at a pint of Guinness. My mind was too busy for me to consider drinking it.

I was too busy working on revenge.

CHAPTER TWENTY THREE

LATER THAT AFTERNOON I found myself driving down Belinda's street and pulling up outside her house. I seemed to have lost a couple of hours and twenty miles. I didn't really want to speak to anyone, but there didn't seem to be any way to avoid it.

I saw her curtains twitch and then her face appeared against the glass. Presumably she'd recognised my car. Moments later her front door opened and she stood there looking quizzically at me. She was fully-dressed this time and seemed to be standing without letting the weight off one leg, as she'd done the last time I saw her.

Eventually she turned away but left the front door open. I climbed out of my car, locked it, and entered her house.

She called out, 'Kitchen!' and I walked down her hallway, over the shiny tiles that seemed more intricate in their pattern than they had a right to be.

I wondered when I'd started noticing decorative anomalies, and took a deep breath. Maybe I wasn't thinking straight.

Belinda was making tea on the kitchen counter, dabbing a tea-bag into two mugs before dropping it into a waste-bin. I was struck once again by how mundane activities could continue after terrible events had taken place. And why not? Belinda didn't know what I'd found so had no reason to be shocked.

'One sugar, wasn't it?'

I nodded, still not sure whether I could trust my mouth to form words. She glanced up at me as she stirred the sugar into the mugs. I felt a sudden need to hold on to her … but instead turned away and went into the front room. Outside, the sun blazed away on the windows of the houses opposite, as though dark deeds and evil-doing didn't exist in such a bright and shiny world.

Belinda came back in with the teas and sat facing me.

I said, 'My client's dead.'

She didn't move. She didn't widen her eyes, drop her jaw or spill her tea. Her expression didn't change and she didn't mutter a curse.

She nodded, once, and looked down. The room had been tidied up since my last visit and I gazed at the banality of the photographs, the wallpaper, the television, the corner table. The slight musty smell of the sick room that had lingered in the air last time had been replaced by the scent of a perfumed straw diffuser on the mantelpiece. It started to give me a headache.

She said, 'How did it happen?'

'They want the police to think it was a copy-cat suicide. Syringe in the arm.'

'And you don't think it was?'

'I'd persuaded her to go away for a few days. She was supposed to be shopping today.'

Understanding landed in her eyes.

'You found her.'

I told her how I'd gone to Midwinter to see Charles Montgomery and been turned away by Jolyon Greif and his muscle. I could still see Mr Bones' sneer as he mentioned Margaret's name.

Belinda said, 'It doesn't make sense. Why would they go so far? Murdering a poor girl like that?'

'The stakes are high. Stratford Greif is an obsessive. He won't want any loose ends.'

'Like you and me.'

'We have to be on the lookout. Don't answer the door unless it's to me. Don't go out at night if you can help it.'

'I never go out at night. Can't get a date.'

'I'm serious.'

'Who isn't?'

She saw I was becoming exasperated.

She said, 'Are you certain that Stratford is responsible for all this? Jolyon and Mr Bones are more like loose cannons than he is.'

'They're yes-men. Jolyon is the one who's been on my case, but Stratford is the leader. You've never met him. You can see the fanaticism in his eyes. I don't know what's behind it but I want to find out. And stop it.'

'I did you a disservice the other day.'

'What do you mean?'

'I said you were like your father, or what you'd told me about him. Wanting to do good. And you think that by doing this job and finding out the truth, whatever that is, it'll help you be a good person.'

'How is that a disservice?'

'It's too simple. I think you've given up on the truth now. You're thinking about revenge, aren't you?'

'Of course not.'

'You're gripping that cup so hard it's going to shatter. Calm down.'

'Don't tell me what to do. Nobody tells me what to do.'

'Okay, you can go now.' She stood up.

'What?'

'Either go or get a grip of yourself. I'm not having you sitting there like an undertaker.'

'I needed somewhere to be.'

'Very flattering, I'm sure.'

There was a pause and then she sat down again. I heard a clock ticking from the room next door, time passing, minutes ebbing away. I was going in a forward direction after all and couldn't prevent the past from happening. I didn't have the time machine that Margaret had mentioned.

I said, 'Regarding what you said just now—I told you, I'm not my dad. I don't think I'm a do-gooder. Besides, he was just an ordinary man who worked down a mine. Our situations are different.'

'In what way? I bet people who did the wrong things for the wrong reasons made him angry, just like they do for you.'

'Why shouldn't I get angry at people's ignorance when they break the law in stupid or dangerous ways? Why are *you* doing this? Is it just a job? Just for the money? Don't you want to catch bad guys?'

She glanced away, towards the photograph showing her younger self climbing onto the side of a Churchill tank, somewhere in Germany.

She said, 'It's not the money. I've worked that way. I've tried ordinary jobs. Office jobs. Partly it's working for other people—I can't seem to do it. I don't mind having clients, but I don't like having bosses.'

'They screw you up.'

'Exactly, then blame you for the mess you've caused.'

I stood up. 'Well I've caused this mess. I pushed Midwinter and they pushed back, and Margaret was caught in the middle. That's on me.'

'Come on, you don't really believe that. You've done nothing wrong except do your job.'

'But maybe you were right.'

'About what?'

I thought for a moment, wondering what I was trying to say. I'd never thought about my behaviour objectively—that was a game for people capable of far more introspection than me.

I said, 'My dad was a good man who was incapable of doing a bad deed. I wanted to be like that. So I went through a shit time in my last job in Customs and Excise because I did what I thought he would do. I was honest. I didn't lie.'

'What happened?'

'Hadn't you noticed? I'm working for myself now. I was negotiated out of the job. I told the truth when I didn't need to, and to the wrong people.'

I could tell she wanted to ask me for the story but I didn't want to tell it, so I gave her no encouragement.

I said, 'But actually I'm not my dad and I don't need to act like him. I don't need to be a good man.'

'You'll find it hard not to be. You're as much a fanatic as Stratford Greif.'

'We'll see.'

'What are you going to do?'

'Come with me tomorrow morning and find out.'

CHAPTER TWENTY FOUR

JOLYON GREIF THOUGHT that Stratford liked the morning meetings because they gave him the opportunity to exercise his power. Although he was head of the unit, he didn't see most of the people in the room on a daily basis, so he had to use these gatherings as a way of keeping control, persuading his young colleagues, who'd bizarrely started calling themselves The Bleak, that they were on the right track and Doing the Right Thing.

He'd often queried his own adherence to Stratford's regime, asking himself whether he was so bereft of direction and character after leaving the force that Stratford's belief system was as good as any other. He'd no doubt that Stratford was a highly intelligent and commanding individual—but he'd seen many of those in the Greater Manchester Police, and many of them had failed in one way or another.

What made Stratford distinct was his burning self-righteousness, his unwavering conviction that his views of the world and its failings were objectively correct and unquestionable. Since he'd renounced the soviet side of his family and come over to the UK he seemed to have a mission, an urgency bordering on fanaticism.

Jolyon remembered the visits to the large house in the Borders where his grandparents had lived, and where the family had gathered periodically during his youth. It was almost a small castle, with a turret and a courtyard and surrounded by tall conifers whose lower branches barely yielded when you ran through them, leaving your ankles, wrists and neck covered with small scratches. On the two occasions Stratford had come with his mother, Jolyon's aunt, he'd refused to engage in any 'childish' games that involved running or jumping or hiding. At ten, Jolyon was sporty and athletic and had teased Stratford about his reading and unwillingness to play with him or the other cousins. Stratford didn't seem to mind being teased and got his own back when they played board games indoors—there being no television—easily winning at Monopoly and chess and Risk, which seemed to particularly excite him.

Thinking back, Jolyon realised there'd been no real friction between them. Stratford was simply uninterested in other people's opinions so couldn't actually be teased or angered or persuaded to do something he didn't want to do.

Even at the age of ten his beliefs were strong and irrevocable.

And Jolyon had come to realise that this was what the younger people in the unit liked. They'd been carefully chosen by Stratford from a pool of recruits who were single, unattached, adrift and without any real convictions—but they had the brains and skills to carry out what he required. They arrived at Midwinter, or specifically at Greif's unit, wanting to be led, wanting to be taught how the world worked. Most of them had been on rigid rails since their mid-teens. They'd had the peculiar type of mind that found science easy, a trick, a series of logic problems to be solved. Their innate abilities had taken them to good universities and then to higher degrees and perhaps a research post here or there. But despite their high levels of intellectual attainment, they were still looking for a purpose, something that excited them as much as solving an equation or seeing the solution to an apparently intractable problem.

And that was Stratford's speciality — imbuing others with a sense of direction and a reason to do as he said. True enough he'd come unstuck a couple of times earlier in his career and had to leave in a hurry … but at Midwinter he'd found a role that gave him resources and independence and a supply of young, malleable minds. Jolyon considered himself to be part of the group but also a detached observer. He'd been asked to do a job and buying into Stratford's endgame wasn't essential. As it happened, he was so disaffected with what had become of his life that he'd taken up Stratford's philosophy anyway. He knew he could give it up when he wanted, unlike the group of youngsters who hung on Stratford's every word.

The last of these, the young man called Preston, came into the conference room and sat down, nodding briefly at Stratford. Apart from him, there were five other young scientists, Harry Tuck, Mr Bones and Jolyon. This was the core group. Jolyon had a couple of other men he used, such as George, but they weren't included because they didn't need to know more than he told them.

Stratford slapped his hand palm down on the table, his usual method of calling the meeting to order. Despite the proximity of the project's conclusion, and the recent problems caused by Nathan Mustow, he seemed to Jolyon to be bearing up well. He was rarely flustered because he was always the cleverest man in the room and could think around any problem.

He said, 'Moving on. Mr Preston, now you've arrived, perhaps you'd like to bring us up to date.'

Preston opened a folder that he'd brought with him and took out a sheet of paper. It would be destroyed as soon as the meeting was concluded.

He said, 'Thank you, Stratford. As you know, final testing was concluded this week. We didn't find anything that we didn't expect, and in fact the targeted enrichment results were a little ahead of our planning ... '

As Preston began speaking, Jolyon tuned out. He'd sat through almost a year of these meetings and had lost interest about one month in. He'd begun to realise that the young men and women were as obsessed about scoring points off each other as achieving Stratford's goals. It was as though they were vying for Daddy's attention. At the after-hours meetings, once a week, the women fluttered their eyes at him while the men drank each other under the table in their attempts to keep up with Stratford's heroic capacity. It all seemed to pass Stratford by. All he wanted was that the project come to fruition at last, after all his aborted attempts to get it going.

Now it was Harcourt's turn up at bat. Jolyon thought that if she did her hair differently and wore contacts instead of those ugly designer specs, she might be passable. Unfortunately, her voice had an awful London twang to it that turned him off completely. He listened as she began to talk about high-throughput sequencing and linear deployment, then turned to look at Bones Bonetti, who seemed as bored as he was. Bonetti would have to go, of course, when it came down to the wire. He was about as trustworthy as a paper knife in an apple peeling contest. There was something inherently flaky in him that was useful when directed properly, but most of the time he set Jolyon's teeth on edge; you never knew what he might do next.

At last all the science was dealt with and Stratford glanced towards Harry Tuck. Jolyon knew that Stratford was beginning to have doubts about the so-called Production Manager. In the last month or so he'd become more and more rattled by Nathan Mustow's behaviour and hadn't been able to keep it in check. Mustow had withdrawn himself from participation in The Bleak before Stratford had steered it towards its ultimate goal, so he had no real idea what its intentions were. However, he'd been a smart man and had begun to worry about some of the research and development projects that Stratford had set in train. Stratford had been able to keep him in line for a while, even using Charles Montgomery as the ultimate sanction— without the Director knowing it, of course. The threat of losing his job had kept Mustow in place and reasonably effective as a project manager, but they'd all known that the time would come when action would need to be taken. It hadn't been easy getting him to that meeting in the hotel. But once there, Bones had done the rest, thankfully.

Tuck had taken it badly, complaining to Stratford that he hadn't signed up for anything like that. Stratford had talked to him and reminded him that he had indeed signed up for it when he agreed to join The Bleak and signed the group charter. Egg on face for Tuck. But it hadn't really settled him down, and now Jolyon was wondering when Stratford would give him the signal and he would have to wind up Bones and set him off again, this time headed in Harry Tuck's direction.

Stratford had been asking Tuck what news there was of that man Dyke and his new colleague, Belinda McFee.

Tuck glanced sidelong at Jolyon. 'I rather deputised that to our security men. The man in charge doesn't get his hands dirty, you know. First rule of warfare.'

Stratford Greif said, 'No. According to Sun Tzu, the first rule of warfare is to know your enemy and to know yourself. I think we can assume we know ourselves. So what do we know about these two meddlers?'

Tuck looked uncomfortable and Jolyon knew why. Tuck had tried to dismiss Dyke and McFee as inconsequential lightweights who he could roll over with his personality. Accordingly, he'd done next to no research on them.

Tuck said, 'They're private investigators, what's to know? One lives in Crewe and the other in south Manchester.'

Stratford's voice went quiet. 'That's it? That's the sum total of your research into these two carbuncles?'

'I asked Jolyon to take care of it!'

'So you abrogated your responsibility as a senior member of my staff to someone else, someone who you well know has a very full plate at the moment.'

Tuck seemed deflated, his cheeks sallow and his shoulders hunched.

'I asked the appropriate member of staff to handle the situation. It's out of my remit, Stratford. You can't expect me to do everything.'

'I don't. I expect you to do *some*thing.'

He turned his attention to Jolyon at the far end of the table. Jolyon felt his pulse quicken a little—he hated being spoken to in front of others he considered more junior.

Stratford said, 'And what have you found out? Do we know Mr Dyke's weight and social security number? Has our research been so thorough?'

'We've spoken to them. They know where they stand.'

'Oh do they? Do they indeed? And where is it exactly that they *do* stand?'

Mr Bones said, 'With one foot in the grave,' then he grinned around the room as if expecting applause. He received blank stares.

Stratford said, 'I understand there was an altercation the other night. What happened?'

Jolyon interrupted before Mr Bones could reply.

'I'll talk to you about that later. Can we move on?'

Stratford stared at him, taking a moment before he said, 'If you insist. Mr Bonetti, how did it go with Miss Sellers?'

Jolyon sat up. He knew nothing about this. What was he talking about?

Mr Bones at least had the grace to look sheepish.

He said, 'It was okay. She's been made aware of our position.'

'Good. No come-backs?'

'No come-backs.'

Jolyon said, 'What's this about? Why wasn't I involved?'

Stratford raised a hand as if to placate him.

'Executive decision, taken when you weren't available. I instructed Mr Bones on a side matter.'

'I'm always available.'

'Not this time you weren't. We'll talk later. Perhaps when we discuss the altercation the other night.'

Jolyon didn't like the death's head smile that flickered across Stratford's face.

Stratford continued, 'As you all know, we'll shortly be entering the final phase. Is everything prepared?'

There were enthusiastic nods from around the table.

'Have you all made your individual arrangements? Once this begins there'll be no opportunity to turn back.'

Murmurs of agreement and one or two of the young scientists smiled shyly at each other. Jolyon couldn't bear it any longer and stood up.

'I'll be outside.'

Stratford commanded, 'Wait!'

He rose from his chair, looking directly at Jolyon, then turned and included Mr Bones by lifting his chin slightly towards him.

'Will you two step outside with me?'

Mr Bones pushed back his chair as though he couldn't get out of the room quickly enough. The three men went into Stratford's office next door and Jolyon found himself moving to the window and forcing himself to calm down.

When the door was closed behind them, he turned and said to Stratford, 'What is this? What are you doing?'

'I need you to get something for me.'

'What? Get what?'

'I think you need to calm down. I'd like you to leave the site for a while and consider your behaviour. As it happens, I forgot something that I need, so I'd be grateful if you could fetch it for me.'

'This is preposterous. I didn't come here to act like a fucking errand-boy.'

'I'm aware of that. I'm trying to calm the situation before either of us says something we'll regret.'

Jolyon glanced at Mr Bones, who seemed to be enjoying the contretemps.

'You can wipe that oily grin off your face.'

'Yes, boss.'

Stratford said, 'Mr Bonetti can go with you. You can amuse each other in the car.'

'It'll take more than this pencil-dick to amuse me.'

Mr Bones said, 'I'm hurt, boss. Size isn't everything.'

'Be grateful I didn't call you a ginger-headed knob-neck.'

'Yes, boss.'

'Now, where the fuck is this thing you want, Stratford?'

Jolyon found himself barely listening as Stratford gave them precise instructions what to look for, and where. He recognised in himself an impatience to move on, to get out of the office and to be outside doing something. Anything. He was discovering that working in security was not as enticing as it had sounded when he'd taken Stratford's offer. There was too much bullshit to deal with.

And he was used to giving instructions, not receiving them.

CHAPTER TWENTY FIVE

AT TEN O'CLOCK Tuesday morning we were parked in my car outside Stratford Greif's house. The weather was still clear and we'd had a good view as he'd left for work at 8.30, pointing his enormous Bentley away from us so that it slid down the suburban road like a duchess making her way through the commoners' kitchen, nose held aloft.

Time passed.

Belinda said, 'He's not coming back. It's been ninety minutes. He's at work.'

'I know. We'll do it. Are you sure about this?'

'I'm the opposite of sure. I think it's reckless and unprofessional. I think you're risking arrest and putting both our livelihoods in danger.'

'And on the down side?'

'I'm not going to stop you.'

'Just be here when I get back.'

'Take the keys if you don't trust me.'

I smiled and shook my head, then climbed out and trotted across the road.

Like most of the houses in the street, Greif's corner plot had electronic gates preventing access to his front drive. I walked the length of the hedge that stretched down one side of his garden until I came to the gap that I'd found when using Google Street View. I slipped into the alley, which was a boundary between his land and the next house in the street, a much more modest location.

At the end of Greif's garden ran a wall about my height with one heavy gate set into it. There was no point trying my bump key because it was the wrong kind of lock.

I glanced left and right, sized up the wall, raised my hands to grip the top row and scrambled up the brickwork and over.

I crouched, conscious that it was full daylight and that anyone could have seen me in the alley. But now, from my position at the bottom of a vegetable plot, I couldn't be seen by the houses to either side, so I waited for a few moments then walked up the paved pathway between rows of leeks and tomato wigwams to the back door. I seemed to be making a habit of breaking into people's kitchens.

This time my bump key worked on the door and I stepped into a large kitchen that was like a space-age laboratory, all smooth black surfaces, curved lines, futuristic gadgets from Germany and Japan. I should have expected nothing less from a scientist.

I walked through to the front of the house, pulling out my phone and dialling Belinda's number.

'I'm in. Text me if anything exciting happens.'

'Be more fun to see how you handle a cleaner turning up.'

I smiled and broke the connection, putting my phone on vibrate.

Now, where to begin?

The room I stood in was a sitting-room dominated by a huge wall-tapestry. It hung on a wall where a more down-market individual might have hung his 50-inch television screen. The tapestry was a mixture of deep reds and blues and seemed to be oriental, depicting old men with pointed beards sitting by flowing rivers and tended by young geishas. The wall facing the window held a long, low bookcase that contained a couple of hundred works of historical and philosophical analysis. I recognised some of the names—Toynbee, Russell, Fukuyama—but many of them were leather-bound and seemed old and arcane. There was a nice glass coffee table in front of the black leather sofa and in the corner a pale Yahama acoustic guitar sat up on a floor-stand. So he hadn't been lying about singing songs to his troops.

I walked out of this room, across a wide hallway and into the room on the other side. This seemed to be a library-cum-study. More bookshelves lining all the walls except the one where the window gave on to the side aspect of the house. I could see down the driveway from here and could make out the nose of my Mondeo just poking out from behind the hedge.

A closed Toshiba laptop sat on the desk—no point opening that. Greif would have some serious security built in, I had no doubt. The computer was perched on a conventional wooden table with drawers and I tried them all. One opened, containing a notebook, but there was nothing written in it. I suspected that even rubbing a pencil over the first page in best private eye fashion wouldn't have revealed a word.

One of the bookcases had glass windows closed over its top two shelves. It was where you might have kept first editions or books you didn't want your children to read. Peering through the glass I saw the same kind of titles I'd seen in the other room—history, philosophy, some biography. Nothing that I would have classified as subversive or anarchic.

But interestingly, there was a row of books by Yukio Mishima. I'd never read anything by him but knew he was a Japanese writer, an ultra-nationalist who'd committed suicide after an attempted coup. What did Greif find so fascinating about him that he had the full collection of works?

I tugged at the bookcase doors but they wouldn't open.

Then I realised that the phone in my pocket was vibrating, and had been for a little while. I took it out. There was a text from Belinda.

CHAPTER TWENTY SIX

SHE HAD BEEN been told many times during her training that breaking and entering was not an option for a professional private detective.

The group she'd worked for in Leeds saw themselves as accountants who wore black polo necks from time to time and, when necessary, would slip down a rope hanging from a helicopter to rescue the client from a fate worse than bankruptcy. But breaking the law in order to gain information was out of the question and, without a doubt, bad practice. If you needed to break the law you were probably not very good at your job.

But Dyke had managed to convince her.

He'd told her that Stratford Greif was unmistakeably a Bad Man working with other Bad Men, and the only way to really get the goods on them was to play them at their own game. What those goods might be, he couldn't say.

She'd said, 'I think the professional term for this is "fishing expedition".'

To which he'd replied, 'No, it's actually covert investigation. Get your terminology right. We *know* they're up to something and we're looking for evidence to support that premise. A fishing expedition is where you *think* somebody might be up to something and try to find out what that might be.'

'That distinction is so fine I can't see any daylight through it.'

'You're not looking hard enough.'

So in the end she agreed that because they'd been set upon by balaclava'd thugs, been close to two mysterious deaths and had been banned from Midwinter, it might be necessary to take matters into their own hands rather than wait for more confrontation with the Greifs.

But she wasn't happy.

Waiting in the car while Dyke broke into a perfectly respectable house in a bourgeois neighbourhood was not how she saw her career developing. If there was any development to come.

She was concerned about that because as she glanced into her rear-view mirror she saw the black Prius that Dyke had warned her about slowing down to swing past her and turn into Stratford Greif's house. There was a brief pause and then the gates opened. She laid down sideways behind the wheel of the Mondeo so that she wouldn't be seen, then sent a rapid text to Dyke and hoped he wasn't so distracted by what he'd found that he failed to feel the buzzing phone.

BELINDA'S SINGLE WORD text read: 'Car.'

Glancing out of the windows I saw that the electronic gates were wide open and that the Prius was already on the driveway. If I were to leave out of the back door now the driver would likely see me haring down the garden path to the gate.

Instead, I left the study and passed into the hallway, then ran up the curving staircase to the upper floor, hearing the front door open as I reached the top.

I was on a thickly-carpeted landing with five doors leading off it. I gently opened the first and it was the bathroom, all glass and steel and black surfaces like the kitchen. No hiding place. There were indistinct voices downstairs now, so more than one person had arrived. I closed the door behind me and padded to the next room. The door was open and I pushed inside. This was a bedroom with a futon-like arrangement laid out close to the floor, an ensuite bathroom, a modern chest of drawers and a row of built-in wardrobes with mirrors attached to the front. The windows gave a view of the side of the house and again I could see my car in the road, now seeming impossibly distant.

Downstairs I could hear an internal door closing and footsteps on the wooden flooring in the hallway. But the front door didn't bang shut so they weren't finished yet. Which meant they might be coming up the padded stairs.

What the hell were they looking for?

I moved quietly into the bathroom and closed the door without engaging the lock. I was just in time because through the crack I saw the door open and Jolyon's bulky figure step in. I watched as he looked at the mess of Stratford's bed and then glanced around. He shook his head. Behind him the door opened wider and Mr Bones came in. The way in which he looked at the room suggested that it was the first time he'd been inside. His eyes were alert and inquisitive.

He said, 'Some gaff, this. Guess he can afford it.'

With almost a protective gesture, Jolyon bent down and re-arranged the bedclothes on the futon so that they were neater than when he'd arrived.

He said, 'Idle bastard. Too used to having things done for him. Where did he say it was?'

'Bottom of the wardrobe.'

Jolyon turned round and opened the first door of the built-in wardrobes.

'Not this one.'

He moved to the next door and opened it, then grunted. 'Look at the junk in here.'

He reached in and came out with a large travelling suitcase in his hand.

'He's had this fucking thing for years. Think he could afford a new one.'

'Sentimental value, boss.'

Jolyon eyed him. 'As if you'd know anything about that. He said the briefcase was behind.'

He reached into the cupboard again and came out with a maroon leather briefcase. He turned and placed it on the bed to open it. There was a pale round patch in the middle of the leather.

Nathan Mustow's briefcase.

Jolyon said, 'I shouldn't have given him this. Why the fuck he wants it here, I don't know. And if you say "sentimental value", you go out that window.'

He undid the catches and lifted the lid, then pulled out the papers that were inside and leafed through them.

Jolyon said, 'We might as well take the whole lot. But I'll have this first.' He brought a smartphone out of the briefcase and stuck it in his pocket. Then he closed the briefcase and laid it on the futon while he replaced the suitcase in the cupboard and closed the door.

'Right, let's get out of here. All this Japanese stuff gives me the creeps.'

He glanced around briefly and then they both walked out, and a few moments later I heard the front door close loudly. I moved to the window and saw that Belinda had driven away. The Prius crunched down the drive and almost before they'd cleared the exit the electronic gates closed after them. Seconds later my car slid into view and I saw Belinda's face peering anxiously up from behind the wheel.

I left the bathroom and crossed to the wardrobes, pulling open the last door that Jolyon had closed. Inside, beneath rows of shirts and jackets hanging from a rail, I could see the travelling suitcase standing vertically. Piled in the wardrobe there was also a clutter of books and magazines that appeared to be stacked haphazardly. I reached down and pulled out the topmost book from the pile.

It was a scholarly history of Aum Shinrikyo, the Japanese cult and terrorist organisation that had released sarin gas on the Tokyo underground in the mid-nineties, killing over a dozen people and injuring thousands more.

I put the book back on the pile and closed the door. I had a bad taste in my mouth and a sinking feeling in my gut.

I'd seen enough.

WHEN HE GUESSED that Mary the gatekeeper had gone home, Jolyon took the lift up to the sixth floor and knocked on Stratford's door. There was the usual imperious order to 'Come!' and Jolyon went inside.

Stratford was sitting at his desk gazing at something on his laptop. He glanced up briefly to see who'd entered and gestured Jolyon to a seat. Jolyon crossed the carpet and sat in the upright chair facing Stratford's desk. It was always the same routine with Stratford—he had to play the little power game before he could give you his attention.

While he waited, Jolyon looked through the windows as the sun set beyond the line of trees that lay outside the boundary fence. He became aware of his breathing, of the weight of his backside on the chair, of the tiredness that pulled at the back of his eyes. All this would be over soon, he thought. There would be nothing more to explain or excuse, no more arguments.

After a couple of minutes he could bear it no more. He leaned forward and pushed down the lid of Stratford's laptop so that it timed out.

Stratford refused to admit to being startled, merely throwing up his hands and leaning back with an exasperated air. Jolyon thought he could have been playing Solitaire for all he knew.

He said, 'Were the papers the right ones?'

'That's not really what you're here to talk about, is it?'

'It's my starting point. It's where I want to start. I want to ensure that I fulfilled your orders correctly. Did I?'

Stratford tapped his fingernail on the lid of his laptop.

'What's this about, Jolyon? Are you having second thoughts?'

'And third and fourth thoughts. I don't like the arrangements. I don't see why we have to change the way things are.'

'It's more than that, isn't it? You're not happy.'

Jolyon almost guffawed. The thought that Stratford might care whether he was happy or not was priceless.

He said, 'If you want to know the truth, I don't like being spoken to like that in front of others.'

'I can't show any favouritism. You're just another employee.'

'I don't want favouritism. I want respect.'

'Then you have to earn it. Do your job better than anyone else.' He let the sentence hang in the air like a physical threat. Then he said, 'Walk to the car-park with me.'

He rose and took a dark coat from the hook on the back of his door. He put it on and opened the door for Jolyon to precede him out of the room. Always formal, always aiming to be thought of as the English gent—something he could never be, Jolyon thought. His genes were too foreign, despite his mother's English blood.

They stood side-by-side in the lift going down, staring at their vague and dehumanised reflections in the aluminium doors.

Jolyon said, 'You didn't answer my question.'

'About the change in arrangements? You always knew this was coming. I don't understand why it's causing you problems now.'

'I suppose I wasn't certain we'd ever get this far. I hadn't confronted the reality.'

The doors opened and they walked out of the building towards the car park, the air cool around them.

Stratford said, 'Did I ever explain to you the origins of the word "strategy"?'

'I'm sure I'd have remembered.'

'It's from the Greek meaning "generalship". In other words, the general is the one up on the hill looking at the whole battlefield, the disposition of troops, the lie of the land and so forth. Tactics, on the other hand, is a far more humble word. It comes from a Greek root meaning to order or arrange. The person responsible for tactics makes the day-to-day arrangements that help the general carry out his strategic plan. I'm not belittling you. What you do is something I couldn't manage, and certainly Tuck doesn't seem capable of doing. I need you to carry on doing that, keeping the others in line, being my eyes when I can't be around. Arranging things.'

He stopped and suddenly seized Jolyon by the upper arms.

'We're almost there, Jolyon. What I've been talking about and planning for years. The ultimate demonstration of our capability—mine and yours. What did Gandhi say?'

'"I want freedom for the full expression of my personality."'

'I'm impressed, you remembered.'

'It was on the reading list you gave us.'

'He also said, "It is better to be violent, if there is violence in our hearts, than to put on the cloak of nonviolence to cover impotence." You and I and the rest of the group are not impotent. This is going to be our shining hour.'

He let go of Jolyon's arms and strode towards his car. Jolyon watched him reverse, turn on his headlights and point them out of the car-park and towards the Cheshire countryside, darkening around him moment by moment.

He thought it was all very well knowing the origin of the word strategy and how it differed from tactics; the difficulty came when your strategy hit the immovable constraints of the real world.

CHAPTER TWENTY SEVEN

I HAD BARELY woken on Wednesday morning when my telephone rang. I glanced at my alarm clock and saw it was 7.15. A call this early usually meant bad news.

It was Isobel Mustow, sounding strained.

'Mr Dyke, I'd like you to come and see me if you can.'

'Of course. Have you spoken to Belinda?'

'Yes, I spoke to her last night. She'll be here too. In fact, it was she who suggested I call you.'

'Sensible girl. Can you tell me what it's about?'

She hesitated. 'I've been clearing Nathan's desk and I found something under the blotter. I think it may be a password.'

'Did your husband have a computer at home or did he just use the one at work?'

'He had one here.'

'I see. What time would suit you today?'

'I've arranged with Miss McFee for two o'clock this afternoon. I have to see a solicitor this morning. About the will.'

I paused. 'Is there a problem?'

'Not as far as I'm aware. Just one or two things to clear up. Nathan left everything to me and there's no one to contest it, anyway.'

'I hope it goes smoothly.'

We said our goodbyes and hung up.

Yesterday I'd told Belinda what I'd found in Stratford Greif's house and we'd decided to do a little more research. She was too young to remember the sarin attacks by the Aum Shinrikyo and was properly horrified when I told her what I remembered.

Last night Wikipedia had told me more: Aum Shinrikyo was a cult started in Japan by a half-blind self-deluding shaman who had begun his career as an alternative therapist. He tried several ways to gather a following before landing on the potent mix of religion and politics that earned him notoriety. Calling himself the new Christ, he stated that the world would end shortly and that only he and a few trusted followers would survive the forthcoming apocalypse.

Of course, he attracted followers immediately, and generally among a young intelligentsia, recent graduates and some lonely and immature scientists. As his influence grew he also attracted critics, and in order to defend itself his organisation began physically attacking them and started stockpiling armaments, including chemical and biological weapons, a helicopter and other military hardware from Russia. He ordered his scientists to attack several targets, first with the botulinum virus and then with nerve gases like VX and sarin. Fortunately his strike rate was risible, at least at first.

None of us in the west had heard of the cult until they released sarin gas on the Tokyo subway system in 1995, hospitalising nearly six thousand people and killing 13.

Belinda had said, 'Seems a bit of a stretch to link Greif to this cult.'

'Are you forgetting the book I found in Stratford's wardrobe?'

'No, but a book is a book. It's not necessarily a manual for revolution.'

'My cynicism about that is growing smaller every day. The way Jolyon and the others have been acting makes me believe they're throwing away the rule-book.'

'So you think they're going to launch some kind of attack somewhere?'

'How the hell do I know? But there's a definite weirdness in Stratford's house, a Japanese influence that I would say is unhealthy.'

'You're over-thinking this. He's a scientist. All of the people who work for him are scientists. They're supposed to be rational. They wouldn't do anything nuts.'

I hadn't replied to her but I'd left her place shortly afterwards. I wasn't usually one to be captivated by the self-deluding lies that people told themselves. But it seemed to me that Stratford Greif was the kind of fanatic capable of twisting the world to suit his own ends, whatever they might be.

LATER THAT MORNING I phoned Dan and asked whether he was free to come with me. He sounded bleary from another late night but was excited by the prospect of 'working on a case', as he put it.

When we arrived at Isobel Mustow's house Belinda's pink Volvo was already there. I squeezed the Mondeo next to it and then rang the bell. Isobel opened the door a fraction but held it tightly.

'Who's this?'

'This is Dan, my son. He's a whiz-kid with computers and might be able to help us. He's worked with me before.'

On cue, Dan stuck out his hand.

'Very pleased to meet you, Mrs Mustow, though I'm sorry about the circumstances.'

Isobel warmed a little and shook his hand, then swung back the door.

'I'm sorry, I'm getting paranoid. Come in.'

We followed her inside to the study that I'd seen on my first visit. Some of the books had gone from the shelves and it had a sadness about it now, an absence of the life that had animated it previously. Belinda was sitting in Nathan Mustow's leather chair, staring at the screen of his laptop. I introduced her to Dan and she raised her chin in acknowledgement then returned to the screen.

Isobel said, 'I'd forgotten about this computer. An odious man from Midwinter came and asked whether Nathan had any of their property, which he wanted returned. I told him no, and I was happy to do it.'

'So this laptop is theirs?'

'As a matter of fact, no. It's Nathan's own machine. I just thought it insulting that they would even ask so soon.'

Belinda had been moving the cursor around the screen but hadn't found anything of interest. She said, 'There was no password to get in to the system, so I don't know what else this might be for.'

She handed me a yellow post-it note over her left shoulder. I stared at the combination of letters and numbers, which of course meant nothing in themselves.

Isobel said, 'Nathan's whole life was password-protected, but with his wonderful memory he could remember them all. He explained to me that he had a system that took the number of syllables in the website's name and then made a code out of them. So he never had to write any of them down. So when I found that note under the blotter on his desk I couldn't think what it might be for. Do you think it *is* a password?'

Dan said, 'Can I have a look?'

Belinda stood up and moved to one side. 'Have at it.'

Dan sat down and looked at the screen for a while, moving the mouse to the Task Bar and the Start icon. Then he went back to the Start icon, clicked into Windows 8 and opened a program from the list.

He said, 'There's a cloud storage aggregator here. He might have uploaded something to the cloud and protected it with the password.'

'Go for it.'

He clicked on the application and it started to open up, then paused as it asked for a password. Dan took the piece of paper and typed in the 8-character code … and the program continued to load.

'Bingo. Let's see what we've got.'

Inside the window that opened, there was one storage application, which Dan clicked to open. This program then showed several yellow directories with cryptic names like 'Bleu', 'Rouge' and 'Vert', and one called Private. He clicked on 'Bleu' and there was nothing in it.

I said, 'Go to Private.'

The directory bloomed open and there was one file visible. From its icon, it appeared to be a movie file, but wasn't titled except with a series of letters and numbers.

Dan double-clicked on it and the software reverted to the Windows 8 desktop and opened the VLC movie player. Then it began to play and Dan clicked the full-screen button so we could see it more easily.

The movie was slightly out of focus, filmed from above and at an angle, and was in colour. A man in a dark jacket and white shirt, with dark hair, was sitting in a chair at a desk. There was nothing on the desk. You could see the man's hands were tied behind him. The room was small and had white walls except for one large mirror on the side opposite the camera—perhaps it was a one-way mirror for observation purposes. The volume on the recording was so low that you couldn't hear any ambient sound, which became more apparent when another man came in from behind, evidently talking. He made a barely-audible mumbling sound. The man in the chair turned and tried to struggle but was bound too tightly.

The man who had come in from behind was Jolyon Greif.

He went to the other man's side, carrying something in his left hand. The man looked up and said something and Jolyon shrugged. Then he placed a small, round object on the desk.

Belinda said, 'What are you doing, Jolyon?'

There was another exchange of words, then Jolyon left the shot. The man stared at the object in front of him, then started rocking in his chair as if trying to back away.

The four of us in the small room held our breath.

After a moment I said quietly to Isobel, 'Do you recognise him?'

'No, I don't think I know him. Is this at Nathan's workplace?'

'Probably. The second man was Jolyon Greif.'

'Ah, Nathan spoke about him.'

Abruptly, a spurt of white smoke emerged from the round object. The man reared back and turned his head from side to side. It was no use. Within seconds he was gripped with convulsions. He twisted his head one way and then the other, and even though the picture was from the wrong angle and you couldn't see his features clearly, you could sense the anguish in his behaviour. He pushed and pulled at the chair to tip it backwards but it must have been bolted to the floor.

After a very short period of time, perhaps ten seconds, he stopped trying to escape. He slumped forward in the chair. Jolyon came in behind him again and undid the straps tying his arms together. Then Mr Bones joined him and between them they lifted the man from the chair and dragged him out of the room.

Belinda said, 'What just happened here?'

I said, 'I think it was an experiment.'

'To do what?'

'To test the efficiency of the material they've been manufacturing.'

She understood what I meant. 'Are you serious?'

I said to Dan, 'Can you make out the time-stamp on that?'

He leaned forward to peer closely at the screen. 'About three weeks ago. Beginning of the month.'

'So two weeks before Nathan's death.'

Isobel said, 'Are you suggesting he had anything to do with this atrocity?'

Before I could reply, Dan interrupted me.

'Look!'

The picture on the screen had continued to play after the man had been taken away. Another figure had entered the frame and was now reaching up towards the camera, which seemed to have been perched high on a shelf.

Isobel said, 'Oh my god, that's Nathan.'

His hand grabbed the camera—doubtless the phone I'd seen Jolyon take from the briefcase—and the picture jumped around before going black. He'd turned it off.

WE ASSEMBLED AGAIN in Isobel's living-room, where we stood facing each other in a small circle. It seemed indecent to sit after witnessing the events of the video. Isobel offered tea but we all refused. She was even paler than usual, her hands joined together as if trying to offer each other support.

She said, 'Should we tell the police?'

'Unfortunately we don't have anything to tell them.'

'But the video …'

'It doesn't prove anything. We don't know what happened to the man, whether he died or not. I think he probably did, but he could have been a volunteer in a test. Something like that. Dan, can you find out if anyone has been reported missing in the last three weeks from this area? Fitting that description, obviously.'

'No problem.'

Belinda said, 'I have to side with my client on this. We're on very thin ice here if we have evidence of a murder being committed. It's not up to us to judge whether it's real or not. We should hand it over and wash our hands of it.'

I realised I had three faces looking up at me expecting me to put them right—or at least argue with them.

In fact, for once I wasn't certain what to do. I guessed the origins of the video would be questioned and that in any case Midwinter and Stratford Greif would have some plausible explanation handy. We didn't have a body, we didn't know who the victim was, we didn't know where it was filmed … it could have been a murder mystery game set up by Jolyon Greif, a bit of fun for his colleagues.

I didn't want to give Midwinter the opportunity to brand us—or Isobel Mustow—as paranoid victims, blaming the company for something they could easily disprove.

I said, 'It's Wednesday today. I suggest I have a conversation with Charles Montgomery about this and see what he says. Let's give it to the weekend before calling in the police.'

Belinda was already shaking her head.

'If they find out we sat on this, even if it's only for a couple of days, then there'll be hell to pay. I don't need any trouble from that quarter. I say we phone them now.'

'It won't be productive if they deny everything, find an excuse, and we're left with egg on our faces. The next time we take something to the police they'll think we're crying wolf again.'

'They'll investigate Midwinter harder, especially after Nathan's suicide.'

I paused, noticing that Isobel Mustow was looking uncomfortable.

I said, 'What do you think, Mrs Mustow? Would you like us to report this video to the police and give it to them, or carry on by ourselves for a while?'

She turned towards me and her eyes were full of a fire I hadn't seen before.

'My husband knew something about this, didn't he? He knew something was going on and was trying to fix it. That's why he made the video. He would do that. That's why he was distracted. That's why he changed. He *knew* something. So no, I don't want you to report this just yet. I don't want those awful policemen here again, asking more questions. If we can find out for ourselves, and by ourselves, then I'd much rather take that route.'

She turned to Belinda.

'I'm sorry, Miss McFee. I don't mean to be siding with Mr Dyke over you. You still have my trust.'

'I understand, but I'd like to make it plain that I don't agree. I think we're storing up problems.'

'Do you want to end the relationship and I'll pay you now?'

Belinda hesitated. 'I'll stay with it, if you don't mind. Someone has to watch his behind.'

Isobel smiled wanly. Then, surprisingly, she stepped forward and gave Belinda a hug. 'Thank you.'

I nodded to Dan to make his way outside. He stood, shook Isobel's hand formally, and left.

When I heard the front door close I said, 'Mrs Mustow, I have something to tell you. I'm sorry to say my client was found dead the day before yesterday.'

Her hand flew to her mouth and she moved sideways to collapse on a sofa.

'Oh dear god …'

'You should know it was Margaret Sellers, Nathan's admin assistant. She hired me because she'd seen your husband's behaviour change in the last year and she was worried about him.'

Now Isobel lowered her head into her hands. Neither of us spoke for a minute. I glanced at Belinda and she shook her head almost imperceptibly, so I continued with the silence.

Eventually she looked up.

'I should have said something, shouldn't I?'

'You might not have been in a position to know.'

'Of course I knew. I saw him change, too. That poor girl. Why didn't she call me?'

'She was embarrassed or thought she might be exaggerating. That's why she asked me to look into it—I can be relatively discreet. Though after your husband died there seemed little point in flying beneath the radar.'

'You say she was found dead ... what does that mean, exactly?'

'I found her. It looked to me as though the scene had been set to look like a suicide, like a copy of your husband's.'

'What do the police think? Do they agree?'

'I don't know. I reported it anonymously. They might find out that she'd hired me but hopefully not.'

She stared at me.

'You run some extraordinary risks, don't you? Why didn't you report it honestly?'

I hesitated. 'I didn't want to get caught up in the police investigation. I'm sure they would have arrested me, if only to keep me in sight while they checked out my story. I thought I might be better employed trying to find out who did it. Assuming it was murder.'

'And now that makes it more certain that Nathan didn't kill himself, is that what you mean?'

'I never really had any doubt. And Margaret was about to leave to spend some time with a friend. And that's why I've told you this now. I don't think you're in any danger, but after what happened to Margaret I don't think you should stay in this house, or even in this area. Is there somewhere you can go?'

I knew she wanted to argue and I saw the battle going on behind her eyes. The comfort of the familiar was keeping her upright at the moment. If she went elsewhere she might collapse.

She said, 'My sister has asked me to go to them, to stay on the farm for a while.'

'Would you feel comfortable being there?'

She looked at her nails, turning over her hands as if she'd never seen them before.

'It might be nice to have no responsibilities for a while.'

'Good, that would be helpful. Take your mobile phone with you.'

Belinda said, 'I'll keep in touch, let you know what's going on.'

'Do you know, I rather wish you wouldn't. I don't think I can take much more of this.'

We spoke for a few more minutes and then Belinda and I said our goodbyes and left. Outside, the cold air was refreshing after the dark images on Nathan Mustow's computer. I hadn't told Belinda or Isobel Mustow about seeing Nathan's briefcase in Stratford Greif's house, nor about the smartphone that Jolyon had taken from it. I didn't know what I'd say once I'd told them. It was proof of a kind but it seemed too hard, too cold, to reveal such information without really knowing what it meant.

Belinda said, 'I disagree about the video but I understand what you're saying. We can't go making accusations until we have real proof. So that's what I'm going to do. I've been sitting around playing second fiddle to you long enough. You're good, but you're not Hercule Poirot. It's about time I did something off my own bat.'

'Just be careful. You've seen what they can do.'

'I'm not the one with the bruise the size of a cabbage on the back of my head. What are you going to do?'

'Like I said in there, I think a well-timed phone call to Charles Montgomery might do the trick right now. It might make The Bleak think twice before they do anything too public.'

But as so often, my timing was out.

CHAPTER TWENTY EIGHT

WHEN JOLYON ENTERED Stratford's office he was surprised to find Mr Bones already there, seated opposite Stratford and apparently in the middle of a cozy conversation. He all but had his feet up on the edge of Stratford's desk.

Ever since Stratford had dispatched Bones to 'deal with' Margaret Sellers without telling him, Jolyon had felt that Stratford was beginning to place more trust in the red-headed man than in himself. He guessed that he liked Bonetti's simple martial philosophy—follow orders and don't ask questions. Whereas he, Jolyon, always had questions. He'd done as he was asked—it was one of the conditions for joining the group and being so well remunerated—but he'd always known that Stratford didn't like to be questioned. He was the smart one, but he didn't want to explain himself and he certainly didn't want to defend his position.

And his position was extreme enough to need defending from time to time.

Stratford said, 'Jolyon, about time. Pull up a chair.'

Jolyon fetched one of the upright chairs lining the far wall and sat next to Mr Bones, whom he'd ignored so far. He wasn't going to even pretend civility towards someone he saw as his inferior.

He said, 'What do you want, Stratford? I've got things to do that don't include chewing the fat with the pair of you.'

'I know. I've been talking to Mr Bonetti here about moving us forward.'

'What does that mean?'

Stratford glanced away. 'I don't like the fact that Dyke and Belinda McFee have been able to operate without censure.'

'Oh for god's sake …'

'I'm serious. What we're doing here, Jolyon, is life-changing. World-changing. But those two ruffians have been running around as if they had every right to question us.'

'Tell that to Charles. He's the one who has to deal with the police. He's having to keep everyone else in the company on track. He thought it was in the best interests of Midwinter as a whole that Dyke should be allowed in. And I don't think he was wrong, as a matter of fact.'

'Really? Why?'

'You know why. I've told you. Until the next phase begins we have to keep our heads below the parapet. What you got this muppet to do to Margaret Sellers was a step too far, in my view. You should have run it by me first.'

Mr Bones said, 'Had to be done quickly. You weren't around. Your brother asked me to step in.'

Jolyon turned to him. 'He's not my brother.'

Mr Bones must have been surprised but his expression didn't change.

'Right, my mistake.'

'And I don't remember asking for your opinion on this. Keep your trap shut.'

'Just pointing out the obvious, boss.'

'Yes, stating the obvious is your *forte*, isn't it? Never shall an original idea pass through your head. Which is why I'd like you to keep quiet until I ask a question.'

'Yes, boss.'

Jolyon stared at him, but the expression on Mr Bones' face remained one of amused tolerance, not the more fearful obedience he'd demonstrated up until now. Jolyon could tell where this was going already. He hadn't worked in regimented bureaucracies for years without learning something about power-struggles.

He said, 'All right. If you want to "censure" Belinda McFee, do it tonight.'

Stratford raised his eyebrows.

'What are you suggesting?'

'Take her out of the equation. Give Dyke something else to worry about instead of bothering us.'

'Why her and not Dyke? I gather from what happened the other night that she can handle herself quite effectively.'

'She's still a woman. Let Bones here show us what he can do. Muddy the waters, maybe even put the blame on Dyke — lovers quarrel, or professional jealousy. Something *obvious* like that.'

A silence fell in the room.

Then Stratford said, 'Well, Mr Bonetti, what do you think? Can you give Miss McFee a severe talking-to? Some advice she's not likely to forget?'

'I think I can manage that. She's only a woman, isn't she?'

Jolyon was pleased to hear a slight edge in Mr Bones' voice, as though he wasn't as sure of himself as he was trying to make out.

Stratford said, 'Good. Now, Jolyon, is everything else ready?'

'What do you think? Have you been down to the labs at all?'

'I leave all that in your hands. You're good at these arrangements, as we discussed the other night.'

'Just make sure you've got everything. There'll be no going back after tomorrow.'

'I know. It's my strategy, after all.'

CHAPTER TWENTY NINE

I ARRIVED OUTSIDE Belinda's house about nine o'clock and parked down the street. It had been dark for about fifteen minutes but there was still a hint of orange behind the houses. The street was quiet with little traffic and I had a sense of normal suburban life being played out behind the lined curtains and Venetian blinds—evening meals, kids being put to bed, a little television. This was an area for young couples getting and spending, trying to establish themselves in their careers in design, IT, marketing, advertising.

By the time I'd got home that afternoon and phoned Midwinter, Charles Montgomery had already left his office. Or at least that's what Mary, his officious secretary, had told me. Perhaps she was passing on a message from Montgomery himself. Maybe he was standing behind her gesturing wildly with his hands while she spoke. Or perhaps she was so experienced at it by now that she was performing her gate-keeper role without supervision. In any case, I planned to call him again the next morning.

I didn't know whether I was going to show him the video from Nathan Mustow's laptop or not. Dan had transferred it to a USB stick that I'd placed in my pocket as if it were poisonous and I'd gone home and transferred it to my own hard drive before sending it to a secure cloud storage drive of my own. My plan was to confront Montgomery, tell him what I'd seen, and if necessary show him the video to convince him that things weren't what they appeared in Stratford Greif's unit. At this point I didn't trust Montgomery but my sense was that he was ignorant of what was going on. How he reacted to the video would tell me something about his position.

But currently there was something else on the agenda.

I took out my phone and dialled Belinda, who answered on the first ring.

She said, 'This could all be a hoax, you know. Someone setting you up.'

'There's an old saying. Better to be safe than flat on your arse.'

'You say the sweetest things. How long are you going to wait out there?'

'I've got a book and Radio 2, I'll be fine. I might stretch my legs in an hour or so.'

'You could come in and have a drink while you wait.'

'The element of surprise would be better if I'm outside. Just stay alert, keep your phone on you. Perhaps you should go lie down in a spare bedroom.'

'You're joking! At this time of night I'd be spark out in five minutes. I think you're taking this too seriously.'

She hung up.

About an hour ago I'd received a cryptic phone call. A voice I didn't know had called my land-line.

It said, 'Belinda McFee should watch out tonight.'

Then the line went dead.

The call-back number didn't register and I hadn't recognised the voice. I'd held the receiver in my hand and tried to recapture how it had sounded, what accent it might have had. All I could tell was that it seemed to be coming through material of some kind—a handkerchief or a scarf. It was male and very low-pitched. Probably someone older— a younger person would have recorded it on a computer and then run it through an application to transform it. This was old school, and somehow more worrying because of that.

I rang Belinda back.

She said, 'You're bored out there, aren't you? What happened to the book? Or the old-time organ from Blackpool on Radio 2?'

'Who do we know who might have called me? What would they have to gain?'

'Well it's obvious, isn't it? One of the scientists doesn't fancy being in The Bleak any more. Getting cold feet.'

'Found out about Margaret, perhaps.'

'Yes, found an ethical brain cell rattling around in there.' She paused. 'If they really are planning something tonight, who would know about it?'

'From the top: Stratford, Jolyon, Mr Bones. Maybe Harry Tuck. Some of the muscle-men, like George. Maybe a couple of the younger scientists.'

'That's not really narrowed it down, has it?'

'They don't all have my home phone number.'

'You're in the Yellow Pages.'

'Damn, a flaw in my logic.'

She laughed. I liked the fact that she could stay upbeat even though she might be in danger. Showed strength of character.

I said, 'Speak to you later.'

IT WAS NEARLY midnight when I saw a car turn into the end of the road and kill its lights. What was suspicious was that no one got out immediately. Not a late-night reveller arriving home. Not a young couple eager to check the sleeping children and send the baby-sitter away.

I found my phone and texted Belinda: 'Someone's here.'

Then I turned off my courtesy light and climbed out of the car, taking my heavy torch with me. I walked away from Belinda's house until I guessed I'd gone far enough, then crossed the road in a gap in the light thrown by the street-lamps, walking as casually as I could. The houses were all semi-detached, pairs of brick-built family homes connected by a party-wall on one side and with separate garages on the other, a short driveway connecting the garage to the main road. At the back, as I'd seen the other day, each house had a medium-sized lawned garden. At the bottom of each garden was a gate leading to an alley between the houses on this street and the gardens belonging to the houses on the parallel road beyond. Belinda had said she'd leave her gate unlocked.

Now out of sight of the car, I ran around the corner and found the entrance to the alley. Although it was darker here there was enough residual light from the street for me to see my way. I counted the houses along to Belinda's and tried what I thought was the appropriate gate. It opened with a rusty creak and I stopped dead for a moment, listening. Just the wind in the trees, the barking of a distant dog and, even further distant, the booming of a car radio. A typical suburban night.

I entered the garden properly and stood still again. Belinda's lawn stretched ahead of me in the pearly dark, a white path snaking towards the house. A faint night scent of wet soil, perhaps an early rose or two. Wooden fences on either side hid the neighbouring gardens from view, but I could tell from the lack of light from the windows that the owners were probably asleep or at least in bed.

I stepped on to the lawn to walk more quietly and headed towards the rear of Belinda's house. Further away I could now hear the roar of Manchester, the dim throb of every major city, but it only emphasised the silence here.

The back of Belinda's house contained her back door and a wide window, both in white uPVC, the usual suburban upgrade for older houses. The set-up reminded me briefly of Margaret's house and the day I found her body. I wondered where the police were with their investigation and whether I'd soon be hearing the heavy knock on my own front door. I put the thought behind me.

I moved to the right, my attention stretching out ahead of me. Between Belinda's garage and the house was the wooden fence that ran down to the bottom of her garden and separated her from her neighbour. You drove into the garage, came out through the same up-and-over door, then entered the back garden through a tall gate in the fence. Or you walked back to the house's front door and let yourself in there. The garden fence was about my height and had broken glass cemented into its top edge. Anyone coming into the garden from the drive would have to find a way through the gate. At the moment it would be easy, however, because Belinda had left it unlocked.

I heard the latch click and moved forward smartly, hiding behind the gate itself as it swung tentatively open.

A tall figure that I guessed was muscle-man George ducked through the opening, wearing the same balaclava-and-dark-jacket outfit that my attackers had worn a few nights before.

I didn't take any risks. I didn't wait. I didn't weigh up my chances. I took a pace and whacked him on the back of the head with my torch.

That would be my rubber torch, which bent him double and made him shout 'Shit!', but didn't incapacitate him or put him on the ground.

He turned towards me with a growl, starting to wind up a lunge, but I took aim and hit him on his right hand with the torch. He drew it back and shook it.

'Bastard!'

I said, 'Am I talking too much now?'

He lunged again, and as he did so I realised that I'd heard footsteps running away, down the driveway towards the front of the house. Then the footsteps had stopped and part of my brain wondered what had happened.

But I had something else to deal with. George's left hand was heading towards me, intent on grasping me around the neck. I stepped to one side and swung again with the torch, this time catching him on his left elbow.

He howled and backed off, breathing heavily. I think I might have broken something, judging by the way he grabbed the elbow with his other hand. All this time I'd been standing between him and the gateway out of the garden. Now I moved away and gestured with the torch.

I said, 'Out. Tell the Greifs what happened. And it's our turn next.'

He stood up tall, ready to prove what a man he was.

'Tell 'em yourself. I quit.'

He ducked his head through the gate and was gone.

I tried the back door, wondering where Belinda was and who the other person had been. The door opened into her kitchen and I saw that lights were now on in the front of the house.

I gently opened the kitchen door and went into the hallway, trying not to make a noise on the polished wooden floorboards.

Belinda's voice came from the front. 'It's okay, Sam, you can come through.'

I walked into her sitting-room and found her standing in the middle of the room with Mr Bones face down on the carpet under her right boot. His hands were behind him, held by handcuffs.

She grinned at me. 'Trying to run away, the little squirt. Caught him a right good one across the chops.'

I said, 'I wonder if he'll sing for his supper. Most cowards do, eventually.'

We turned him over and propped him up on Belinda's sofa. His red hair was mussed and he had a bruise forming under his left eye. I noticed how yellow his skin was against the black outfit that came up to his neck. I'd seen his balaclava on one of Belinda's armchairs.

I said, 'So what was all this about? What did you intend to do?'

He looked away as though finding Belinda's curtains terrifically interesting.

Belinda picked up his balaclava and stuck her fingers through the eye-holes, then sat down in the chair.

She said, 'You're not very good at this, are you? Lumbering around like dinosaurs in the jungle.'

Mr Bones looked at her, his eyes glittering. 'Miss Sellers wouldn't have that opinion.'

Belinda glanced at me, then hauled off and hit him across the cheek with the flat of her hand. He fell sideways across the sofa.

'I don't usually approve of torturing people who can't fight back, but in your case I'll make an exception.'

'Only way you'd beat me, bitch.'

'Says the man handcuffed and sitting on my sofa with a bruise the size of Cuba on his face. Nice try.'

I said, 'Someone phoned me, said you'd be coming tonight. Who do you think that would be?'

'I don't believe you.'

'Our guess at the moment is that it's one of the young geeks. Getting a bit worried about all this real world stuff, murder and poisoning people with gas.'

His eyes met mine and there was humour in there.

'Is that what you think it is?'

'We've seen the video. Someone rather like yourself, strapped to a chair. He dies, then you and Jolyon take him away. Who was it?'

'I've no idea what you're talking about.'

'Okay, we're in no hurry. We've got you and an attempted break-in. We've got video of what looks like a murder being committed. We've got a pretty good idea you killed Margaret Sellers and probably Nathan Mustow. Want to hold on to your ignorance? Or would it be a good chance to talk?'

He turned his head away again, a muscle working high in his cheek.

Belinda said, 'Hey, these houses, you know—they're great. Built in the nineteen-thirties. Cellars and everything. What do you think, Sam?'

'Great idea.'

We stood Bonetti up and Belinda led the way to a door in the kitchen. She reached in and turned on a light, then walked us down a set of concrete steps with me holding Bonetti from the back. At the bottom there was a rough concrete floor and some red plastic boxes piled in one corner.

She said, 'There are pipes over there.'

Bonetti had started pulling away from me, rolling his shoulders as though he might make a dash for it. Not that there was anywhere to go. I held him tight while Belinda undid the handcuffs briefly, passed them around a solid metal pipe and re-cuffed them. He was forced to sit on the concrete floor.

He said, 'I need a piss.'

Belinda kicked him on the shins.

'Be my guest, but you wipe it up afterwards. Like anything else you do.'

We left and Belinda turned off the light at the top of the stairs before closing and padlocking the door behind her. She turned towards me.

'Now what?'

'Now the fun begins. We'll see if Greif wants his man back.'

CHAPTER THIRTY

SINCE FOUNDING MIDWINTER twenty years previously, Charles Montgomery had seen it go through many changes. The rapid development of technology had driven its growth more than any desire of his own. Not that he was slow to latch on to new ideas, but rather he liked the ideas to grow organically from painstaking research. He liked the accumulation of detail and evidence, the working out of a new hypothesis and then the devising of experiments to prove it. It seemed to him that recently the technology drove the research. The belief had grown that because you *could* do something different with a sparkling new piece of kit, you *should* do it.

That wasn't his idea of science.

Of course, his backers—that secretive coven of potentates and magnates back in South Africa—didn't really care. What they wanted was something they could bring to market— *now*. He'd tried his best. He'd brought in some of the brightest minds he could find, and they in turn had recruited young and urgent blood who wanted to break new ground. Don Pastor's work on graphene-based solar cells was looking promising, as was Gloria Duhamel's research into micro-machines manufactured from strands of DNA. Within a year he hoped that both of these units would be at the point of productising the research, or at least filing patents.

His biggest disappointment had been Stratford Greif's unit. He'd had high hopes of Stratford, who'd come with an interesting and varied CV and seemed cleverer than any three of his other managers put together.

He'd acceded to Stratford's wishes to recruit his own people—he wouldn't have expected anything else, in truth—and he'd even allowed him to introduce his own security team because he was fearful that his group's work might be the victim of some kind of espionage. Locked doors Montgomery was happy with; not so with doors that were completely inaccessible to him.

Which was why he'd ensured that whenever Stratford put in a new locking system, he'd asked the contractor to provide him with the means of entrance. As he was footing the bill, he'd had every right to make the demand. He respected Stratford's wish to have control of his environment and its product, but there were limits.

Today he'd have the conversation with Stratford that he'd been dreading. The secrecy had gone too far. The actions of Jolyon Greif and that Bonetti character were beginning to frighten the other members of staff. They seemed to think they were untouchable and walked around the site as though they owned it. And Harry Tuck seemed to be out of his depth, kowtowing to Stratford at every turn.

What's more, he wasn't seeing any results. The weekly reports were a joke, promising startling advances and amazing levels of development with one hand while asking for more money for new machinery and supplies with the other. And whenever he'd cornered Stratford about it, he was casual and dismissive, saying that work of this nature went in fits and starts, that you could never predict the breakthrough moment, that a project timeline and milestones were inappropriate.

Well, enough was enough. It was time to put some regularity back into everyday life on the site. Nathan Mustow and the Sellers girl seemed to have had some kind of suicide pact—at least that's what the police had told him—but all that was finished with now. Things should be back on an even keel.

It was time to have a word. Stratford would have to get his act together or his unit would be closed.

Once he reached his office he asked Mary to make him a cup of tea, and when she came in carrying his World's Best Dad mug and his usual two digestive biscuits on a tray, he asked her to phone Stratford Greif and put him through.

Two minutes later his desk phone rang and he replied. It was Mary.

'I'm sorry, Mr Montgomery, but no-one's answering. I've tried a couple of other people down there and no-one's picking up.'

Montgomery glanced at his watch. 'What time do they think it is? Someone should be in by now.'

'Yes, sir. Shall I try again?'

'Don't bother. I'll go down and see for myself.'

He finished his drink while reading the headlines of the Telegraph on-line, then folded down the lid of his laptop and headed out of his office. In the lift he straightened his tie and pulled down his suit jacket. It had never quite fitted properly once he'd started putting on weight around the middle. But this was no time to be vain.

Out of the lift, he crossed the foyer and headed down the series of corridors that led to Stratford's unit. It seemed quiet down here. There were usually one or two people shuttling between labs or talking in the coffee areas.

He arrived at the heavy entrance door to the unit's suite. Peering through the latticed window he could see no activity, so he swiped his pass through the reader. There was no 'click' of acknowledgement from the door's mechanism but that didn't deter him. He lifted the lid on the electronic keypad and typed in the four-number code that unlocked every door in the unit.

This time the mechanism responded and he pushed the door open.

He knew almost immediately that something had changed. There was something indefinably different in the atmosphere—he couldn't tell whether it was a smell, a texture, a density, a sound. But perhaps that was it: the acoustics were different. He walked down the carpeted corridor and paused at the first door. Looking through the window, he could see no one.

He moved down to the next door and looked through its window. Again, there was nobody inside. This time he turned the handle and went in.

What he saw astonished him.

CHAPTER THIRTY ONE

I WAS ON my way to see Charles Montgomery when he called me. Good citizen that I am, I pulled over by the side of the road to take the call.

'Dyke, you've got to get here.'

'Hello, Charles. How are you?'

'Don't be clever, Dyke. How soon can you be here?'

'About five minutes.'

'I said don't be clever.'

'I wasn't. I'm actually on my way to see you. There's something you should know.'

'I don't care about that. Just get here. I'll tell them at the gate to let you in. I'll meet you in the science block.'

He hung up rather abruptly, I thought. His tone of voice had been peremptory but with an edge of worry. I had no doubt it was connected to Stratford Greif and wondered what he'd been up to now.

Within a few minutes I arrived at the security lodge and the usual uniformed man with the iPad came out. When he saw who it was he went back inside and the white pole lifted. I drove through to the car-park and nestled the Mondeo amongst its more glamorous siblings. I ignored the signs to report to Reception and headed quickly up the short tarmac path to the science block.

Montgomery was waiting for me. He came out to operate the full-body turnstile with his pass, then led us both back inside. He had a dazed look in his eyes and he was sweating despite the air-conditioned evenness of the temperature.

I said, 'What's up?'

'Follow me. I can't make sense of it.'

I followed him down the corridors that I'd walked along before until we arrived at the entrance to Stratford Greif's laboratories. Montgomery typed a code into a numerical pad then opened the door. Inside he took two paces then stopped and pulled open another door to one of the laboratories. He waited for me to join him so I approached and looked inside.

It was empty.

Not only of people, but of equipment. Where I guessed there'd been gleaming white scientific instruments there were now only faint shadows on the benches, probably created by the running temperatures of the missing equipment. All that was left were these workbenches, three brown plastic chairs and a long cabinet built into the wall, one of those where you put your hands through openings to manipulate dangerous material inside.

Montgomery saw me looking. 'They couldn't very well take the BSCs, could they? Biosafety cabinets. If they've taken the materials, Lord knows how they're going to handle them.'

He took me down to the next lab. The same again. An echoing empty space. There were tall glass-fronted cabinets that I supposed would have once held petri dishes or glass bottles of gloop, and were presumably too hefty to take on a moonlight flit, but these too were empty. There was a kettle on a small table and five sad-looking mugs. Normally when a room is stripped there are dust-lines or paint-marks that have been obscured by furniture. In this gleaming environment there were no such signs, just pristine white benches and clean walls. The whole place stank of ammonia or bleach where they'd wiped everything down.

'Is it all like this?'

'Every lab in this unit. No people, no instruments, no materials, no supplies, no computers. Oh, except one.'

He walked past me and led us to the room at the end of the corridor. Inside, a single laptop sat in the middle of an empty bench, its screen dark.

Montgomery rubbed its pad to wake it from hibernation and after a moment a large smiley face appeared on the screen. Beneath it was a message:

'SEE YOU IN HELL, BOYS!'

Montgomery gestured to the screen.

'What's going on? Where's my equipment? Where are my staff? Where in buggery is all the research we've been paying for over the last eighteen months?'

'I'm flattered that you ask but of course I haven't a clue.'

'Well isn't that your *job*? Isn't that what somebody hired you to *do*? What have you said to these people that's made them vanish into thin air? What are they playing at and why are they doing it in my company?'

I could tell he was angry.

I stepped out of the room on the pretence of looking in the other laboratories but it was actually to give myself time to think. All the laboratories were the same and there was nothing more to see. All the vital equipment seemed to have gone, leaving only everyday supplies like tables or chairs or tea-pots. When I found him again, he was on his mobile. He hung up.

'Mary's tried both Greifs, Harry Tuck, three of Stratford's team. No replies from any of them. They've vanished.'

'Okay, calm down. Let's look at this sensibly. When did this happen?'

'It must have been last night. Overnight. I think I would have noticed a lorry-load of scientific instruments leaving by the front gate in daylight.'

'Is anyone here overnight? I mean, anyone working in any of the other labs?'

'No, just security.'

'That's Jolyon Greif's security, I suppose.'

The realisation showed in his face. 'Yes, of course. He must have been involved, and his men. It wouldn't have been easy to move all of this lot. But if you had a dozen people I suppose you could do it in a couple of hours.'

'What about the man on the gate today? Would he know anything?'

'No, that's Jimmy. He's been here since before the Greifs arrived. He's not in their group and he probably wasn't on duty last night because he's on now.'

'Okay. So this equipment, doesn't it need specialist removers and padded trucks and so forth?'

'Some of it, not all. There are specialist lab moving companies that will do the whole thing for you. But that takes ages to set up and dozens of meetings and project management and so on. This was done so fast I think they've probably just kitted out a normal van with some harnesses and done a bunk. Completely against all sorts of regulations. Jesus, what am I going to tell my people in South Africa? They'll go ape-shit.'

'The bigger question is, where will they have gone? And why have they moved?'

Montgomery shook his head. 'Greif could have gone back to the Ukraine for all I know, and taken his gang with him. And as to why, I have even less of an idea. I thought they were close to having something to show me.'

'What did you mean, "gone back to the Ukraine?"'

'It was just a phrase. I don't think he's going to sell any secrets to anyone behind the Iron Curtain, if that even exists any more. Stratford Greif's family came from Odessa. After he got his undergraduate degree he worked there for a while before coming over here to research his doctorate. Didn't you know?'

'Apparently there's lots I don't know. I might have to sack my researcher.'

'He didn't talk about it and it's not in any of the public records. I only know because my backers insisted that I do a thorough check on high-profile recruits.'

'What did he do when he worked there, in Odessa?'

'Pharmaceutical research, if I remember right. Something for the Ukrainian government. It links to what he was doing here on air-borne pathogens and how we might be able to filter them. You know, make the world a safer place and all that. It's a big market. Where are you going?'

I was heading for the exit. I turned back to him.

'I want you to shut this building down, lock it up. And I'd also advise that you close the whole site until after the weekend. Tell everyone they've got an extra day's holiday tomorrow, courtesy of you.'

'I can't do that! They'll worry.'

'I don't care. But you have to get people away from here and away from Stratford Greif's influence.'

He stood to his full height and straightened his tie as if about to perform a public duty. In his own way he had a kind of tragic dignity, despite the fact that everything he thought he knew was turning out to be wrong.

He said, 'Why were you coming here, anyway? What did you want to tell me?'

'It doesn't matter. Greif has trumped us now. He's working up to something bigger than I gave him credit for.'

'Such as what?'

'I think he's preparing an attack of some sort in a public place.'

'What! Why on earth would he do that?'

'To show how clever he is. And how stupid the rest of us are. At the moment, I'm inclined to think he's right.'

CHAPTER THIRTY TWO

MONTGOMERY HAD TOLD me they'd had no reply from Greif or any of his unit when he and Mary had tried to contact them. None of them had wives or girlfriends or boyfriends at home to answer the phone. Even the security team were single or divorced. Stratford had been extremely clever with his recruitment tactics, finding people without responsibilities or ties to do his dirty work.

So the next best thing was to go visiting. I could have asked Belinda to do it as she was closer, but I wanted to see things with my own eyes. That's why I'm best working by myself—I find it hard to trust other people will do a good job. Some people have called that trait controlling. I prefer to think of it as being careful.

I drove up to south Manchester and knocked on Stratford's door, then twenty minutes later on Jolyon's. No reply from either. Looking through the windows I could see no activity but by this time I wasn't expecting any. Whatever they'd decided to do, they'd co-ordinated their actions and removed themselves from sight. I got back in my car and drove out to Harry Tuck's house and found nobody there, either.

It was late afternoon by now, a cold and cloudy March day. I sat in my car outside Tuck's house and stared through the windscreen as kids from a local school skittered and jabbered by, herded by a couple of young mothers who were well wrapped-up against the wind. I thought back to that first morning when I'd met Margaret Sellers. This had seemed a simple job back then, probably involving a bit of tracking, an interview, a little surveillance and a whole lot of educated guesswork.

How had it turned into a search for a group of nuts who, it seemed, were building up to something catastrophic? And for no apparent purpose other than the self-aggrandisement of one man who took himself too seriously.

I took out my phone and called a policeman I knew.

HOWARD MET ME at the Farmhouse Beefeater, a new redbrick bar and diner linked to a Premier Inn on the edge of Crewe, just past the Queens Park municipal golf course. It was dark inside in that fake-plush look that new pubs often have, but at least you could find a corner where a television didn't force itself on your attention. The barman offered us a plasticated menu of various pre-formed meals but we refused and found a table on a raised dais in a dark corner. Two youths played pool in a room opposite, the balls clacking together periodically.

Howard had filled out since I'd met him a few years ago but his hair was still black as coal and his eyes shrewd. When you looked at him straight on, his head was a kind of oblong, with a very square jaw and a narrow brow. He reminded me of a cartoon character but I could never remember which one. We didn't really like each other but it was useful for me to know someone in the local police. I don't think he had any use for me at all. He cultivated a cynical demeanour but at least he listened and in my experience he paid attention without too much pre-judging.

He said, 'This is after hours for me, Dyke. It better be worth it. There's a football match waiting for me to watch it when I get home.'

'You're not going to believe half of what I tell you anyway. But I'll buy your drink and keep you entertained for a while.'

'I doubt it. What have you got for me?'

So I told him. I started with meeting Margaret in Costa Coffee and went all the way through to that morning at Midwinter and the apparent disappearance of all of Stratford Greif's team. I didn't tell him about seeing Nathan Mustow's briefcase and smartphone at Greif's house. I'd been there illegally at the time and there was no point making things more difficult for myself.

When I finished he was about half-way through his pint. He took a swig and set it on the table without letting his eyes meet mine.

'So where is this place?'

'Up past Congleton, on the way to Alderley Edge.'

'And it's called Midwinter?'

'Midwinter Enterprises. Very American, though I think the money comes from South Africa.'

'Really?'

'Don't get excited. As far as I can tell it's not a means of getting gold out of the country. It's lots of smaller investors clubbing together. Charles Montgomery went on a tour there twenty years ago and drummed up the money. A lot of people wanted to invest in foreign research so they were happy to hand it over.'

He finished his beer and placed the empty glass on the table.

'So what do you expect me to do with this information?'

'I expect you to spring into action, call in the Flying Squad and MI5 and scour the country for these ne'er-do-wells.'

'And failing that?'

'I just thought you'd be interested. Knowing how high terrorism is on the general agenda these days. I thought a word to the wise might be appreciated.'

'Do you know how many tip-offs like this we get every day.'

'Of course not.'

'Neither do I. But I bet it runs into the dozens. I appreciate what you're saying about this man Greif. He sounds like a nasty piece of work with a chip the size of Iceland on his shoulder. But you have to admit you don't have any evidence of any wrong-doing and no suggestion that they might be planning something.'

I tried to keep the exasperation out of my voice.

'You could at least look at Nathan Mustow's and Margaret Sellers' so-called suicides. No notes for either of them. No reason for Mustow to be at the airport hotel and no way that Margaret could have got hold of whatever it was she was supposed to have injected. If it was the same as Mustow used, how did she get hold of it? Also, Mustow's briefcase and phone are missing. Your boys don't seem to have them, according to Mustow's wife. Aren't they suspicious circumstances?'

'Suicides can be resourceful buggers when they've made their mind up. And remind me, how did you get into her house again?'

'I told you, the front door was open. If you check phone records you'll find I called that morning and got no reply. When I turned up the door was ajar and she was dead at the table inside.'

'So you called it in.'

'I could have been more forthcoming, I grant you. But I didn't have time to get caught up with all the interviews and paperwork that would have been thrown at me had I hung around.'

He shook his head.

'Whenever I meet you, it's usually because you've gone it alone and got yourself in some kind of trouble. Then you want me to clean up behind you.'

'I see you as public servants performing a valuable service to the community. Of which I'm a member.'

'You're close to being an upright member. A dick, in other words.'

'Are you going to do anything or not? All of Stratford Greif's unit are missing. For all I know he might have killed them as part of the master plan. I'd start by getting into the houses of Harry Tuck and Jolyon Greif, see if they're in there. Tied up or worse.'

'That's what you'd suggest, is it? A little light house-breaking? And what are you going to be doing?'

'Finding some laurels to rest on. I think my work here is done.'

'Knowing you, I find that hard to believe.'

'So you'll look into it?'

'I can't say yes, I can't say no. Police work is an infinitely vague activity, constrained by unreliable information and the behaviours of people who don't know their own limitations, intellectually or psychologically.'

'You should have that printed on a mouse-mat.'

'I've got it on the wall in my bathroom. I read it every morning while I shave. Helps keep my spirits up.'

CHAPTER THIRTY THREE

WHEN I LEFT the pub I called Dan and Belinda, asking them to meet me at my house later that night.

Belinda said, 'Hey, I don't even know where you live. And you're talking a thirty-minute drive. What do I get out of it?'

'Indian take-away?'

'What was your number again?'

I asked her how Mr Bones was doing and she told me she'd fed and watered him—allowing him to pee in a bucket—and that he actually seemed reasonably content, which was strange.

I said, 'Perhaps he likes the idea of being led round like a dog. Perhaps he likes being subordinate for once.'

'Ew. Now that's an image I won't get out of my head for a while.'

Dan was more reluctant to come because he had a big deal going through. But I managed to intrigue him.

'I want you to do a search on Odessa, in the Ukraine, and see if there's any connection with the kind of work that Stratford Greif might have been doing at Midwinter. Check out these people too.'

I then gave him the names of the scientists I'd met, the members of The Bleak who'd also gone missing.

Dan said, 'What am I looking for as far as they're concerned?'

'History, past associations, previous employment, if any. What is it that Greif wanted them for?'

'You think they had specialist skills?'

'I'd bet the house on it.'

I ARRIVED HOME ten minutes before Dan and a half hour before Belinda, which gave me time to order some chicken and lamb curry dishes from the take-away just past the station. I sent Dan to fetch them while I showered and got the kitchen prepared for its spice invasion. When they had both arrived and settled down, we started in on the food as though we hadn't eaten for a month.

The last to finish was Belinda, who mopped up the final drop of her tikka masala sauce with a piece of naan bread and folded the end into her mouth.

'Of course you know south Manchester is the Mecca of curry, so this doesn't really rate.'

'I could tell that by the way you were holding your nose as you forced it down.'

'One has to try when one is with the peasantry.'

'Well, this peasant has got something to tell you. Stratford Greif and Jolyon and Harry Tuck and the whole Bleak unit have gone missing, taking their stuff with them.'

'What do you mean, "missing"?'

'Just as it sounds. Didn't turn up for work, and when Charles Montgomery went downstairs he found that they'd packed up the whole of the lab and taken it with them. Equipment, materials, computers, everything. An overnight bunk.'

Belinda said, 'When did you find out?'

'This morning.'

'And you've waited till now to tell me?'

'It gets worse.'

'How?'

'I've brought the police in. Through a side-entrance.'

'What the hell are you talking about?'

'I know a man in the local fuzz. I had a word in his ear, just to protect us. He can't say they didn't know if things start to go haywire in the next few days.'

She stared at me. 'I thought it was your idea to keep them out of it. We were supposed to be keeping a low profile. Anything else I should know?'

'When I was in Stratford Greif's house I saw Nathan's briefcase and his smartphone. The one he probably made the video on. There were some papers inside the briefcase that Jolyon had come for, and he took the briefcase, the papers and the phone back to Stratford. Maybe because he had the papers and the video was the reason they got Mustow to the airport hotel and then killed him. Perhaps he agreed to talk to them, like a mediation or a bargaining discussion, but they did him in anyway.'

'You think?'

'It's an idea I'm formulating.'

'Isn't everything? I'm beginning to think you're making this up as you go along and you don't care what I or anyone else says.'

'I'm doing what I think's best.'

'Who for? You?'

'For all of us. This could get really dirty soon.'

'I think you're forgetting that Isobel Mustow is *my* client and currently there's no one paying your bills. I think I deserve a bit more say in what decisions you make.'

'You may be right.'

'I *am* right. This isn't your case any more, you're just a passenger. You're doing that thing again.'

'What thing?'

'The seeker for truth and justice—even if it means trampling over everyone else's rights.'

'Bullshit. I just like to finish what I've started.'

'And you feel guilty about Margaret. Tell me you don't.'

I couldn't exactly say that, so instead I stood up and started clearing away the dirty plates.

Belinda said, 'See, your feelings are getting in the way of us working together on this thing, and you can't even admit it.'

Dan had been watching the back-and-forth between us in silence. I wondered briefly what he thought about his old man being harangued like this. Even though he deserved it.

I shouldn't have worried. He responded as though he couldn't care less about the argument. He was probably just impatient to get back to his Bitcoin deal.

He said, 'Can we stop all this bickering and get on? You'll like this.'

'Let's go into the sitting room, it's not as messy.'

We went through from the kitchen, leaving an apocalypse of silver-foil trays by the sink.

Seated again, Dan said, 'You asked me to look for any links between Stratford Greif's line of work and Odessa. Well, Odessa is one of the places the Russians had set up a plague station.'

Belinda and I looked at each other, our argument forgotten.

'What the hell is a plague station?'

Dan had some papers he'd printed out. He gave us several sheets of text and photos each but talked us through them anyway.

'During most of the last century, the Russians were worried to death that plague in some form might be introduced into the country. Like, on purpose. By their enemies. They'd already had epidemics of different diseases so they had experience of trying to deal with hundreds of sick people and they didn't like it. So they started to set up these "plague stations" to monitor any unusual illnesses that turned up in the populace, then hopefully deal with them.'

'Russia's massive. How could they keep track of what was going on miles from anywhere?'

'They built loads of these places. Eighty-eight facilities in total, including smaller stations and regional operations. They were scattered all over the Soviet Union, including Moscow, Leningrad, Kazakhstan and the Ukraine. Crimea, to be exact. Quite early on they'd established a program to use the results from the stations. Now it wasn't just a case of gathering info to help cure people. They began to think they might as well use what they found out. This was well before the second World War, the late twenties. There were two parts to the program—one to find ways of preventing plague or other biological threats from getting in and killing people; and the second, to do research and find ways of weaponising the diseases.'

Belinda said, 'What, like biological warfare?'

'Exactly. And like the Brits and the Americans, they were at it for decades. Until they all got together and decided they'd make an agreement to stop doing it. It was too dangerous for everyone.'

'What, so they all stopped making biological weapons?'

'Allegedly. Get this, at the same time as the Soviet Union signed the treaty against biological warfare in 1972, they were getting ready to ramp up their research into how to make it work. They were shamelessly two-faced about it. The Americans and British had completely stopped their development of biological weapons by 1970, but the Russians just carried on. They set up this huge pharmaceutical organisation called *Biopreparat* to research and produce biological weapons. They were very keen on bubonic plague and cholera, with a side order of anthrax. One group, called *Ferment*, looked at making weapons to kill humans, another looked at methods of killing off animals and plant-life. They called that the *Ecology* program. Nice twist.'

I said to Belinda, 'If you were wondering, this is why I asked Dan to help out.'

She ignored me, concentrating on what he was telling us.

She said, 'But then I suppose the Berlin Wall came down and the Soviet Union started to fall apart. What happened to these stations? Are they still in operation?'

'Good question. Apparently, when the Soviet state began to crumble in the nineties, the funding started to be cut. You can imagine. You had all these research stations containing all this dangerous material and the buildings it was kept in were falling down around their ears. Low security, minimal safety regulations. Most of the scientists who worked there left and were replaced by younger models who didn't have the proper training but would work for peanuts, happy to have a job.'

I said, 'And Odessa?'

'Yep, you got it. There was an outbreak of plague there in 1910 and a cholera epidemic in 1970, so it was a good place to establish a station. It was still going in 2005 — an American journalist wrote an article about it for the *Washington Post*. He said one of the biggest problems the authorities had was making sure that strains of the disease weren't stolen or sold off. And he said the scientists working there often operated without proper safety equipment and with the windows wide open. In the middle of town.'

'Jesus.'

'And your man Greif ...'

'What about him?'

'Guess where he worked when he was in Odessa.'

'Not on the docks.'

'Nope. Right in the station. Security was so lax he could have walked out of there with a strain of bubonic plague in a jar in his pocket.'

IT WAS A lot to take in, and Belinda and I buried our heads in the print-outs for a while. I went back over everything I knew about Greif and his team. It seemed fantastical that he could be working up to something shocking, something that might injure or kill hundreds or thousands of people. Didn't it?

But I'd been reading about the Aum cult and the sarin attack on the Tokyo subway in 1995. The fanatic who established Aum Shinrikyo had managed to persuade many thousands of people that he knew the truth, and this truth called for the death of those who were persecuting him. His followers included many intelligent students from Japan's best universities, together with dozens of scientists whom he inveigled into working on his doomsday projects. Why did they do it? What did they see in this half-blind, geeky messiah that made them give up their presumably rational beliefs in favour of some kind of religious martyrdom? I'd known some charismatic leaders in my time and while I'd never fallen for the cult of personality myself, I could understand—just—that the certainty that leaders like this offered was comforting.

So perhaps this was what Greif offered, too. A respite from the vagueness and doubt of modern living. The confidence to assert that his intelligence was all that mattered and that he *must* be revealing the Truth because he was always right.

Dan broke into my reverie by saying, 'You also asked about the members of his team.'

'Are they all fanatics, too?'

'You wouldn't think so. You think I'm nerdy, you should meet this lot. None of them seem to have any friends, no Facebook or Twitter profiles, no membership of any clubs. It was like Greif dug up these clones who had no life and gave them one.'

'And what do they do? What are their specialities?'

'A real mix, as though he was covering all the bases. A couple have published papers on fluid dynamics, one gave a speech at a conference on the use of pathogens in medical research. Lots of stuff in their various Ph.Ds about climate change, weather patterns, cloud formation. Lots of big words that kept me and Google busy for a while.'

Belinda said, 'Where did Greif do his Ph.D?'

'Manchester University.'

'Do you happen to know who supervised it?'

I glanced at her. 'Is that important?'

'When I was in Germany I knew someone, a trainer, who'd completed his doctorate. He was still in touch with his supervisor, said the guy had had a big influence on how he thought and was a kind of mentor. I just wondered whether we could talk to Greif's supervisor, see if he could shed some light on what Greif was like.'

Dan had found the name with a quick search on his laptop. 'Doctor Joseph Roberts. I've got an email address from the university site.'

He read it out and Belinda made a note.

'I'll send him a mail later, see if he'll talk.'

Dan said, 'I've had an idea.'

'Go on.'

'The way you've been talking about Greif, he sounds like he's really arrogant and big-headed. When I was looking into him I found his entry in Wikipedia. I was wondering whether we could change it, make him seem stupid or something. I bet he's the kind of guy who Googles himself all the time to see what's being said about him.'

'Do people do that?'

'Yeah, Dad, people with a life.'

'Point taken. So how do we do it?'

'So long as his entry's editable I can get in and add some things. What kind of stuff should I put in?'

I thought for a moment.

'Make it look as though no one takes him seriously. Undermine him, you know, little phrases like "People thought that he'd stolen most of his ideas from his Ph.D supervisor", or, "He was fired from this job because he was thought to be lazy and not intelligent enough to handle it". That kind of thing. Really get his goat.'

'Is it dangerous?'

'Probably. But if it gets him to come out of hiding it'll be worth it.'

WE BROKE UP about eleven and I cleared the kitchen, stuffing the empty curry dishes into the waste bin and washing the plates and cutlery before rinsing them. There's nothing worse than orange curry stains on your washing utensils. And nothing more persistent.

Besides, it gave me some downtime to think about everything that we'd discussed. I'd been giving some thought to what Belinda had said to me days before, the impression I gave out that I was some holier-than-thou seeker for truth and justice. One part of me was horrified that people might see me as a goody two-shoes, some saintly knight who considered himself above other people. Another part wondered whether she was right—perhaps I gave myself airs and graces by calling my stubbornness 'persistence' as though it was a virtue. When in fact it was just a refusal to admit I could be wrong. I tried to think back to the last time I'd apologised to anyone or said that I was wrong.

I couldn't remember.

I'd resisted any sort of self-analysis ever since the personnel department at Customs and Excise had put us all through an exercise designed to establish our strengths and weaknesses as part of a reorganisation. All the members in my department had been sent on courses where we'd completed a series of exercises while being observed by psychologists, who sat around the outside of the room like visitors to a zoo, making notes. We'd then been given 'feedback' by these people, who didn't know us, didn't know our jobs and had no idea of the stresses and strains we worked under.

I'd nodded politely and said the right things, then ignored them and got on with my work. While I was sure there were certain constants in human behaviour, I didn't see how these observers could claim any objectivity in describing our traits and failings. It seemed to me that my actions were dependent on who I was dealing with and what the situation was, not just on my own preferences for how I liked to behave.

So the thought that I might have a messiah-complex of my own didn't feel good. It put me in the same company as Stratford Greif, though coming at the world from a different perspective. I felt he wanted to teach people something because he felt he knew better: his version of the truth. By contrast, I wanted to dig down and find the truth about the people I dealt with because I felt it was the only way I could understand them and therefore do my job. I'd lied to myself too often in the past, with less than stellar outcomes, to think that everybody else should believe what I said as if it were a commandment from on high. Stratford Greif was helping me to see that 'truth' was only what we called those things we were willing to believe in.

I was still turning all this over in my mind when my land-line phone rang. It was eleven-thirty and I thought it might be Dan pulling another all-nighter on his dealing, or perhaps wanting to run his Wikipedia entry on Stratford Greif past me.

But no, it was the same disguised voice that had called me before with the warning about the attack on Belinda. It still sounded as though he were talking through a cloth and probably lowering the pitch of his voice as well. He didn't bother with pleasantries.

'The people you're looking for are at the old adhesive factory on the Torrington Estate, Altrincham. The entrance to the estate is wide open but there's a new locking system on the door to the main building. Code 20031995 for the door. Password to every computer is Satyan. Capital S, spelled as it sounds. Do your worst.'

I scribbled down the code and the password on a pad I kept by the phone.

'Who are you?'

'I'm not your friend.'

'Are you one of The Bleak?'

'You should find Harry Tuck. Maybe he can tell you.'

'Tuck? Why Tuck? Where is he?'

'Just find him.'

'Call it in. Tell the police. I can't trust what you tell me.'

The line went dead.

I recognised the password 'Satyan' from my reading about the Aum Shinrikyo cult and hoped I was wrong about its implications. Also, the code my informant had given me for the main door, 20031995, referred to the 20th March, 1995—the date of the sarin attack on the Tokyo subway.

Tomorrow was 20th March.

CHAPTER THIRTY FOUR

IT SEEMED THAT everyone wanted to talk to me.

The next morning my mobile phone rang before I was even out of bed. I stretched for it and sat up, seeing a pale light filtering through my bedroom curtains telling me it wasn't yet eight o'clock.

'Ah, Dyke, Stratford Greif here. I was wondering whether we could talk.'

I came alert. 'Talking is never out of the question.'

'Glad to hear it. Actually, I'd like to talk to you face-to-face. I'm not very good on the telephone. I don't know why, but they scare me a little. Odd, that, isn't it?'

'We all have our little foibles. I get migraines from time to time.'

'Really? I'm sorry to hear that. Of course you've given up dairy and chocolate.'

'One out of two.'

'When I was growing up my mother wouldn't allow milk in the house. She couldn't understand how anything that had been inside a cow could possibly be good for you.'

'Was this in Odessa or Edinburgh?'

A slight pause. 'Yes, very good. The private detective at work. So, to business. Where shall we meet?'

'The Manchester Exchange theatre has a café inside on the right. We can have a nice cup of tea and a piece of cake.'

'Very good. Let's make it noon today. Come alone, won't you? Or I simply won't turn up and you'll miss the opportunity to hear what I have to say.'

'What *do* you have to say?'

'Hear it in full later.'

He hung up.

I rang Belinda immediately, got the same bleary voice that Greif must have got from me.

I said, 'It's me. I've suddenly become very popular. I've had two phone calls.'

I went on to tell her about the call from the informant the night before, then the call from Greif.

She said, 'Very good, a sturdy effort. You haven't won the private investigators gold shield, though, because I win. I'm meeting Greif's supervisor this afternoon. That trumps you because you didn't do anything, just answered the phone. I actually had to make a call.'

'You're so petty.'

She was waking up now and a sense of liveliness entered her voice.

'How are you going to play it? Do you want me there?'

'Not necessary. I'm meeting him in the centre of Manchester. He won't try anything in the middle of town. Though I suppose he could try to bludgeon me to death with big words.'

'Then you're a goner.'

I smiled to myself. I liked her optimism.

'Afterwards, I'm going directly to the place the first man told me about last night.'

'Which is where?'

I hesitated. 'I'll only tell you on condition that you promise not to follow me.'

'For Christ's sake, what are you, twelve? We're supposed to be working together on this. I'm the one with the client, remember?'

'I don't remember signing a contract stating that we'd share all our information. My view was that you were the apprentice, the side-kick to my Indiana Jones. The Friar Tuck to my Robin Hood.'

'You could at least have made me Little John.'

'You're too butch.'

'You bastard. Now tell me where this place is or I'll come over there and beat it out of you.'

I gave her the location, the door code and the password. I thought it best that this information, at least, be shared.

She said, 'What the hell does "Satyan" mean?'

'When the scientists who worked for the Aum Shinrikyo cult were building facilities in which to manufacture their nerve gases, they gave them the names Satyan 1 through to Satyan 7. Satyan 7 was where they made the sarin gas. Apparently "Satyan" means "Truth" in Sanskrit.'

She took this in, then said, 'You're right.'

'About what?'

'These people are nuts. I was beginning to think we were exaggerating because they beat us up and we didn't like them. But I've been reading up on cults and they usually go like this, don't they? Some forceful person at the centre who's very persuasive and a bully, too, who convinces people that he's special in some way. They have to devote themselves entirely to him and give up their other lives, then do exactly as he tells them. Whether that means having people killed or injured—anything to prove that you're worthy. Do you really think Stratford is that bad, that he's lost contact with reality?'

'As soon as they killed Nathan Mustow and faked the death as a suicide, which I'm convinced they did, everyone else was drawn in. That's another characteristic of the cult leader—they get others to do the dirty work. That keeps their hands clean while at the same time implicating others, who have to be loyal afterwards because they're criminals and could be thrown to the dogs.'

'So do you know who your informant is yet? Have you recognised the voice?'

'Male, slightly cocky and full of himself. Given how implicated all the senior people are—Jolyon, Harry Tuck, Mr Bones—I'm still guessing it's one of the scientists who's had enough. Doesn't like the direction it's gone in. Liked it when it was a drinking club, doesn't like it when it's a murderers' den. He may even have quit by now and left them to it.'

'But then he wouldn't have been able to give you the door code and password to the new premises.'

'Good point. Which means that if I'm being fed this information by someone who's still in the group, then I might be being suckered in.'

'They wouldn't have given up Mr Bones as a pawn, though, would they? Let him come to me but then give him up to you, knowing you'd race over to save me.'

I said, 'They weren't counting on your Friar Tuck fighting skills, cooking karate or whatever it was. Perhaps they didn't expect Bones to be captured. How is he, by the way? Toilet trained yet?'

'He's docile. You know that sort of aggressive look he had, like a ten-year-old trying to look tough?'

'I do.'

'It's worn off. He's beginning to look more like a human being. Should we hand him over to the cops yet? This is kidnapping, you know. He could sue the arse off us.'

'He won't. Anyway, he'll be in such trouble himself we'll be seen as public heroes for keeping him locked up.'

'Be careful this lunchtime. Don't let Greif slip you a mickey finn.'

'Your detective references are so dated.'

'It's the company I keep.'

She hung up while I was still smiling.

CHAPTER THIRTY FIVE

WHEN HE LOOKED out of Preston's patio windows at the mundane back garden, graced with the presence of a medium-sized trampoline, apparently so that Preston could keep fit, Jolyon felt his heart sinking. Had it all come to this? Hiding out in a terraced house in Altrincham? There'd been a time when he'd commanded men, organised crime hunts, dealt with the elected representatives of the region. He'd once been put in charge of the unit detailed to safeguard the Queen's passage through Manchester on her way to an exhibition of national treasures. People jumped when he spoke. Did as they were told. Looked to him for guidance and advice.

Now he was the proverbial spare dick at a wedding. Stratford didn't listen to him. Bonetti did more or less what he wanted. Even Harry Tuck seemed to have vanished, perhaps giving in to his fearfulness about what they were planning to do ...

When Stratford had persuaded him to join him at
Midwinter it had seemed like something of a coronation to
him. All their lives they'd stayed apart, barely spoken.
There'd been the unspoken assumption that Stratford's life
was simply more important than his own, and that Jolyon
was just filling in time until Stratford achieved his
apotheosis, whatever that was going to be. Jolyon had
assumed that it would be something in politics because on
the few occasions they had met, Stratford was always
arguing, always convincing, always advancing ideas that
were more or less unspeakable in polite conversation — ideas
about the differences between people being genetic, though
not based on race or class; or proposing concepts that would
supposedly energise the intellectual elite so that they
worked together to fulfil their potential instead of fighting
each other like cats in a sack; concepts of a revolution based
on purity of thought, not class interest or social division.

Jolyon had never really been interested in any of this
chatter. What he wanted, in truth, was excitement. He'd
never married, didn't read much, didn't have time for
culture of either the high or low variety. He'd come to realise
a long time ago that he was someone who was bored after
five minutes if something new hadn't happened, something
different, pulse-quickening, challenging. It was movement
and change that interested him, not ideas, so it was fun to set
up the security system at Midwinter, fun to put into
operation Stratford's ideas about the elite club of scientists,
fun to be part of something that was *going somewhere.*

But now the destination was approaching, he wasn't sure
he wanted to be on the bus.

Stratford had come through from the kitchen and was
standing behind him, looking out at the same hideous
garden, a cup of coffee in his hand.

He said, 'Petty and trivial, isn't it? The ordinary world. You catch a glimpse here of what Hindus call *samsara*, the unending cycle of birth, misery and death.'

'It's enough for some people.'

'Perhaps, but why are you taking their side? Do you feel some pity or perhaps regret for what's coming?'

Jolyon turned to face him.

'We never really knew each other, did we? All those years apart, your mother not speaking to mine, even though they were sisters. I never even knew what the argument was about.'

'Would you believe me if I told you it was about you and I?'

Jolyon saw that Stratford was serious.

'What do you mean?'

'Your mother wanted to keep us separate. She told her sister that I belittled you and looked down on you.'

'Was that true?'

'I might have belittled you. I belittle everyone. But no, I never looked down on you. I read books but you were engaged with the real world. The world of running and jumping and playing physical games. I wouldn't say that I admired you, because I admire few people. But there was an extent to which I envied you.'

'I didn't know that.'

'Of course not. I couldn't do what you did, so I buried myself in books and knowledge, and then those brought their own rewards.'

Jolyon realised that a strange sensation was gathering in his chest. He couldn't identify it but felt it was connected to an emotion that he'd never felt before, something that was new and a little scary.

He said, 'It's funny that everyone thinks we're brothers because we're completely different.'

'In what way?'

Jolyon knew that Stratford would be expecting a compliment at this point, having bared what little soul he had, so he refused to give him one.

'I've always worked amongst people whereas you've busied yourself with facts and ideas. You can spend hours reading one paper while I'd be finished after the first paragraph. But most of all, you're bothered by what people say whereas I couldn't give a shit.'

As Jolyon knew he would, Stratford took his meaning. He sipped from his drink and then grimaced at it.

He said, 'An article in Wikipedia is very influential. You shouldn't dismiss it.'

'You wouldn't have seen it if Preston hadn't been bored last night and looked you up. He's changed it back again, so what does it matter?'

Stratford's face was darkening.

'People would have seen it. At this stage of the game I can't allow my reputation to be belittled.'

'It was midnight, for god's sake!'

'Which is the middle of the afternoon in California.'

'Where all the loons live.'

'Influential loons, thinking loons.'

Jolyon tried another approach, seeing as Stratford's ego-sensitivity was apparently inflamed and not to be impugned.

'I don't trust Dyke. What if he turns up mob-handed with half the local fuzz with him?'

'Then you'll be able to renew acquaintance with old chums, won't you?'

'You know what I mean. It could interfere with the plan. Even if they don't turn up to the meeting, they might follow you. I just don't know what purpose it serves to put yourself in plain view of Dyke again.'

'I enjoy our chats. He amuses me. It's like looking at myself in a mirror, if the mirror took away about half my IQ and all of my dress sense.'

'You're not like Dyke, and he's not like you.'

'You're wrong. We share certain … qualities. Tenaciousness. Persistence. The ability to believe strongly in our own version of reality.'

'Reality is the same for all of us. That's why it's called reality.'

Stratford moved away and put his cup down on the kitchen table.

'Reality is a construct that each of us creates to serve our own best interests. If you don't know that yet, then you haven't been paying attention to what I've been saying to you for the last eighteen months. I believe I can change the reality that the world perceives is fixed and stable. Its premise and its underlying principles are flawed. Dyke believes that he can keep things the same, preserve them in aspic. Each of us has our own truths.'

'Where's Harry Tuck? I haven't seen him for a few days.'

If Stratford was fazed by the abrupt change in subject, he didn't show it.

'I sent him on a mission. He was grateful to get away, as you probably know.'

'What mission?'

'I can't tell you that.'

The silence that Stratford let hang in the air was as heavy as a barrage of kettledrums. The cousins stared at each other. Jolyon had a bad feeling for Tuck.

Then Stratford said, 'Talking of missing persons, where's Mr Bonetti?'

'I haven't seen *him* for a few days.' Jolyon added with a sarcasm he enjoyed, 'Perhaps he went with Tuck on his mission.'

'Do you know whether Bonetti accomplished his mission with Miss McFee?'

'He never reported back. But I had a text from George. He quit. Didn't say why.'

Stratford looked at his shoes and stood like a penitent for a minute.

Then he said, 'Doesn't matter. Too late now. If they've both gone, we're lighter. If they didn't succeed with Miss McFee, hopefully she'll at least be out of the picture or too frightened to show up again. If she dealt with them we're not really in any worse situation. They wouldn't talk, would they?'

'They didn't know anything, so nothing to say.'

'Ah, your military tactics at work again.'

Jolyon bent down and picked up his rucksack from where he'd left it on the floor.

'We should get going if you want to be in central Manchester for twelve.'

'My coat's in the other room. Tell Preston to stay here now, and the others. I've done the final load myself and they'll know what to do afterwards. Is everything ready?'

'Where you left it, upstairs in the third bedroom. I kept a couple of men at the factory to keep an eye on the rest of the stuff. Don't want any kids breaking in before you get there.'

'So you have got a brain ticking away up there, tick, tock.'

'It helps me work on the tactics. Still shit at strategy, though.'

CHAPTER THIRTY SIX

THE ONLY TABLE I could get in the theatre café faced away from the entrance, so when Greif arrived at my side at exactly midday it was a shock. He looked as calm and possessed as he had the first time I met him, though now he was even more well-dressed. He wore a navy suit with a carnation buttonhole, a bow-tie and a striped shirt. I wasn't certain, but I thought the suit jacket had tails. It was as though he'd stopped off on his way to a society wedding. But he was as expressionless and controlled as ever. I looked behind me to see whether he'd brought anyone with him as muscle, but if he had they weren't visible.

He sat down without preamble and gestured to my coffee, raising his voice above the cultured hubbub that surrounded us.

'You started without me. How impolite.'

'I wasn't sure you'd come, I didn't want it to go cold.'

'Well I'm sure good manners aren't important to someone in your job. So, no doubt you're wondering what's going on. You're a private investigator, after all, and you and Miss McFee have been charging around like the fabled bull, smashing porcelain wherever you go. It must be heart-rending to have no clue what it is you're looking for.'

'We know enough. We've had a long talk with Mr Bones about the situation. He turned out to be a very willing talker, once the legal position he finds himself in was outlined in words of one syllable.'

'Ah, you've found him. We were wondering where he'd got to. He didn't tell us where he was going or what he was doing.'

'He was clear enough about what *you* were doing.'

Greif smiled, which was like a coffin opening.

'Oh, please forgo all that nonsense. Bonetti knows nothing about what's going on, even less than Harry Tuck, if that's possible. You know that perfectly well. I daresay you've got him locked up somewhere to keep him out of harm's way, but if you'd taken him to the police it would have been all over the media and I would have been arrested before I set foot in this fine establishment.'

'Are you saying you don't believe that he talked?'

'I'm disappointed in you once again. This is turning into a habit. I expect rather more from a seasoned investigator and all-round tough guy.'

I was on the verge of telling him I knew about the factory in Altrincham and the code number to get in—but that would have tipped my hand when I still had a hand to play.

Instead, I said, 'So tell me what you wanted to tell me and then we can both go home.'

He leaned back in his chair and looked at me speculatively, his eyes roving over my face as though searching for something, some sign.

He said, 'I think you've got the wrong idea about me and my little group. You seem to have created a playful scenario in which we're responsible for several Bad Things, and you're the knight who's going to ride in and return the world to its balance.'

'Am I wrong?'

'Of course you are. My group does research, Mr Dyke. That's all. We've come together under the aegis of Midwinter Enterprises to create new products that will change the world. We're working on a biological filter that will prevent pathogens of many kinds from entering the water table. We're creating a process to seed clouds where previously that's not been possible, for instance in arid climates. We're investigating ways of using bioaerosols to seed inaccessible locations with flora that will be beneficial to local insects and wild-life.'

'So how does bubonic plague and cholera and anthrax figure in this noble work?'

He frowned, then converted this expression into one of surprise.

'Not for the first time, I don't follow your line of argument.'

'Your work in Odessa, at the plague station, must have sparked an interest for you. How did you get the bacillus back to the UK when you came over?'

He laid the palm of his hand flat on the table between us. It was slender and well-manicured.

'I see, you're taking the part-time job I had in the kitchens of the research centre and fabricating a narrative in which, as a master criminal, I steal dangerous material for my own uses. What did I do, stuff the microbes into a cigarette packet before walking to the docks and boarding a freighter?'

'It's a compelling story, isn't it? Highly intelligent man develops an abiding dislike of the less intelligent and creates a fancy rationale to justify his own cruelty. Despairing of the inability of other humans to think as cleverly as himself, he decides to establish a cult to promote the aforementioned rationale which, incidentally, very few people take seriously. He persuades his cult members that the only way out of this vale of tears is to participate in some kind of attack on the general public, itself an idea he borrows from a self-styled messiah figure who's failed at everything he's ever tried to do. Our hero then plans an event that will put many lives at risk and even perhaps kill hundreds of innocent people. How does it sound so far? Are you gripped?'

'Slightly bored, actually. Sounds as though you've been indulging an appetite for science fiction.'

I leaned over the table and he recoiled slightly, as though I might punch him.

I said, 'Why is it that a high degree of intelligence often seems to go together with a cool attitude towards life? Can't you get excited about anything? Let's face it, you're a petty dictator who likes showing off your superior intelligence, befuddling more stupid people into believing that your rational understanding of how things work gives you a better apprehension of what the truth is.'

'Ah, the truth. That arbitrary criterion by which we judge the moral value of our actions. Are we acting according to what is objectively true, or what we subjectively believe is good? Which is it for you, Dyke? Which side of the truth-goodness scale do you fall on? Do you do your thing because you're looking for the truth for your clients? Or because you want to be a good person and want everyone to know it? Would you rather discover the truth even if it meant doing something bad? Or would you always do something good, even if it meant the truth remained concealed.'

'That's too fanciful for me. I deal in facts and things, not ideas.'

'All right, let me give you an example. If you had a client that wanted you to do something morally wrong—let's say, torture someone—in order to discover a truth that led to a greater good, would you do it?'

'No.'

'So *you* make the choice to be good rather than pursue a truth that might benefit other people. Because the person you're torturing, in my example, knows the formula for a cure for cancer but is unwilling to reveal it, for whatever reason.'

'What would be your choice?'

'One might argue that I'm already making it. The truth is that a proportion of the population is more gifted intellectually than another proportion. I'm willing to do something that is morally reprehensible for that truth to become not only visible, but completely understood. When that truth is acknowledged we'll be able to move on as a species.'

'But the validity of your argument depends on everyone agreeing that intelligence is the only factor that leads to progress, to the right decisions being made.'

'Good comeback. You've been thinking about this in your weekly philosophy classes, haven't you?'

'So do you have an answer? Or is it bad form to disagree with you?'

Greif looked around at the other people in the café as though seeing them for the first time and disliking what he saw. He licked his lips delicately then turned his black eyes back to me.

'If you ask me you're just an example of that wonderful phrase, a plaster saint. You accuse me of being cold and rational—because I don't possess the dreaded emotional intelligence that is apparently the mark of successful human beings—while at the same time you sift evidence and follow clues like a scientist. How's *your* emotional intelligence? Have you empathised with anyone lately? Or are we all tools in your detective toolbox, only useful insofar as we can help you solve the case?'

'Say what you want, Stratford, the game's up. Whatever you try to do, you'll be stopped.'

He unfolded himself from his chair and stood looking down at me.

'I'm working to change the world, Dyke. To make it a better place. Your fantasies are just the creations of a mind that's become hyper-active by being exposed to IQs that are higher than your body temperature. Goodbye. We won't meet again.'

He strode past me to leave. Then stopped and came back.

'I was offended by what you wrote in Wikipedia. But I'm not going to get angry. I'm too cool for that.'

He walked away again. I stood up and followed him to the door but as I got there two large men I hadn't seen before stepped forward from the shadows to block my way. Through the wide entrance I saw Jolyon Greif across the pedestrianised street. He raised a hand and waved a single finger side to side at me, telling me No.

CHAPTER THIRTY SEVEN

AFTER SHE'D PARKED in the NCP multi-storey, Belinda walked down Whitworth Street, past a row of high, smoke-darkened Victorian redbrick buildings and turned into Sackville Street. She'd said she'd meet Greif's supervisor, Dr Roberts—'Call me Joe,' he'd said on the phone—by the Vimto statue. This was a huge statue of a bottle of Vimto soft drink, carved from wood, standing next to outsize wooden replicas of the fruit that were its alleged ingredients.

He'd arrived there before her, a man in his mid-fifties with long grey hair that tumbled over his ears, wearing a white parka against the chill that had turned up that morning. She watched for a moment from the corner. He stood perfectly still with his head down and she realised he was reading from a tablet. Although she understood technology she couldn't see the value of having something that was less flexible than a laptop and larger than a phone, which did everything she wanted to do anyway. She decided he looked harmless and went towards him.

He looked up as she approached and she saw his face acknowledge and appreciate her in the same instant. It was nice to be appreciated by someone with brains.

She stuck out a hand, which he shook with a strong grip.

She said, 'You're early. That makes me look bad.'

'I'm always early. Character flaw. Says something about my potty training, probably.'

She laughed. 'Is there somewhere we can go? A bit cold out here.'

'Sure, there's the pub over there.'

He led her under the railway viaduct to a pub that looked as though it dated from the sixties. It was full of young people who she guessed were students having lunch. Roberts asked what she wanted to drink and she told him just a tonic water.

She watched him at the bar while he bought their drinks, and wondered why she never met men like that in her private life—a bit bohemian, intelligent, quick-witted. Then she wondered where this so-called 'private life' was. One of the problems of being an investigator was that there was no off-switch. Evenings and weekends were not out of bounds if someone had to be followed or a report had to be written. Her diary was a mess and she couldn't forward plan anything further than a fortnight ahead. Was it any surprise that she never met a man she could pursue?

Roberts sat down and raised his glass.

'To Stratford Greif, you little bastard. I hope you're giving someone else hell now.'

Belinda raised her glass mutely.

Then she said, 'Was he difficult, then? As a student?'

'Look, I need to get some things straight. First off, who are you, exactly?'

'I'm sorry, I thought I explained it on the phone.'

'That was early this morning, you caught me unawares and half asleep. So, what's going on?'

Belinda told him what she thought she could. Stratford Greif was being investigated in relation to some irregularities in how a research unit was being run. The owners wanted her—and her colleague—to put together a report on what Greif was doing.

He said, 'Let me see if I've got this right. Greif is running a research unit somewhere and the people who own it don't know what he's doing?'

'Sounds barmy when you put it like that, doesn't it? In fact he's been telling them one thing and doing another. It's come to light in the last week. There's a company director over here but the investors are mostly from South Africa, so they're worried.'

'Weren't there checks and balances, ethics committees, all the usual stuff?'

'It's a small company. They seem to have let some things slide.'

Roberts breathed in deeply, then shook his head.

'I'm glad I stayed an academic. It's bad enough having to justify your existence through research and return-on-investment in the faculty here. Christ knows what it's like in the rough and tumble of private science.'

'So can you talk to me about Greif?'

'I can put a cautious toe in the water. I suppose it's not strictly private as his research is available if you want it.'

'Actually it's not. He seems to have taken it out of circulation.'

'Oh did he? Well that's an option he had when he submitted. But it doesn't make your job any easier, does it, because I've got to be even more careful now, haven't I?'

Belinda sipped her drink and looked at Roberts over the top of her glass, letting her eyes do some work on him.

'Why did you call him a little bastard?'

'Did I? Probably an emotional response to the memory of listening to him rave on. Have you met him?'

'No, but my colleague has.'

'What does he say?'

'That Greif is an egocentric who sees himself as some kind of messianic leader with a mission to educate us all into his way of thinking. Something like that.'

'Sounds about right. When I first met him he was rough around the edges but evidently extremely clever, one of the cleverest people I've met. He'd not long come over from the Soviet Union, and while he didn't have an accent because one of his parents was English, he didn't exactly have the manners. I don't mean etiquette and how to drink a cup of tea. I mean he didn't understand Western Europe. He had an Eastern European sensibility and a confidence that came from being intelligent in two languages. You remember Garry Kasparov, the chess player? He was like that on speed. If you disagreed with him you were a fool, and he didn't mind telling you so. He had no restraint. Pissed off a lot of people.'

'He seems to have gone through several jobs.'

'Yes, he *would* argue. He couldn't bide his time, play the long game, compromise. He even got into an argument with one of his assessors on his *viva* for his doctorate. He was lucky to get it after that. Fortunately the other assessors overrode the old prof Greif had antagonised. Am I talking too much? You seem to have got me going—either I'm drunk already or you're a very skilled interviewer.'

'I couldn't possibly say. So can you tell me what his research was actually about? We have information that it's possible he worked with biological weapons when he was in the Ukraine.'

Roberts sat back in his chair.

'Where is this going? I thought you were investigating him because of irregularities in his management.'

'That's true. He kept secrets from his immediate superiors and seems to have recruited a group of people around him who are acting like cult members. We're worried there may be something more serious going on.'

'Like what?'

'That's why I'm talking to you. To find out what his own work was focused on.'

Roberts' demeanour had become serious and less sociable in the last couple of minutes, and Belinda felt herself tightening up, becoming more dogmatic and insistent.

She said, 'Look, I don't want to put you in a difficult position, professionally, telling me stuff you don't feel comfortable with. And likewise there are things I can't tell you because we don't have absolute proof yet. But what I can tell you is that Greif and his team have vanished. They've taken nearly all of the equipment from their employer's laboratories and done a bunk.'

'This is beginning to sound crazy.'

'Tell me about it. I was hired to look into a suicide and I'm now investigating the disappearance of a dozen people. That's a bit of an escalation.'

'I don't know what to tell you. Most of his work looked at atmospherics—my own field—analysing data related to the creation of bioaerosols. How biological material becomes suspended in liquid in the first place, what the mechanism is. But his final work wasn't really about that.'

'What *was* it about?'

'It seemed to me he was more interested in how you could *use* bioaerosols.'

'What do you mean?'

'Put it this way, while he pretended an interest in how the packages were made, he was actually more concerned with how they were delivered. How do you deliver seeding to a wide area to produce the required fall-out?'

CHAPTER THIRTY EIGHT

EARLY AFTERNOON TRAFFIC on Friday, in Manchester, is a good kickstarter for road-rage. I wondered why I'd driven into town instead of taking the train but there was something about having your own transport that suggested freedom.

A freedom that I wasn't experiencing as we slogged out of the city centre and I tried to orientate myself south.

When the traffic had thinned a little, I pulled into the side of the road and phoned Midwinter. Charles Montgomery answered the phone himself without the call going to Reception or even to his gatekeeper, Mary.

I said, 'I take it you're in the office alone?'

'Dyke? Yes, I did as you suggested. Sent them all home. No one was doing any work anyway. As soon as it got out that Greif and his team had gone missing they did nothing but gossip all day. I've told them not to come back until Tuesday.'

'Good. It will all be settled by then.'

'What will? Do you know what the hell is going on here? I'd like to know what I can tell my investors, in the unhappy event that they call me and demand to know what one of my best unit managers is doing.'

'To be honest, Charles, I don't know. I have some ideas but I'm not going to tell you because they're completely without foundation.'

'I could become your client, then you'd have to tell me.'

'Only the results of investigations after you became a client, not before.'

'I'll make it worth your while.'

'I'm sure, but there are some things worth more than money.'

Montgomery laughed, a cruel sound that was probably the result of his frustration.

'A private investigator turning down cash for work? It strikes me you're probably not very successful at running a business.'

'Ah, but I have my honour.'

'Do you? Really? I don't think anyone in your profession can legitimately say that.'

'Charles, you're tired and emotional. Go home. You'll read all about this in the papers on Monday morning.'

'No, I'm staying here. The company needs some kind of front. Why did you ring?'

'Just checking in.'

'Are you sure it wasn't because you were worried about us? Worried how I was getting on? Are you sure you weren't emotionally invested, just a little?'

'Don't talk nonsense, Charles. Have a good weekend.'

AS I CONTINUED south through Manchester I found myself putting things together in my head. One perspective might be that Stratford Greif was a highly intelligent man whose sense of his place in the world was skewed. He tried out several jobs but each time managed to get himself sacked—he was probably overbearing, a bully, and no doubt belittled the people who worked for him. He couldn't hold down a job and became embittered over time. Finally he got a position at Midwinter and was going to take his revenge, using all the resources at his disposal.

Another view might be that he knew full well what he was doing from the beginning. The reason for his moving from job to job might be that he'd tried his world-building schemes before, tried to recruit people to his way of thinking, his view of what people needed. He was taking his time, looking for the right environment to start his mission. Asahara, the leader of Aum Shinrikyo, had himself attempted various professions before becoming a guru in order to assert his megalomaniac intentions. Then he concluded that in order for mankind to be pure again, according to his philosophy, it would first have to be destroyed—hence his use of biological and chemical weapons, starting small but with the intention of ramping up the attacks until they were worldwide in their effect.

Greif would have known through his reading of the Japanese writer Mishima that it was useless to attempt revolution with blunt force or through the ballot-box— something Asahara had tried, too—but he was arrogant enough to believe that he could change the world not with logical argument but through a demonstration of intellectual might. No one, he thought, would be clever enough to outfox him. So he sailed close to the wind at Midwinter, recruited disaffected but clever youngsters to do the drudge work and got rid of obstacles or troublemakers like Nathan Mustow and Margaret Sellers. It was the Aum Shinrikyo model all over again, without the pretension to religious thinking.

Now the Bleak was re-grouping somewhere, perhaps putting the final touches to their master-plan away from the prying eyes of Charles Montgomery, Midwinter and myself and Belinda.

And currently all I had to go on was an address given to me by a disguised voice in a mysterious telephone call. I wondered what I could have done differently. Perhaps I should have spent more time looking at paperwork—Greif and his unit must have bought their supplies from somewhere and must have corresponded in some form with whoever it was that was letting them their current laboratory. I had no doubt they were in commercial property somewhere: the environment they needed was too specialised to be somebody's front room in Chorlton. The address of the factory that the mystery voice had given me might be real … but what if it wasn't? What if it was simply a bluff to prevent me looking for the actual place, the real laboratory?

I turned into Harry Tuck's street and braked immediately. Further down the road I could see a couple of police Volvos and an ambulance, together with what looked like an unmarked car parked at an angle across the road. Uniforms with bright yellow waistcoats were shepherding onlookers around.

I parked, put on a wind-cheater with a pull-up hood, shoved my hands in my pockets like a true Mancunian and sauntered down the road as though I lived there.

When I got closer I saw two paramedics shunting a gurney out of the front door and through the sitting-room window, where once I'd seen Harry Tuck talking on his phone, I saw Inspector Howard's dark hair and his oblong head. He was talking to someone I couldn't see, pointing a finger at him and becoming very animated.

I turned and went back to my car before he saw me staring up at him.

It seemed that Harry Tuck had joined Mustow and Margaret Sellers amongst those who had dissatisfied Stratford Greif. I hadn't liked the man much but he had energy. I guessed that he was planning to take that energy and move it somewhere that Greif couldn't compromise it. But he'd waited too long and Greif had had the last word.

The mystery voice had told me to look for Harry Tuck and ask him what was going on. Maybe he was pointing me in this direction, knowing that Tuck was dead.

So perhaps his information about the location of the Bleak was also accurate.

With this in mind, there was only one place left for me to go.

CHAPTER THIRTY NINE

IT TOOK ME forty-five minutes to get out of greater Manchester and find the Torrington Estate in Altrincham that the mystery man had told me about. Altrincham isn't that big but my GPS didn't have the Estate in its database and I was reduced to driving around the the town looking for likely candidates.

It was now getting on for 3.30 and the town was gathering itself for the rush-hour push, commuters getting ready to head out towards the M56 motorway or to the A556 connecting link to the M6. Altrincham has one of the highest per-capita spending figures outside of London's poshest areas, though it always looked a little seedy and run-down to me, as if it were waiting for a good makeover. House prices in Altrincham and nearby Bowdon and Hale Barns were still ludicrously high but the public and commercial buildings were decrepit.

So I wasn't surprised when I found the Estate to discover that it was an old industrial zone containing decidedly low-tech brick warehouses and offices, similar to the ones that Tuck had lured me to a few days before. Greif seemed to have a knack for finding buildings and sites that were on their last legs, the final sparks of industry or commerce having been squeezed out of them when the latest Crash came down the line.

As with the other estate, it looked as though the site was deserted. From a parking bay opposite the entrance I counted twelve units and in the half hour that I sat and watched no one went in or out. There was a board by the front gate that listed the businesses you might once have found on the site, but most of them had been scratched out or marked over with heavy black pen. Only three businesses seemed to be still going—a computer accessories warehouse, a cheap kitchen outfitter, and an adhesives manufacturer and supplier—U-Stick. I guessed the first two were probably now defunct as well, given the state of the economy, and that the unit used by the adhesives manufacturer had been sub-let to Stratford Greif or whoever had signed the letting agreement for him.

I was about to get out of my car and cross the road when my phone rang. Belinda.

She said, 'At last you answer.'

I never answered the phone when driving and now recalled guiltily that it had rung twice while I was en route. I'd forgotten to check my messages when I arrived at the estate. I must have been excited.

I said, 'How was Doctor Joe?'

'Very nice, just my type. Clever, good hair, very calming influence.'

'But was he informative?'

'Never mind me, where are you? What happened with Greif?'

'You first.'

'Jesus ... okay. Roberts told me that Stratford was very difficult, very Eastern European in his outlook.'

'What did he mean by that?'

'He said Greif developed all the trappings of the calm and considered British gentleman, but he had a fiery personality. He can hold a grudge, he takes against you if you argue with him. And he can't be at all diplomatic.'

'And this helps us how?'

'He also said that his research interests were a bluff. He seemed to be looking at how these bioaerosol-things worked, so they could be filtered out before they carried disease into places we wouldn't want them to go.'

'But in fact ...'

'In fact it seemed to Roberts that Greif was more interested in how you could make them go where you wanted, carrying the diseases that you wanted. In other words, how you develop these things so that they can spread diseases for a long time over a wide area.'

'How on earth would he get away with that as a research topic for his Ph.D?'

'It's science, Sam! As long as you can get the funding, and approval from the university, you can do it. He disguised it, though, according to Roberts. Pretended he was looking at *how* bioaerosols worked, when he was in fact researching what you could do to *improve* how they worked.'

'So what do you think?'

'Wow, you want my opinion? What have I done to deserve this honour?'

'You have learned well, grasshopper.'

'As it happens, I don't know what to think. Worst-case scenario is that he's got plague or anthrax or something that he's going to let loose somewhere. But I did some reading of my own last night. It seems that getting these biological weapons to work isn't easy. Your man at Aum Shinrikyo tried it first, didn't he, before they settled on chemistry and made the sarin gas instead.'

She was right. Asahara's scientists had attempted various ways of weaponising botulinum, with limited success. They'd tried growing the bacterium in huge fermenting tanks but it hadn't worked properly. That didn't stop them from using three converted trucks to spray what they had into two US Naval bases, Narita airport, the Japanese parliament and the Imperial Palace.

No one came down with so much as a cold.

They also produced over twenty tons of a medium containing anthrax and sprayed it from trucks at various locations in Tokyo, again with no result.

Only when they got their science right and started producing VX nerve agent and sarin did they begin to have success, injuring and killing a number of specific individuals who were causing Asahara legal problems.

I wondered whether Stratford Greif was targeting people who'd irritated him—like me—or whether he was going straight for the grandstand effect.

Belinda said, 'You've had my news, so what happened with Greif?'

I told her briefly what Greif and I had said to each other— that Greif more or less denied knowledge of what we were accusing him of, while at the same time insisting that he was going to change the world.

Belinda said, 'And how's he going to do that? By killing off large swathes of it from a cosy bunker in Manchester?'

'Don't look for reason, Belinda. The reason is in his head, made up of nine-tenths superiority and one-tenth resentment.'

'Against what?'

'Who knows? It doesn't matter. But there's always resentment against something. For bad guys like this it's almost always about revenge at some level. They can't let go of stuff and it eats them up. Anyway, where are you now?'

'On my way.'

'Yes, but where to?'

'That would be telling.'

'I hope you're not coming here. This is going to get dangerous soon.'

'Sorry, line's going, can't hear you ...'

The connection was broken, and I had little doubt who had broken it.

THERE WAS NO option now.

I climbed from my car and walked briskly between the two rusted pillars to which the estate's fence was attached. Now I was out of the car I could hear the distant roar of the motorways and the closer hum of Altrincham's town centre, the shunting traffic, the beep of pedestrian crossings, the slamming of car doors. This estate was only a short walk from the heart of the town and I could have just turned around and gone shopping in George Street.

There was a skeletal map on the board containing the list of businesses and I worked out where the adhesive factory was. It was in a far corner of the estate, backing on to the railway line that ran through the heart of the town. I zipped up my leather jacket and started walking in that direction, keeping as close as possible to the line of the warehouses and office buildings as I could so that I wasn't immediately visible to anyone watching.

I don't know what I expected to find. If today was the day that Greif was going to make his big statement, it was possible that the factory would be a hive of malicious activity, with the members of The Bleak scurrying back and forth with big drums of poisonous material. On the other hand, whatever he planned to do might already be in train, with the team members scattered far and wide and nothing but tumbleweed blowing through their latest location.

It began to rain as I turned the final corner and saw a square building with 'U-Stick' written on a large hoarding attached to it. Presumably stuck on with adhesive.

The building, like the others, was painted a dull grey and seemed to be in two parts. There was a front entrance which was neatly made from red brick with large windows and a double-glazed door. This was doubtless an entry to some kind of Reception area. Behind this concession to human scale, the rest of the building bloomed out like an enormous hangar, window-less and obscure, and I expected that either at the back or on the far side, which I couldn't see, there would be a loading ramp of some kind.

I watched for five minutes and saw nobody, so I decided to use the direct approach.

I walked up to the door and saw a keypad set into brickwork to the right. I entered the code of 20031995 and turned the handle—the door opened.

CHAPTER FORTY

MONTGOMERY HAD NO idea why he was in the car with this woman. He didn't even know how she'd got hold of his number. But at least he felt as though he was doing something. He'd spent the previous day after Dyke's visit going round the buildings telling people to go home, then passed the afternoon in his office answering the phone. He'd found himself in a quandary. He felt somehow responsible for the people who hadn't turned up that morning—Greif's team, and the security group—but he didn't want to admit defeat and get the police involved. For all he knew, Greif might have taken his team away for a motivational trip somewhere and had failed to let him know. It wouldn't be the first time something had been kept from him.

But knowing Greif, motivation was probably the last thing on his mind. He was certainly good at inspiring loyalty from his team; however, his motivational techniques seemed rather crude and dependent on belittling and punishing those who didn't come up to scratch. And of course there was the question of the missing equipment …

So when this young woman had called an hour ago and asked whether he'd help her in the search for Greif and his unit he was only too glad to lend a hand. It would distract him from the larger implications of what was happening at Midwinter.

She'd picked him up from the office at four o'clock, driving this revolting pink Volvo, and they were now battling cross-country, seemingly headed for somewhere south of Manchester. She'd told him on the phone that she was helping Dyke, and she certainly seemed both confident and competent. He was used to working with people who were slightly restrained and cautious, given to thinking through their actions and being emotionally cool. This woman oozed life and certainty, and drove as though she travelled these roads every day and knew every lump and curve in the tarmac. He realised that he had one hand on the door handle and the other threaded through the seat-belt. He breathed deeply and let go of the seat-belt.

The movement seemed to attract her eye.

'Sorry, Charlie, am I going too fast? Got to move, you know. Sam's on his own and I don't like what he's doing.'

'Where is he?'

'Someone phoned him with information about where Greif and his people are. But it could be a set-up, like the other night. I don't believe he's just walking into it again.'

'Why would he do that, if it's dangerous? And what do you mean by "the other night"? What happened?'

'Sam and I had a little contretemps with a couple of Greif's boys. That's who we're assuming it was. I got away but he got a bump on the head.'

'Good Lord! How do you know it was anything to do with Greif?'

'Hell of a coincidence otherwise.'

'Did you report it to the police?'

'Nothing to report. Four blokes in balaclavas, two for Sam, two for me. Nothing taken, no I.D. possible. Water under the bridge now.'

Montgomery felt himself tightening up even more and gripped the seat-belt again. He'd known as soon as he'd met Dyke that he was someone who attracted ill-feeling and probably anger. He was too … unforgiving. Too direct and non-negotiable. Like this young woman, he seemed to have a confidence that was based on cynicism and probably too much contact with the seedier side of life. His assumptions about right and wrong were quickly made and implacable.

He said, 'Have you any idea what Stratford is up to? Did he really have something to do with Nathan Mustow's death? Or the Sellers girl?'

'Charlie, Stratford Greif is a piece of shit. Get that into your head. I've never met the man but from what I've heard he talks a good talk and acts like the superior English gent. But deep down he doesn't much care for us. His heart's still with the mother country.'

'Russia? But he left there years ago and never went back, so far as I know. Are you saying he's on some anti-West crusade?'

'Too many questions, Charlie, and I don't have any answers. All we really know is that he's not what he seems and he's got some very strange ideas about his place in the world. Plus, he seems to have recruited all these boffins into his world-view, which is particularly unhealthy.'

'But they're all very clever and rational people! They wouldn't do anything malicious or evil.'

'Think again. They're all young, relatively inexperienced, blinkered in how they think and convinced that they belong to some kind of elite. They're like bankers but with fewer morals. If that's possible.'

Montgomery stiffened. 'My son's a banker.'

The woman laughed. 'My mistake. Foot in mouth yet again. Christ, can't these cars go faster than thirty?'

Montgomery focused on the road, his mind a whirlwind. He couldn't believe that he'd missed all of this. There must have been signs, people in the company must have noticed. But they didn't say anything. The worst thing he'd heard was a couple of ribald comments about the after-hours drinking that Greif seemed to encourage at his get-togethers every week.

All this time he'd wanted Midwinter to grow and develop into a prime destination for the best research minds. They didn't have the resources of the university departments that were his main competition, but his backers had been generous and they were all hopeful that at least one of the projects that were coming to term would get back some of the investment and demonstrate that it was possible to make money with private research. Academic papers in prestigious journals were all well and good, but in the end his tenure at Midwinter—his legacy—would be judged on its turnover and eventual financial success.

Acting as a breeding ground for Stratford Greif's off-centre ideas, or possibly worse, was not what he'd had in mind.

He said, 'Tell me again where we're going and why.'

The woman glanced at him and he sensed an appraisal in her eyes, as though assessing how much to tell him.

'Sam thinks he's found your missing team and he's going to talk to them politely. We're going to help.'

'What help can I possibly be?'

'I'm beginning to wonder the same thing. I thought you might know how to operate the computers or something, or defuse the switch that sets off the bomb.'

Montgomery knew that his mouth had opened slightly and hoped that she hadn't noticed.

She looked at him again.

She turned away and said, 'In hindsight I'm beginning to think that Sam and Stratford speak different languages. How are you at translating?'

CHAPTER FORTY ONE

ONCE I WAS in the empty Reception office I stood still for several seconds, listening.

I was in a small space occupied by a desk, a filing cabinet, a chair and a thin carpet. A flipover paper calendar on the desk showed a date from a year ago—presumably the last time it had been used for manufacturing and distributing adhesives. Next to the calendar was a plastic gizmo that held office stationery—a wooden ruler, a pair of scissors, pencils. I expected there to be a stapler in one of the drawers. There was a round clock on the wall whose red second-hand was still turning. It read 4.10.

The air smelled musty, and I recognised it as the smell of paper going mouldy, overlaid with a strong odour of the chemicals presumably used in the manufacture of glues and now soaked deeply into the walls.

Facing me was the door into the main body of the factory. Another calendar hung on it at head height, this one showing pictures of classic British cars. The month on view was a 1951 Bristol 401, very sleek looking.

I put my ear to the door and listened. Nothing to hear. No faintly threatening hum, no orders being barked to willing hands, no sounds of barrels being rolled into the rear of waiting trucks.

I tried the handle and it turned, so I went inside.

The space behind was far larger than it looked from the outside. It was three-quarters the length of a football pitch and half as wide, with a high metal-beamed roof stretching overhead. Vast skylights let a feeble grey light trickle through, illuminating a drab concrete floor that was discoloured here and there from oil and chemical spills. In the furthest corner I could see steps going up to another office and a loading bay next to a massive door that looked as though it would roll up. There was an ordinary door cut into this larger one.

I could also see what looked like most of the laboratory equipment that they'd taken from Midwinter. Most of it was piled haphazardly on the floor, white instruments leaning over, spilling out of cardboard boxes, a table piled with laptops sliding over each other, a couple of tall glass-fronted cupboards. I saw a mound of blue cloth that I realised was a pile of the lab coats I'd seen some of the scientists wearing at Midwinter. There were eddies of black waste bags, cliffs of polystyrene sheets, presumably used to pack some of the instruments safely, swirls of files that lay on the floor and had been kicked to and fro. In one area it looked as though a work-space had been set up. A neat desk with a cantilevered lamp, a proper office chair on castors, some vials and retorts. It was an ordered space in a scrap-yard. If they'd been handling biological toxins they must have forgotten everything they ever knew about safety procedures.

Surrounding all this detritus there were several plastic chairs gathered together in groups, as though people had moved towards each other to talk or eat a sandwich. They couldn't resist the human touch, whatever it was they were up to.

But I was afraid. It seemed to me that things were speeding up: they'd been in and out of this location in the space of a day. Long enough to do what?

It looked as though they'd expended all that energy to come here and do one thing. They left nothing behind except the items they no longer needed.

And except for the two men who stepped out from the shadows either side of me and pinned my arms.

One of them said, 'Hello, Dyke,' and when I looked I recognised the man with the pockmarked face and short hair who Jolyon Greif had called Spike. The last time I saw him he was wearing a thick band-aid across his nose. It was gone now and I could see that the nose was bent. Belinda's work. He had a couple of inches on me and although he was thinner in the chest, his colleague was solid and looked strong. I might have been able to take them but as long as they weren't about to shoot me or knock me out I thought I'd see how we went.

I said, 'So they left you to sweep up, did they? While they went off and played cowboys and indians.'

Spike said, 'Let's sit him over there, Dibs.'

They walked me to one of the plastic chairs and then the short one found a piece of binding twine from a pile of wrapping on the floor and tied it around my wrists.

Spike said to his colleague, 'You better call Jolyon, let him know.'

Dibs wandered down the vast hangar, pulling out his phone, dialling and then talking quietly into it. Spike stood in front of me with his arms folded like a disappointed parent. His jacket was too big for him and his trousers were too short, as though he'd kitted himself out from a jumble sale without trying on the clothes first. His shoes looked like Doc Martens and were dusty.

He said, 'If you were that girl I'd kick you in the nuts. That really hurt the other night.'

'Girls don't have nuts, Spike. You must have been dating some strange women. Did any of them have deep voices and a beard?'

He frowned. 'Jesus, all these so-called scientists are up their own arses and think they're being funny at my expense. Don't you start. You're in no position to piss me off.'

'Sorry, it's not your fault you're as tall and green as a beanpole.'

He was about to take the bait on that one when his partner came back and laid a hand on his arm.

'Stratford's already in his car. Leave Dyke alone.'

'What did he say?'

'Wants a word with Sonny Jim here. Says we're to strap him down tight. Don't let him get away.'

As they took a step towards me I stood up, but they reached me and shoved me back into the chair. Spike held me down while Dibs took more twine and tied my legs together, wrapping it around quickly. I tried to keep my knees apart but between them they had the advantage. Spike looked wiry but he was strong.

When my ankles were bound they strapped the whole bundle to the legs of the chair, then fetched more twine and ran a line between the ankle bindings and my wrists.

Spike stood up. 'Trussed like a turkey. We should have done that to you before.'

'You could have tried. Wouldn't have got you far. After all, you were beaten up by a girl. Did you tell your mate that, or was he there with you?'

Dibs looked up at Spike.

'What's he talking about? You said you duffed up the girl but banged your nose on her car.'

'That's right, that's what happened.'

I said, 'Ask him why his nuts are sore.'

'Shut up, you! She never touched my nuts!'

'She didn't need to because she broke your nose. Own up, Spike, you're not really a fighter.'

'Got you wrapped up, didn't we?'

'All part of my plan.'

Dibs took Spike's arm again and led him away. Like Spike, I wondered why Stratford was coming in person. I would have thought he had more important things to do. If what I thought was correct, today—20th March— was the day for the master plan to be carried out, so why bother with me? What would giving me another tongue-lashing achieve?

I didn't have long to wait. The guards left me alone and after ten minutes I heard the door to Reception ping open at the front of the building and a loud buzzer ring at the far end. No wonder Spike and Dibs were able to nab me—the opening of the door warned people in the factory that someone had come in, so that if the person meant to be working on Reception was in the hangar he or she could dash back and be welcoming.

After a few seconds, the door through to the hangar opened behind me and I heard Stratford Greif's measured steps as he walked round to look down at me.

He was still wearing the smart suit and tie that I'd seen him dressed in almost four hours ago. I was saddened that perhaps he hadn't dressed up for me earlier and this was perhaps his habitual off-duty costume. His hair looked impeccably cut and combed and I even thought there was a whiff of after-shave in the air. In his right hand he carried Nathan Mustow's slightly battered maroon briefcase. From the way he gripped it in his fingers it seemed to be heavy.

His expression was grave and unforgiving, his dark eyes intense, as though he were trying to see through to my inner motivations and character. It was more than a little creepy. Despite the fact that I was wrapped like a Christmas present, I didn't feel threatened.

Perhaps I should have done.

He smiled thinly and said, 'Wait there.'

Then he turned and walked to the far end of the hangar, to the cleared work-space that I'd noticed before. I counted seventy steps. Spike and Dibs watched him but said nothing. Greif set the maroon briefcase on the table and opened it so that its lid concealed from me what was inside, though I was too far away to see anyway. He looked intently at something inside and reached in a hand, then closed the lid and placed it on the floor. He straightened his tie and walked back to me, each step of his highly-polished shoes ringing on the concrete floor.

When he reached me he stopped and pushed his hands into his pockets. He could almost have been waiting for a bus.

He said, 'You know, when I instituted the weekly meetings of my group, it wasn't my idea to call it The Bleak. One of the young men suggested the name but I thought it was too … obvious. "In the bleak midwinter", all that Christmas carol nonsense. I acquiesced anyway. And shortly afterwards I came across a quotation that I thought would be much more relevant to our project. It's like a secret motto for our group. Do you want to hear it?'

'Do I have a choice?'

'We always have choices, Mr Dyke. Anyway, I'll assume you've agreed. It's a quotation from Kahlil Gibran, the author of that awful collection of cod philosophy. Do you know him?'

I shook my head.

'You haven't missed a thing. Anyway, the quotation is this: "Rebellion without truth is like spring in a bleak, arid desert." Do you get it? Our usage of The Bleak is a reference to the desert of ignorance and stupidity that is the great unwashed public. You might say that what we're doing, or about to do, is a rebellion of a kind. But as Gibran says, if it's only rebellion for its own sake, without a bedrock of truth beneath it, then it's like pretending that spring will nurture and nourish the desert. It won't. Truth is needed to help underpin the rebellion, to enable the public to see the virtue of the rebellion, to help them understand its underlying cause and its necessity. *We* are not The Bleak. It is those who fail to know their place in the natural order of things. The common man, and woman, of course.'

I took a deep breath and stared at him.

'And how are you going to teach them?'

It was as if I'd prodded him with an electric wire. He took his hands from his pockets and walked briskly to fetch a plastic chair and then sit facing me.

He said, 'In just over an hour's time there will be a change in the public consciousness. An event so cataclysmic will take place that the old order of things will vanish. Existing values and morality will be challenged. Our ways of formal governance will be questioned. The usual institutions—the police, the judiciary, the scientific and religious establishments—will all be buried beneath the weight of criticism and disdain that will come their way. People will look for new leaders, a new moral charter, a new philosophy of being.'

'It didn't work for Mishima or Asahara at Aum Shinrikyo—why should it work for your pathetic little band?'

For the first time ever, I think I'd surprised him. He looked at me warily and glanced over his shoulder as though checking whether Spike and Dibs had heard my apostasy.

He said, 'You're more enterprising than you look. You're correct that Mishima tried brute force to overthrow the Japanese government, but was compelled to commit *seppuku* when he failed. A sword in the belly and then beheaded by a colleague, who was himself then beheaded. Asahara only failed because he was largely an amateur and the people who worked for him were barely graduate students, hardly scientists at all. And yet he still had a measure of success.'

'And was sentenced to death for his pains. Why do you think people will listen to you afterwards? After whatever it is you plan to do.'

He stood up. 'Nice try, Dyke. I'm not going to tell you anything. This isn't a Bond movie. But I do expect you to die.'

He turned and gestured to Spike and Dibs, who hurried across from the other end of the hangar.

He said, 'Leave him tied here. I want you two to stand outside the building until I call and tell you to leave. That will be later tonight. Whatever you do, don't come into the building until after I tell you to. There's going to be a little surprise for Mr Dyke.'

Spike said, 'Where's Jolyon? I thought he'd be coming.'

'He's with me. Dibs, is it? Go out through the hangar door and stay there. Spike, you go out the front.'

They both looked at him dubiously but eventually separated and walked away. Greif watched as Dibs reached the loading ramp and opened up the cut-away door, then stepped outside and closed it behind him. I heard the door at my back open and close as Spike made his way to the front of the building.

I felt myself beginning to sweat. I didn't like the look of this. I had no doubt that Greif would do whatever he had set his mind to do.

He said, 'Well, Mr Dyke. We say our farewells. It looks like they've done a good job with wrapping you up. You won't be going far.' He glanced at his watch. 'Ten to five. In ten minutes time you'll have a little surprise … although I suppose we might say I've spoiled it for you now. And then later, when you'll be in no position to do anything, there will be considerable consternation somewhere else not a million miles from here.'

'I should say something about you not getting away with it.'

'You should, you should. It plays properly into the script I'm sure you'd like to believe. But you'll never know, so I wouldn't bother saying it, if I were you. Goodbye.'

He strode past me to the door and left. I didn't hear his Bentley leave. I stared at the empty hangar, wondering how long I could make ten minutes last.

CHAPTER FORTY TWO

BELINDA SAW DYKE'S car parked opposite the entrance to the industrial state and thought she wasn't going to pussyfoot around like that. Pausing only long enough to read the plan by the gate to see where the adhesive factory was, she drove through the gates and then between the deserted warehouses and offices until she thought she was close enough to find the place on foot.

She slowed to a halt, then glanced at her watch before opening the door of her Volvo and climbing out.

4.53.

Montgomery had got out of the passenger door at the same time. She said to him over the top of the Volvo, 'You coming with me or staying here?'

'Try and stop me.'

'Good on you, Charlie. But stay behind me. I give you permission to watch my arse but don't go mad.'

She got her bearings on the estate, glancing at the series of industrial units marching evenly down the road towards her, each one shuttered, graffiti-laden and desolate. She started jogging towards the last but one building on the grid, running on the overgrown grass verge in order to keep silence. She heard Montgomery huffing behind her and hoped he wouldn't keel over before they got there.

At the corner of the building she paused and lifted an arm to keep Montgomery back. The drizzle of rain had stopped and the tarmac glistened in a sudden burst of sunshine. As she peered around the corner she saw a tall, skinny man standing with his back to the Reception office, smoking a cigarette. There was something in the way he stood that reminded her of the big man she'd hit the other night. Good. She'd like another go at him.

She turned back to Montgomery. 'Stay here. I'm going around the back of this place to have a crack at the man over there. Don't move, you understand?'

'I'm not a child.'

'To be confirmed. Stay here.'

She went back past him and ran down the side of the metal-sided building, which seemed to be a defunct tyre depot. Stacks of dirty tyres were piled higher than she could reach against the building's walls. Some had escaped confinement and lay around haphazardly on the grass. Rounding the corner she was now parallel to the railway line, which gleamed wetly beyond a rusted metal fence, and she slowed to a rapid walk, letting her breathing calm before she arrived at the bottom corner.

Once there she peered around the metal siding, still slick with rain, and looked back up towards the front of the adhesive factory. She could see the thin man's bony arm sticking out from the side of the Reception office, tapping ash on to the pavement.

Then her heart sank as she saw Charles Montgomery emerge from the corner of the tyre depot and walk towards him. He strode purposefully, like the company director that he was, and she caught the faintest hint of his voice as he called out to the man on duty. She saw the thin man stand to attention and walk towards Montgomery, then hesitate. Perhaps he'd recognised the person who'd been his nominal boss until a couple of days ago.

Montgomery stopped a few yards short of the building and manoeuvred himself so that the younger man, still walking, had his back to where Belinda was hidden.

She saw what Montgomery was doing immediately and thought, *You're a very silly boy, but you might have just made this easier.*

She crossed the road and ran cat-like up the grass verge beside the road. As she came closer she heard Montgomery talking at the top of his voice, presumably to cover the sound of her approach. His arms were waving and his face was pink. She thought that before she got there the thin man would punch him rather than have to put up with such provocation.

The last ten yards were the hardest. The younger man must have finally heard her pounding feet and began to turn just as she prepared to strike.

It had the effect of shifting his face into a perfect target. As she saw the plaster on his nose, and knew for certain that he was the man she'd struck before, she raised the side of her hand and, still running, chopped it hard across his face.

The man yelped and fell backwards like a step-ladder collapsing, his legs and arms an awkward tangle. Belinda landed on top of him and clubbed him twice with her clenched fist, the knuckles hardened through constant practice. Her instructor in Germany would have laughed at her technique, but the man stayed down, his hands rising slowly towards his nose, a faint whimpering sound bubbling from between his lips. Belinda crouched over him for a moment but knew he wouldn't fight. She quickly checked him for weapons, then stood up. She'd come away with a wooden baton about eighteen inches long and thick as a baseball bat.

She said, 'Charlie, you're very naughty, but you did good. Now, let's see what's inside.'

When they got to the Reception door, Belinda saw that she needed to enter the code Dyke had given her on a numeric pad. She did so and swung the door handle, which turned and let her step into the small room, Montgomery close behind. Although she was breathing hard, she thought she heard a buzzer of some kind ringing in the warehouse behind the office. It stopped when she closed the door.

Shit.

A clock on the wall facing her read 4.57.

CHAPTER FORTY THREE

THE BUZZER SOUNDED and I wondered why Spike would be coming back in. Greif had given him specific instructions to stay outside. I'd been trying to squirm out of the bindings on the chair but had done nothing but chafed my wrists and ankles against the plastic twine that Dibs had used. I'd also been counting down ten minutes in my head and knew there were only three left before something happened. I didn't like to think what it might be. Something poisonous. Something involving disease …

But there were two sets of footsteps heading towards me.

I turned my head just as Belinda came into sight, with Charles Montgomery behind her looking red-faced and more than a little flustered.

Belinda stood in front of me with her arms folded.

'Well, and I thought of you as my mentor.'

'You need to go, now. You've got less than three minutes to get away.'

She unfolded her arms quickly and pointed to Montgomery.

'Charlie, get back to the car. I'll be there as soon as I can.'

'Belinda!'

'There are scissors back in the office, hold on.'

She was already running back to the front of the building. Montgomery hadn't moved.

He said, 'What's going to happen? What has Greif done?'

'I'm not certain. Greif set something up.' He must have seen my eyes flicker to the far end of the factory. He turned and started to run. I called after him, 'Where are you going?'

Behind me I heard the door open and then Belinda was in front of me, forcing the scissors between my wrists and sawing at the twine.

I pulled as she cut and the ties fell away.

'My legs.'

She bent down and started to cut again. Over the top of her head I saw that Montgomery had stopped and was looking around at the debris from his laboratories. He noticed the maroon briefcase under the table, probably something he didn't recognise, and placed it on the table.

I shouted, 'Charles, leave it alone!'

Belinda said, 'What's he doing?'

'Trying to be a hero.'

'Doesn't he know that's your job?'

'He's going to get himself killed.'

I looked at my watch. There was less than half a minute to go. I grabbed the scissors from Belinda and started cutting as fast as I could.

I said, 'Get out of here. No point all of us being infected.'

'I should go help him.'

'Don't you dare. It's too late. Get out.'

She stood up. 'When you go.'

I swore and was going to swear even harder when the plastic ties around my ankles suddenly fell away. I stood up and was facing her. Fifty metres away Montgomery was staring at the inside of the briefcase as though he didn't know what he was looking at.

At that moment, the door cut into the loading bay opened and Dibs stepped inside.

I said to Belinda, 'We can't help him. Move.'

We turned and ran towards the front office.

MONTGOMERY STARED AT the confusion of wires and the two red canisters they surrounded. When he was running down the length of the hangar he was aware how stupid he must look. What on earth did he think he could do? If Greif had rigged up some kind of infectious weapon, what would he be able to do to contain it? Although he had begun in science, he had largely been an administrator for fifteen years and his expertise was beyond rusty.

The wiring in the case was multi-coloured and seemed to loop in and out of several small boxes. There were two dials, or were they gauges? Or even timers? He found that he couldn't think straight, couldn't calm his mind to follow a logical thought process, to start at one end of the puzzle and finish at the other. Ever since this nightmare had begun he'd realised that he was out of his depth. He was good at setting out a plan, a course, and persuading people that it was the right direction to go in. He was persuasive, without a doubt. But he couldn't think on his feet. He got flustered and then he got angry and then he got frustrated, so his only course of action was often to thump a wall or pound a table.

He didn't think that would be a good idea right now.

He dimly heard Dyke shouting something from the other end of the factory. And a moment later the light changed as the door in the loading bay swung wide. A man was standing in silhouette facing him, and he was saying something that Montgomery was too occupied to hear.

Perhaps that woman, Belinda, would deal with the man while he carried on puzzling out this mass of wires and timers and canisters and switches …

It was only at the last moment that he realised where he was going wrong. He'd been looking for some kind of valve that would be opened in order for the poison or the infection to be released into the atmosphere. That was what Greif worked with. That was what he would use if he wanted to end Dyke's investigation into his misdeeds—and end his life, too.

But where Montgomery had gone wrong was in his belief that it would have been Greif who put together this device, using his own particular expertise.

When of course it had been one of his men, someone with military experience, perhaps, or at least with enough knowledge to use a completely different kind of expertise.

Montgomery smiled at his own stupidity at the exact moment he realised what the device was.

It wasn't a device containing canisters of nerve gas or plague or anthrax.

It was a simple bomb.

The understanding came to him in a dazzling light that suddenly consumed his whole world.

CHAPTER FORTY FOUR

WE AGREED AFTERWARDS that we felt it before we heard it.

The explosion inside the massive warehouse blew out most of its metal cladding, punched a hole in the wall behind the Reception office and as a result sent glass and bricks hurtling towards us.

Belinda and I had run about forty yards from the building when we felt ourselves thrown forward by the air-blast a moment before the sound caught up.

I landed face-down on tarmac and immediately covered my head with my hands, waiting for bricks or beams or sheets of siding to come clattering down. Fortunately, the major force of the bomb had dissipated before it hit the walls, so although the blast hurtled through the building and tore most of it down, by the time it reached us with enough strength to knock us over it was too weak to carry with it any of the building's materials. A few slivers of glass and some pieces of shattered uPVC window-frame fell on to our backs.

I glanced over at Belinda and she was in the same position as me, face down on the road, hands on head.

After the echoing noise of the blast had drifted away I said, 'You all right?'

She turned over and looked up at the sky.

'Montgomery must be dead. Poor Charlie.'

'He tried to do the right thing but at the wrong time. How are you?'

'A bit deaf but okay. You?'

'Torn knees in my jeans. I'll survive.'

We stood up slowly and looked at the wreck of the adhesive factory. There was a chemical smell in the air that was more than the odour of explosives—it was the indefinable and pungent smell of glue. It had been trapped in the bones of the building and was now released into freedom. The building itself looked as though God had tried to open it with a can-opener, its roof split at the apex and peeled back, the front office reduced to complete rubble, the walls distended in most places and absolutely collapsed in others, leaving only the bare metal skeleton of its construction visible in twisted beams and exposed electrical wiring. Small fires were already breaking out here and there, though there was nothing much to sustain them and they didn't burn fiercely.

Belinda said, 'Oh my god.'

I followed her gaze. The man called Spike had survived too, though he'd been closer to the explosion. He was standing woozily to his feet and looked like the risen dead, his hair burned, his clothing scorched and hanging off his shoulders. He looked to his left and right as though checking to see if anyone had noticed him, then he picked a direction and started shambling out of the estate as though he'd just woken from a nightmare and needed to get home.

I said, 'The other man, Dibs, is probably dead too. He was close.'

'Do we stay for the cops and the fire brigade?'

I looked her over. She was a little ragged around the edges but otherwise seemed okay. It was starting to rain again and I steered her towards the entrance to the industrial estate.

'Where's your car?'

'Just there.'

We'd turned a corner and now I saw the pink Volvo.

I said, 'Greif told me that something was going to happen in just over an hour's time. That was before five, so he must have meant six o'clock. The thing is, I have no idea where he was going or what they intended to do.'

We arrived at her car and climbed in. I felt the beginnings of one of my migraines and tried to will it away. I lay back in the passenger seat and closed my eyes, trying to unknot the tension at the back of my head.

Belinda said, 'Didn't he give any hint at all? Do you think it'll be another bomb or what they've been working on all this time?'

I shook my head slowly.

'That bomb was a special, a one-off. He intended to plant it whether I was there or not, to get rid of any evidence. Maybe the idea was to draw attention over here, to Altrincham, while setting off the main event elsewhere. But where?'

'What do we know that might help?'

I thought back over what we'd learned, my mind racing even while I was trying to keep calm in order to minimise the migraine. There was no doubt that Greif had been influenced by Asahara and his Aum Shinrikyo group. Asahara was a manipulative charlatan who used his influence to try to extract revenge against people who denied him success or threatened him in legal proceedings. He enlarged this initial vengefulness to aim at Japanese society as a whole.

As for Greif, he took a philosophical rather than a religious or apocalyptic stance. It was about the superiority of his thinking compared to the rest of us, the common herd. He intended to teach us how skewed our thinking was so that we'd stop and listen to his views. I wondered whether Greif knew what an under-achiever Asahara had been. But then realised that he must have known. Unlike me, he'd read more than a couple of Wikipedia entries.

So what did he really think about Asahara's strategy and his actions? Was he really wedded to the idea of mass-murder as political statement? Or was it simple revenge for the perceived slights he'd thought were aimed in his direction? For all his faults, Greif wasn't naive. He seemed worldly-wise and shrewd.

I opened my eyes. I felt an idea building.

I said, 'How quickly can you get to Piccadilly Station?'

'On a good day, about forty-five minutes, I would think. But it's Friday rush-hour. It could be an hour.'

I glanced at my watch.

'You've got forty minutes. Do you want me to drive?'

'Don't be ridiculous. Fasten your seat-belt.'

CHAPTER FORTY FIVE

HE WASN'T SURE that he could take the noise and the bustle for much longer.

So many people, all of them leading pathetic and miserable lives, none of them knowing what real power felt like. Only when you had real power could you understand what it was to be alive.

Since he'd lost his power-base, Jolyon had been searching for a way to feel that buzz again. Leading a bunch of second-rate losers as part of his 'security' team hadn't really done it. He'd hoped that involvement with Stratford's project would help, but apparently not. There was a word to describe what he felt—a word that he'd seen in a television programme and had to look up because he hadn't recognised it.

Anomie.

Feeling alone and anxious because of a lack of control.

Control is what he'd once had and now had lost. Stratford had given him the illusion of having it again but it was exactly that: an illusion, without foundation in fact. So whatever happened in the next twenty minutes or so didn't really matter. There was no way he'd be able to get back the feeling of control that he'd had when eighty people reported directly to him. Those days were gone.

He shifted his position slightly. The rickety chair was uncomfortable and he was getting tired of the dismissive looks that came his way from people who were no better than he was, but thought they were because they were travelling somewhere. If they only knew.

Stratford came back, phone in hand, and sat next to him. It was odd to see him dressed this way. He had always been so particular in his dress-code, as though it were a personal affront if his tie didn't match his socks and his trousers weren't perfectly pressed. But he'd explained that things had to change if the world was to change.

Stratford said, 'It happened. Enormous explosion. Just hitting the websites now. Keep watching the screen up there and you'll see it.'

'Anyone killed?'

'Nothing mentioned yet. It's probably too soon. There was no possible way for Dyke to escape, though. I had Spike and that other one watching the doors.'

'Did they make it?'

'I have no idea and you should know me by now, Jolyon: I don't care.'

Jolyon turned away. Of course he knew that. He'd just hoped that something might have awakened in Stratford at this pinnacle of his career. He wondered if Stratford had really thought through the consequences of what he was about to do, what it meant to the thousands of people in the station at that moment, and maybe to their friends and families beyond. Did he ever think about other people in that way, their fears, their expectations, their worries?

But of course he knew the answer to that.

Stratford said, 'How long?'

Jolyon looked at his watch. 'Two minutes. Where are the others?'

'I told them to go back to their various safe-houses. We'll meet up later.'

'Montgomery might find them, give them an ear-full. You know what he's like when he's angry.'

'And do what to them? Sack them? I hope you don't think we're going back to Midwinter after tonight.'

'If he finds them he'll probably just tell the Law. Even if he doesn't find them he'll have to get the police involved eventually, when he realises everyone's gone missing.'

'It won't matter. The Law won't matter after tonight. You haven't been listening, have you?'

'We'll see.'

Stratford turned towards him, his dark eyes even more shadowy in the bright overhead light of the station.

'Listen, Jolyon. I know you find it hard to be committed to this. If you want to go, leave now. I can manage. It's not difficult. You'll see, it'll be for the best.'

'Will it? I wonder.'

'You've been sitting here with me for ten minutes now. Watching these people, like me. Don't you feel ashamed to be part of the human race? The inconsequential nature of their transactions. The inability to follow a logical argument. The willingness to ignore most of what they learn in their lifetimes in exchange for taking the easy way out and watching television.'

'I watch television.'

'Of course you do. Everyone does. But you don't believe it, do you? That's the difference. Now, what's the time?'

'Another minute.'

Jolyon had the sense that there was a flurry of activity at the entrance to the station. From where he was sitting he couldn't see around the corner, past the large electronic timetables in the concourse. It was probably someone running for their connection. Another train had arrived at the platform behind them and now its passengers were beginning to come by, streaming past completely oblivious of them, heading outside or searching for a board that would tell them the platform for their train home. He realised that the noise in the station was loud, almost deafening, the sound of announcements merging with the clatter of thousands of feet and the tumult of conversation between passengers, this noise in turn mixing with the clamour of the interactions between customers and staff serving food and other goods in the shops in the concourse. A harsh, insistent, vibrant racket. The sound of human communication.

Still seated, Stratford pulled one of the two cases towards him across the floor and opened it up, then leaned towards him.

'Have you got your mask?'

'Of course.'

'Put it on. Show time.'

CHAPTER FORTY SIX

I DON'T KNOW how she did it but Belinda got us to the taxi-rank outside Piccadilly Station with a couple of minutes to spare. I'd called Howard but there was no reply and I had to leave a message. I could have called 999 but thought there was little chance of the police doing anything without more information than I was able to give them. And they'd be inundated with calls about the explosion in Altrincham anyway.

We hadn't spoken much en route, each of us perhaps going over the narrow escape we'd had in the adhesive factory. Every so often I felt a shudder pass through me and recognised it as a sign of shock, as though my body was working to hold me back or calm me down.

But I didn't want to be held back. I wanted to find Stratford Greif and beat him to a pulp for what he'd done to Charles Montgomery, Margaret Sellers and Nathan Mustow. There was a rage coursing through my veins that I hadn't felt in a long time and I wondered where it was coming from. I had a suspicion that Greif had got under my skin because what he'd done seemed … unmotivated. Usually the bad guys I came across had a genuine sob-story — bad parenting, bullying, social exclusion: all the reasons why making wrong decisions seemed reasonable from their perspective.

With Greif it was an intellectual exercise. He did bad stuff as an experiment in social division, trying to push groups of individuals into agreeing or disagreeing with him based on their values or their view of society as a whole. He was like a politician without a conscience, imposing his will on people who had no power to argue back.

Perhaps Belinda had been right in the end and I was trying to emulate my dad, attempting to do the good thing if only because I couldn't bear the thought of the bad one.

I came out of this reverie when I lurched forward in the seat as Belinda braked fiercely.

She yelled, 'Go, goddamn it! I'm behind you!'

I'd already undone my seat-belt and now I flung back the car door and ran through the wide entrance hall of the station, dodging between the hundreds of people who were heading home, looking forward to a quiet weekend. The clock ahead of me showed 5.59. I had one minute to find Greif and disarm his weapon, and I had no idea where to start.

Manchester Piccadilly — end of the line from Edinburgh, York, Birmingham, London. A central hub for one of the largest cities in the country. And it was Friday night, the busiest night of the week.

It was chaos.

Running through the entrance I came out into the wider concourse and a couple of people fluttered out of my way. The collection of shops stretched out to my right, behind the ticket office, which was crowded with snaking queues. To my left were Boots the chemist and Burger King, together with the amusement arcade rattling out its insane electronic jabber.

Directly ahead of me hung the huge overhead timetables and beyond them, the first row of platforms visible behind floor-to-ceiling glass, accessed through gaps for every pair of platforms. A train had recently arrived because passengers were heading towards me in broken ranks, some on phones telling the wife or husband they were on the way, others still engrossed in the evening papers. I dodged through them and looked around the enormous space, glancing at each platform down to the furthest, number 10.

Where would I begin? How would I spot Greif? Would he even be here? He was wearing a smart suit and tie the last time I saw him, but that wouldn't mark him out in this crowd.

I walked down the concourse, staring at everyone: the man eating a burger and licking mustard off his fingers, the woman arguing angrily with someone at the other end of the phone, the young man pushing a bicycle, steering it by holding the seat and leaning one way and then the other.

I stopped and looked around.

Hundreds of people, and I couldn't do a thing. We were probably all going to die.

I turned and stared at the people sitting on the benches beside each entrance to the platforms. The businessman reading his paperback, a young Asian woman trying to control an unruly child, a couple of buskers dressed as clowns and setting up their amplifiers, a white-haired old lady staring into space, a student reading a text-book, a couple of teenagers entwining their fingers.

Where would Greif let out his infection? Could I get to the air-conditioning units? Where were they?

Helpless, I started to run towards the far end of the echoing hall, the memory of the factory explosion replaying in my head. If only I could catch a glimpse of Greif or any of his other men …

I stopped as an image came back to me.

Guitars.

There were two men about to play guitars. Dressed as clowns. Two large, heavy amplifiers on the floor in front of them. Why did they need amplifiers when their guitars were acoustic? Yes, they could have used pick-ups, but where would they plug the amps in? I remembered Stratford and Jolyon playing their guitars and singing for The Bleak…

I turned and ran back towards the clowns.

They both looked up at me as though they'd sensed that I was coming towards them. One of them reached up a hand and lifted up his mask.

Stratford Greif was smiling at me beneath it.

Then he pulled the mask down—it wasn't just a clown mask, I realised: it contained a breathing mouthpiece—and reached for the back of his amplifier. I was still twenty yards away and I watched impotently as he pulled down a switch.

Nothing happened.

But then I didn't expect a blinding flash or a hiss of escaping gas. I knew that the infection, the plague or anthrax or whatever they were using, would seep gently into the air, borne on whatever bioaerosol transport that Greif's team had created.

Greif didn't seem so certain.

He looked down at the amplifier and worked the device again, and again.

By now I was on him and crashed him backwards over the bench, landing on top of him and wrenching his mask from his face. If we were all going to die, so was he.

But Greif was laughing in my face.

'Did you expect bugs, Dyke? A touch of the plague? Think modern medicine will be able to cure you? Well the joke's on you. Let me introduce you to sarin. Already it's seeping into your pores. Soon your nerve endings will stop working and shortly afterwards asphyxia will set in because your breathing will be out of your control. You'll be dead in less than ten minutes. Enjoy the ride.'

My hands were around his neck.

'How many, Greif? How many will die?'

'Dozens. Hundreds. And there's nothing you can do.'

I drew back my fist to punch him when a hand caught my arm. There was voice in my ear. Jolyon Greif's voice. And he was trying to pull me up.

'Dyke! There's nothing. There's nothing there. Let him go.'

I stood up and hauled Stratford to his feet with me. I was breathing hard. I saw Belinda running through the mass of people, many of whom had stopped and were staring at me. Jolyon Greif had stood up and taken off his own mask. The pair of them looked ridiculous, their costumes contrasting vividly with their neatly combed hair.

I said, 'What do you mean?'

'I disarmed the device. Took out the sarin canisters while Stratford was dealing with you in Altrincham.'

Stratford let out a howl and tried to leap on Jolyon, who stepped back. I held Stratford away, twisting his right arm behind him.

Jolyon talked past me to Stratford, 'You could have been my brother but you never let me forget.'

'Forget what, you treacherous pig-fucker?'

'That you had the family brains. Tough shit—the family idiot has seen through you.'

Stratford tried again to launch himself at his cousin but I held him back again. Then the life seemed to drain from his body and he slumped.

I said to Jolyon, 'You were the one who called me, weren't you?'

Jolyon inclined his head but said nothing, and in that moment Stratford surged back to life, yanked his arm from my grip and dashed through the entrance to Platform 6.

Belinda said, 'Go, I'll watch Jolyon.'

I was only fifteen yards behind Stratford as he raced up the platform, which was full of commuters waiting for their incoming train. He sliced through the crowds who quickly became aware of this madman running towards them and stepped back out of his way.

I couldn't see what he thought he might do. There was no escape and eventually the platform would end, leaving nothing but bare tracks for him to run on.

And then I saw the train that they were all waiting for, just entering the covered portion of the station. It was a fast train that I knew would reverse out when full and head south towards Birmingham and then on to London. Now it was slowing and getting ready to stop before disgorging its present load.

Greif had seen it too and changed the direction of his flight, moving closer to edge of the platform and scattering more people as he ran.

Then he did it.

He leaped from the platform and on to the train tracks, running towards the oncoming train. I heard some screams and calls around me but I was in pursuit and couldn't stop now. I ran on the platform parallel to Stratford who was still five yards ahead of me. His clown's outfit fluttered around his thin body as his legs pumped him along the track.

The train was fifty yards away, its brakes beginning to graunch and grind as the driver saw the apparition on the track and tried to slow even further.

Greif had a surprising turn of speed for someone who had seemed so leisurely. He was now thirty yards from the train and it was obvious that the driver couldn't stop.

Greif had reached the point where he was parallel to the extreme end of the platform. There were no passengers this far down and he finally halted and turned, as though he knew I was close behind. I reached the edge of the platform and looked down at him. We were both breathing hard.

I said, 'Give me your hand. Come up.'

He shook his head.

'You don't deserve to save my life. I have no respect for you. Why would you do that?'

'Because it's in my nature.'

'It's not in mine to give up.'

He turned as the train began to cast its shadow over him, barely ten yards away and moving in slow-motion though still too fast to stop.

I watched as he stared at his approaching fate. He seemed resigned to it, almost calm, ignoring the calls and the shouts from the people who now surrounded me on the platform's edge.

We could smell the burning metal and heated oil as the train tried its hardest to avoid hitting the stationary man. It loomed huge and monstrous and unforgiving. I became aware of the vast space around me, the air beyond the glass roof, the thousands of people who would go home tonight and lie safe in bed.

At the last moment, Greif turned towards me, said, 'Okay,' and raised his hand to be lifted from the tracks.

I didn't take it.

CHAPTER FORTY SEVEN

BY THE TIME I got back into the concourse—ignoring the wide-eyed stares of the commuters who'd seen Greif's end—Inspector Howard had managed to organise his troops. He must have got my message and contacted the British Transport Police, who in turn would have run their procedures in the station. Now I saw flashing lights outside the entrance and could hear the two-tone wail of approaching police-cars.

Two policemen had Jolyon Greif between them and Belinda was talking fast. She broke off when she saw me arrive.

'What happened?'

I glanced at Jolyon.

'He jumped in front of a train.'

I turned to the older of the policemen.

'You should clear the platform. The driver will have radioed it in and there's a mess to clean up. You'll need an ambulance.'

'And who are you?'

Belinda said, 'He's the man who stopped this whole bloody station from being infected. I think you should call someone before people start throwing up at the sight of gore.'

The policemen glanced nervously at each other then the older one stepped away and got on his radio. More policemen were coming through now and the commuters had stopped what they were doing to watch the entertainment.

Jolyon said, 'How did you know we were here? Lucky guess?'

'Stratford had to be somewhere that was less than an hour from Altrincham. He had to get there for six. And I thought of Asahara's attack on the Tokyo underground. Trains. I guessed Stratford would want to outdo him, show he was cleverer. Have a bigger impact.'

Jolyon said, 'He was always in competition with someone though he wouldn't admit it.'

'You went to the trouble of swapping the canisters. Why did you let him carry on with his plan in the first place? You got him killed, and for nothing.'

'I wasn't the one who chased him down the platform till he jumped. Does that make you feel happy, big man?'

I stepped towards him.

'Sam!' Belinda pulled me away.

Jolyon said, 'He was a failure anyway, just like the Japanese guy he was so keen on.'

'How?'

'All those brains, all that money and time, and he still couldn't get the botulinum toxin to work. In the end they thought Mustow had changed the data, led them all to think that such-and-such a mixture would work, but it didn't. The toxin kept dying off too soon, before it could be used. Drove them mad.'

I pointed to the square electronic amplifiers that were still standing in front of the passenger bench.

'So what did he think he put in the canisters?'

'He told you—sarin. He went back to what that Japanese nutcase did and got his people to develop sarin. It was easier. A couple of stages. Christ, they bought the chemicals they needed on-line. That's what they needed the glue factory for—somewhere to mix the chemicals away from prying eyes, and just before the attack so it didn't degrade. Apparently it's a simple thing to do if you've got the precursor chemicals and you don't want to make tons of it. If you buy small quantities you're not breaching the Chemical Warfare Convention so you can buy it more or less with a credit card. Stratford did his research.'

For the first time since I'd met him he seemed relaxed. It was as though explaining Stratford's actions had made it easier for him to behave like a normal person instead of a swaggering bully.

I said, 'So what happened to you? Why the change of heart and the phone calls to me? Why did you want him to fail?'

Jolyon looked away, watching more police pour through the entrance and start to herd people outside.

He said, 'He was never family. He took my mother's name when he came over from Russia but he never really wanted to know me. And the odd thing was, he thought he *did* know me, because I was a policeman. He thought I was a pig. But he knew nothing about me. Despite what you might think, I'm not a monster.'

'We've got you on video. There's a man dying in a chair. Seems like he was exposed to poison gas. Looks pretty monstrous to me when you and Bonetti cart him away.'

Jolyon pulled down the corners of his lips.

'He was an experiment, someone we found on the street and gave a meal to. No one missed him. No one came after him. He wasn't dead, just ill. We gave him the antidote and five hundred quid and let him go a week later.'

'You'll have to prove that.'

'Bollocks. I know how evidence works.'

The older of the two policemen came back to us. He looked at his colleague and gestured towards Jolyon with his chin.

'What's he been saying?'

'Couldn't follow most of it. But there's going to be a big conversation back at the nick.'

Jolyon said to the older policeman, 'Don't I know you? Didn't your brother work over in Didsbury?'

I glanced at Belinda.

'This isn't going to be easy.'

She patted my arm. 'The other scientists in The Bleak will cough up, try to save themselves.'

'I wouldn't be so sure of that. They were pretty fanatical to go this far.'

'But we've got a secret weapon.'

'What's that?'

'Mr Bones is still tied up in my cellar. And he's really pissed off with the Greifs.'

Journet, France, May 2014.

ACKNOWLEDGEMENTS

Thanks to the usual supportive folks, and especially to those who continue to buy the Sam Dyke books.

Special thanks this time to Mary Danks for specialist knowledge ... I can say no more.

Now go to the next page to read the first chapter of the next Sam Dyke Investigation, *The Strange Girl.*

CHAPTER ONE

DESPITE WHAT MOST people think about private investigators, I don't spend all my time waiting in my office for beautiful blonde women with mysterious eyes and long legs to walk in and offer me money to find their missing relatives.

And the first time it happened, it was just my luck she was brought by a cop.

His name was Howard, and I'd had a couple of dealings with him over the years. He was the very embodiment of the word Plod - although he was thin, almost bony, his demeanour was so heavy you felt that if he stood still long enough he'd grow roots.

So when he knocked and poked his head around my office door I wasn't expecting much in the way of entertainment.

He glanced around the empty room and nodded.

'You're in, then.'

'Apparently.'

'Got a job for you.'

Perhaps I should have sat up straight and showed some enthusiasm, but to be honest I don't have a lot of enthusiasm these days. My son, Dan, had traded Bitcoins online for me during the last three months, and I'd done surprisingly well. In fact, the income I'd made in the last three months had outstripped my investigation earnings for the last two years.

Not so good for the motivation.

Now Inspector Howard opened the door wide and stepped back. A young woman walked past him and into my life.

Is that too corny?

Possibly, but that's what it felt like. She was tall and slender, with the kind of walk that placed one foot in front of the other, like a catwalk model on a tightrope—not that kind of splay-footed amble people usually adopt when entering a space they don't know. She moved into the room as though she owned it, looked for a seat and commanded it, placing slender hands on either arm of the chair as she sat. It looked grateful to receive her.

She shook her head to release her hair and it bobbed once and settled. It was long and ebony black, framing a pale, oval face with hazel eyes at its centre. She crossed her legs, but she was seated on the far side of my desk so I couldn't see them. I didn't need to see them to know they'd be great.

I hadn't realised I'd stood up until I found myself sitting down. Howard had also come in by now and moved the other client chair to take his place beside her.

I said to the woman, 'You're not blonde.'

'Is that a problem?'

'We'll find out. I'm Sam Dyke.'

'So I've heard. Inspector Howard told me that while he wouldn't trust you, you'd probably do a good job. He said you'd be persistent. Was he right?'

'Yes. He never trusts me.'

'But are you persistent?'

'I keep trying to be. Every now and then I give up.'

She turned to Howard.

'He thinks he's funny. Will you tell him, or shall I?'

As she turned, I caught a glimpse of her profile. I've seen worse. Straight nose, delicate chin, earlobes like porcelain shells. Long eye-lashes, too, beneath a high and gently-sloping brow. I've already mentioned the black hair, but I'll add the fact that it seemed to fall in natural waves to her shoulders without any help from product or styling.

Howard leaned forward in his chair and placed a hand on my desk.

'This young lady needs your help, Dyke. I've told her you'd do the job. Don't let me down.'

'Or what, you'll never talk to me again? I can live with that.'

He didn't move and kept staring at me, his lips slightly pursed in irritation.

I shifted my gaze to the woman. 'You have the advantage of me. You know my name. I don't know yours.'

'Let me explain the situation first. Then you can tell me whether you want to hear my name.'

'I'm all ears.'

She relaxed into the chair, uncrossing her legs and reaching for her handbag. Howard leaned back and looked out of the window behind me, into Crewe town centre, as though trying to demonstrate that he wasn't going to listen to what she said. Either that or he found shoppers fascinating.

The woman had opened her handbag. She said, 'Can I smoke?'

'I'd prefer it if you didn't. It might set off the fire alarm. I don't like fires.'

She placed the handbag on the floor again, every action precise as though it had been considered for several minutes beforehand.

She said, 'My father is Lorenzo Strano, and he was a policeman. Several years ago he was found guilty of selling steroids and was sent to prison. He served eight years and was released last month.'

She paused and I wondered if she was going to cry. She'd given no sign of emotion but there was an intensity in her expression that led me to think she might just burst into tears.

I said, 'Must have been bad for a policeman in prison.'

'Probably. I wouldn't know. Since he's been released I haven't seen him.'

Howard said, 'That's where you come in.'

The woman glanced sharply at him then turned back to me.

'When my father was sent to prison my mother took me away. I was seventeen and didn't argue. I was angry with her and I was angry with him. Can you understand that?'

'Of course.'

'After that first year I went away to university and I've been away until the last few years. Now I'm back in the area and I'm something I never thought I'd say—I'm a business-woman. I have a good life with good friends and a fancy office.'

I said, 'But the simple version is that you want me to find your dad?'

'Your first deduction, I'm impressed.'

'And what do you want me to do when I find him?'

'I want you to tell me where he is.'

'And what will you do then?'

She stared at me. 'That's up to me, the client, don't you think?'

'Not if you go round to his place with a sawn-off shotgun because he abandoned you and your mother. Not if you set a gang of thugs on him. Do you see my point?'

'Not entirely. This is a financial transaction, isn't it?'

'My point is, what if he doesn't want you to know where he is, possibly for very good reasons of his own?'

She turned to Howard again.

'This isn't going well. Do you have another investigator on your list?'

I said, 'Look, I'll find him for you, if that's what you want. But you have to be prepared for the fact he might not want to be found. You might have a conversation with him and then he vanishes again. Why else do you think he hasn't been in contact?'

Her lips tightened and her hazel eyes found a touch of steel, and the atmosphere in the room gained a little electricity.

She said, 'Not that it's any of your business, but relations between my father and me weren't always good. You have to remember I was seventeen when all this happened. I daresay I blamed him for breaking up the family. And I daresay I didn't hide it.'

'What does your mother think?'

Howard brought his attention back into the room as though a code word had triggered him.

'Maria died a couple of years ago. Anjelica nursed her but the cancer took her in the end.'

A grateful look passed between the young woman and the policeman, as though he'd said something she couldn't. And now I had a name - Anjelica Strano. I liked it, though its owner was turning out to be rather spiky.

I said, 'So now your father's out of prison and you think he's steering clear of you because you weren't getting on. Did it occur to you he might be embarrassed or ashamed? Perhaps he doesn't want you to see him after eight years in a prison environment. Perhaps he's got tattoos or was beaten up. Perhaps he wants to be the one who decides when you actually see each other again.'

'I understand that. But I don't know for certain, do I?' She hesitated briefly. 'I don't want him to think I bear him a grudge. I've grown up. I've lost my mother … I don't want to lose my father as well.'

There was no doubt it was tempting. I would have liked Anjelica Strano as a client. I would have made sure we had regular client meetings, probably in a more relaxed environment than my uncomfortable office.

But her father was an ex-cop. Which meant that to learn anything, I'd probably be talking to other policemen—something neither they nor I would like. Moreover, it seemed like a fool's errand. If he wanted to talk to his daughter it was his right to choose when and where to do it. There was no reason for me to be mixed up in this, nothing I could use to defend my involvement in the case—if it was even a case.

I said, 'I appreciate your situation, Miss Strano. But I don't think there's anything I can do for you. If I were you, I'd talk to some of his old friends and see if they know where he might have gone.'

Howard interrupted again. 'We've tried that. No one knows anything. That's why we thought we'd use a professional. But we came to you first.'

I ignored the jibe and so did Anjelica. She said, 'Don't you want to know the real reason he was sent to prison?'

'I don't see what difference it will make.'

'He gave up.'

'You mean he admitted it?'

'It was a big trial, lots of pressure. TV and newspapers. He was accused of buying and selling steroids from a man working in a gym. There seemed to be no doubt he was guilty. They found steroids in a suitcase in our house and there were witnesses who saw him talking to his supplier and other witnesses who allegedly bought from him.'

'Sounds open and shut.'

'But my dad offered no defence. For the first time in his life, he had nothing to say. Just took it, day after day in the dock, saying nothing. Didn't defend himself.'

The intensity had returned to her face, sharpening her features, putting a light in the back of her eyes. She'd laid a hand on the desk between us. Her fingers were long and slender and tipped with pink.

I said, 'So why do you think he was silent?'

'Isn't it obvious?'

'Explain it to me.'

'He was either guilty or he was protecting someone.'

'So he put himself in jail? Hard to believe, for a copper. What was his defence team doing?'

'Nothing. They barely questioned the witnesses and seemed bored most of the time.'

'You watched it?'

'A few days. Then I couldn't stand it. He'd given up, so in the end even *I* thought he must be guilty. I was young, I didn't know anything.'

'Why have you changed your mind?'

'Because I'm my father's daughter, and I don't give up. Like you, I'm persistent.'

TWENTY MINUTES LATER I'd agreed to look for Lorenzo Strano. I didn't want to and I didn't need the work. But I couldn't argue with the strength of the young woman's conviction and the fact that Howard agreed with her. He was as cold-hearted as they come, so if he'd seen enough to bring her to me, there was probably something in it.

After we'd arranged terms and she'd given me some photos of her father, they both got up to leave.

I said to her, 'How did you find the Inspector here? Why him?'

'He knew my father and was the only one to send me a Christmas card every year. Sounds silly, but it meant a lot to us. Everyone else acted as though he'd never existed.'

Howard had turned away but I thought I saw some colour in his cheek.

I said, 'That's tough. Coppers usually stick together. It doesn't bode well. If they didn't want to speak to you then, it's not likely they'll want to speak to me now.'

As if in reply, she handed me an index card on which she'd written two names and telephone numbers.

'Talk to them. They knew my dad. They wouldn't talk to the Inspector but then he's still an officer of the court, as they say.

They wouldn't talk to me because … well, because they know who I am. They're probably embarrassed.'

'And you think I can bully them into talking.'

'I'm sure you'll find a way.'

I said to Howard, 'What's your opinion? Why do you think he's gone into hiding?'

'I don't have an opinion. You're on your own with this. I've done what I can because I know the family, but I can't do any more.'

I understood. He was probably acting against policy by steering the young woman towards me in the first place. It was harder these days for individual policemen to act independently, whatever their rank. His hands were almost certainly tied.

He looked as though he might add something but instead just nodded at me and led her to the door. Before she left completely she came back into the room, shook my hand and almost as an afterthought gave me a business card.

She said, 'About my name. I don't use Strano any more. There was so much publicity about the case I changed it.'

'So what do I call you now?'

Before answering she walked back to the doorway then turned to look at me from within her cloud of long black hair. 'Strano is Italian for "strange". It was my nickname at school. The Strange girl. You can call me Anjelica Strange.'

Also by Keith Dixon

The Sam Dyke Series

Altered Life
The Private Lie
The Hard Swim
The Bleak
The Strange Girl
The Secret Sharers
The Innocent Dead
The Second Guess (short story)

The Paul Storey Thriller Series

Storey
One Punch
The Song of Geneva Chance

Standalone Novels

A French Darcy – a Romance
Actress – a Contemporary novel

Essays on Writing

The Idle Writer
Crime Writing Confidential

Blog

www.cwconfidential.blogspot.com

Webpage

http://www.keithdixonnovels.com